I0609738

MURDER
SO HEARTLESS

MURDER
SO HEARTLESS

A Merry March Mystery

Eileen Curley Hammond

Twody Press

Murder So Heartless Copyright © 2019 by Eileen Hammond. All Rights Reserved.

All rights reserved. No part of this book may be reproduced in any form or by any electronic or mechanical means including information storage and retrieval systems, without permission in writing from the author. The only exception is by a reviewer, who may quote short excerpts in a review.

Cover designed by SelfPubBookCovers.com/ RLSather

This book is a work of fiction. Names, characters, places, and incidents either are products of the author's imagination or are used fictitiously. Any resemblance to actual persons, living or dead, events, or locales is entirely coincidental.

Eileen Curley Hammond
Visit my website at www.eileencurleyhammond.com

Printed in the United States of America

First Printing: Feb 2019
Twody Press

ISBN-978-1-7325460-5-9

Library of Congress Control Number: 2019901638

AUTHOR'S NOTE

Thank you to my readers. I appreciate you wanting to spend your time with Merry in the town of Hopeful. I hope you enjoy this latest book. And if you do, please let others know about it through your favorite social media platform or a review on Amazon.

I'm so fortunate to have friends who are willing to give of their time to make my books more readable. In particular, I'd like to thank young adult writer, Jenna Grinstead, for being a key touchstone and especially for her feedback on the short synopsis that describes this book. Eric Henderson graciously fit me in with his seminary studies and pointed out things that made the book more understandable. And, as always, the Buckeye Crime Writers group (a Sisters in Crime chapter), is a community that provides a continual source of inspiration and support.

I'd like to thank my editor, Lauren Pan, who challenged me to be more descriptive and asked great questions that made be me more thoughtful in my writing.

Thank you to my contractor, neighbor, and friend, Ray Parker (and his wife Kathy) who put up with endless questions at what was supposed to be a fun, non-work related, dinner.

My family continues to be a great source of inspiration and support. Specifically, I'd like to thank my Uncle Kevin Curley, who as a playwright approaches things from a different perspective and gives me new ideas. I'd also like to thank my husband, Robert. He is a great first reader and cheerleader for my efforts.

I'm so blessed to have such a great team to help me.

For Dad.

PROLOGUE

The road stretched endlessly toward the desolate horizon, banked by sand on both sides. A line of tanks and armored personnel carriers crawled along, like ants marching home to their nest. One vehicle lagged behind the main convoy. Nearby a camouflaged Iraqi transporter-launcher laid in wait. Without warning it leapt into action, releasing a Scud missile. It hurtled toward the unsuspecting caravan. However, instead of hitting its targeted destination, it hit near the dawdler. The armored personnel carrier leapt toward the sky, tossing its human cargo onto the unforgiving road below.

CHAPTER 1

She looked beautiful. Her dress was blushing pink, a teensy bit shorter than I would have liked, but with good coverage on top and three quarter length sleeves. Her blond hair was styled in long ringlets and was topped with a sparkly rhinestone barrette. She finished accenting her bright blue eyes with a lavender liner and moved back from the mirror. I gave her a side hug. "Perfect. Absolutely perfect."

"Careful, Mom. I know you don't want me to spend another three hours on my makeup." She smiled in the mirror at me. "You look terrific too. I love the emerald green; it really brings out the color in your eyes." She blew me a kiss. "The roses Mr. Jenson sent are beautiful. It seems kind of mean that you have to spend Valentine's Day with us. Thanks for being a chaperone."

I patted my own auburn curls and touched up my makeup. "Rob and I can celebrate later. Jacob should be here any minute. Almost done?"

"Yes." She fiddled with her hair.

"Let's go downstairs." We descended, arm in arm. "We clean up pretty good."

She smiled, "Yes, we do. I can't wait for you to see Cindy's dress. It's an electric blue."

There was a staccato knock at the door, and three laughing teens barged in: my daughter's best friend, Cindy, her boyfriend, Michael, and Jenny's new beau, Jacob. The girls fell on each other gushing about how fabulous they both looked. The boys stood slightly apart, shifting from foot to foot, eyes wide, probably because of the decibel level in the room.

I shook Michael's hand, then Jacob's. "Jacob, have you and your parents finished unpacking yet?"

"We're almost done, Ms. March. We still can't get a car in the garage, but with my dad being in the military, we've gotten pretty good at moving."

"Well, I hope you'll get to stay here through graduation next year."

He smiled at Jenny. "I hope so too."

The front door opened, and my best friend, Patty Twilliger, hustled in, her long brown hair looking like it had been pulled hastily into a ponytail. "Pictures." She pulled on Cindy's arm. "We need pictures. Of the whole group."

Patrick, Patty's husband, stepped in behind her, iPhone at the ready.

Cindy sighed. "Mom, you already took like a hundred pictures."

Patty frowned. "Someday you'll thank me, young lady. I need pictures of Jenny too. Plus, Ms. March is going to want pictures of you, won't you, Merry?" She gave me a stern look.

I piped up, "Of course! I want pictures of everyone."

Patty shot me small smile, then sprang into action, issuing orders to the teens.

My boyfriend, Rob, turned the corner to the hallway. He raised his hand as if to stop Patty. "Wait, I'm not ready yet!" He hurried over, the digital SLR camera around his neck bobbing up and down. He quickly found a spot and began clicking.

Patrick guffawed. "Oh, the expensive camera comes out for the photo op."

Rob's mustache twitched, and then he turned back to the group. "Now the couples. Cindy and Michael first. Pose by the fireplace."

After photos were taken of what seemed like every possible arrangement, Patty and Rob started to put their cameras away. I nudged Rob. "We need to get going."

Jenny shook her finger. "Not so fast. We're not the only ones dressed up. Now you and Mr. Jenson."

Rob and I acquiesced and posed by the fireplace. Jenny chortled. "You may want to stand on the hearth, Mom. That way you'd be almost as tall as Mr. Jenson."

I stuck my tongue out, but hopped up on the hearth. Rob winked and brushed his fingers through his wavy blond hair.

Patty chuckled and took the shot. "Now let's get a real picture."

I stepped down and stood in front of Rob. He wrapped his arms around my waist. I sunk into him, enjoying the warmth of his embrace.

Patrick called out, "Smile!" Before I could, the front door opened with a bang. My ex, Drew, waltzed in. I grimaced.

Patrick glanced at the viewer. "Not keeping that one."

I crossed my arms over my chest and grit my teeth.

Jenny pranced to her father and gave him a hug. "Hi, Dad. I'm glad you're here."

He held her at arm's length. "You look beautiful, smart stuff."

"Thanks. Do you want Jacob and me to pose for you?"

I took a deep breath as he took a few shots. Drew and I divorced four years ago after he swindled the town and went to prison. When he was released, he rented the house next door. Our relationship could only be described as rocky.

Michael pushed his hair back from his forehead. "We need to get going or we'll be late for the Valentine's Day dance." Air kisses ensued and they filed out the door, followed by Patrick and Patty.

We waved as they drove away. I turned to Rob. "We need to be leaving too. It won't look good if one of the chaperones and the newspaper's photographer-owner are late."

Drew stared at me, his blue eyes misty. "You look wonderful, Merry."

My cheeks reddened. Rob's fists clenched.

I put my hand out to restrain Rob. "Thank you, Drew. We need to leave now, so if you don't mind." I gestured toward the door.

He opened it.

"Oh, and don't forget to fill out the annulment paperwork I gave you two weeks ago. Father Tom is waiting on it."

Drew smirked as he sauntered out. "Yeah, I guess I still need to do that, don't I?"

Rob scowled. "What did that mean? Is he going to fill it out or not?"

"You heard what I heard. I'll have Father Tom talk to him." I reached out and stroked Rob's cheek. "Don't worry. We'll get through this."

He took my hand and kissed it. "We will, but I'm can't promise the same for your ex."

I stood on tiptoes and gave Rob a quick kiss. "Thanks for being so understanding." I picked up my purse and we left.

When we arrived at the high school, the parking lot was packed. Rob found a spot and grabbed his camera. He opened my door. "Promise me we'll get at least one dance tonight?"

"Depends on what's playing, but I'm game if you are."

I left him by the door taking photos of the arriving kids. A large red heart with a lacy white insert had been set up for them to pose in. Hearts of all different hues of red were affixed to the linoleum floor showing the way to the gym. Following the trail, I opened the door. My mouth dropped. The students had stretched a net from one set of bleachers to those on the other side. Dangling from the net were

Cupid's arrows interspersed with scores of hearts that formed daisy chains. Red carnations spelled out 'Love' and decorated the walls.

Barbara Ziebold approached, her arms spread wide. "Isn't it beautiful? The kids did a super job."

"That they did. I'm sorry I'm a few minutes late. There was a flurry of picture taking before Jenny left the house."

"Don't worry. I just got here myself. Jay and I were doing the same. I can't believe how old they are. It seems like we were just changing their diapers two minutes ago."

"Probably shouldn't bring that up tonight."

She chuckled. "You're right." She pointed at the refreshments table. "Do you mind being stationed over there? I want to make sure no one slips anything into the punch."

"I don't mind, although I do think your husband, Jay, would be more of a deterrent."

"Because of his size? Or because he's a detective?"

"Both."

"He did it last year. Our son was mortified. He said he'd never go to another dance if Jay was there."

I grinned and started filling cups with punch.

Barbara turned to the rest of the chaperones, "Everyone ready?" We nodded in unison. The DJ began playing and Barbara flung open the doors.

My foot tapped to the rhythm of a Taylor Swift song as I handed out cups of punch and greeted the kids I knew.

Jenny was dancing with Jacob across the gym. Seventeen. How did she grow up so fast? It was only yesterday that I knelt, bandaging her knees, after her first rollerblading adventure.

Rob broke my reverie. "Can you spare a glass of punch for a thirsty photographer?"

"Of course. Did you get some good photos?"

"Yes." He slurped the punch and grimaced. "Too sweet."

I pulled a bottle of water from under the table. "Chaperone special."

"Much better." He took a sip. "I'm going to get candid shots now." He walked off, appearing to zero in on Jenny and Jacob.

There was another rush at the punch table, and I hurried to keep up. Before long, Barbara joined me. "Need a break?"

"Thanks. I'll take a quick one." I made a beeline for the ladies room. The area by the mirrors was packed with girls adjusting their makeup and gossiping about who was dancing with whom. I wove through to the sink and washed my hands. A quick swipe of some lip gloss, and I was back out the door. As I returned to my post, I noticed someone behind the bleachers. He was lifting a flask to his lips. I strode up to him. "Stop." I held out my hand. "I'll take that."

He turned beet red. "It's not what you think."

"Uh huh." I motioned for him to hand me the flask.

"You're not going to tell my parents, are you?" He placed it in my hand.

"Yes, I am."

His face fell.

"But not till tomorrow. Enjoy the rest of the dance."

His face brightened, and he held out his hand for the flask. I shook my head. "You don't need this. I'll be sure to return it to your parents tomorrow."

He slunk away.

I unscrewed the flask and sniffed. My eyes watered. *What is this?* I strolled back to the table, slipping it into my purse.

Rob snuck around the tables to join me. "Stopped two kids who were getting frisky at the end of the bleachers. They thought no one would see them."

"Nice work. I caught someone with his own refreshments. One hundred proof."

"Can you take a break? I'd like to claim that dance."

My eyes widened. "Dance to this?" A very energetic song was playing. It had no discernable rhythm.

Rob grinned. "One of the great things about being an adult is that you have money to bribe the DJ."

I waved Barbara over. "Do you mind if I take a quick dance break?"

She stuck her fingers in her ears. "If you think you can dance to this, go ahead."

Rob took my hand and led me onto the floor. He waved to the DJ. *Bless the Broken Road* by Rascal Flatts started to play. Pulling me into his arms, we began to dance and the gym fell away.

I looked up into his beautiful green eyes. "I love this song." He pulled me closer, and I closed my eyes, warm against his chest.

✻ ✻ ✻

I groaned as I massaged my feet the next morning. *Why do women wear heels?* Between guarding the punch bowl and stolen moments on the dance floor with Rob, my feet had gotten a workout. I donned my sweatpants, hoody, and warm fuzzy slippers and padded my way downstairs into the kitchen. In short order I was sitting on the window seat, a cup of hot java in my hands. One of my cats, Courvoisier, jumped up next to me. I petted her and stared at Drew's house. *Maybe he'll move on now that he's been cleared of murder charges.*

A taxi pulled up and deposited a tall brunette on the sidewalk in front of Drew's house. She was striking. Cheekbones you could cut a knife on, brown almond shaped eyes, and legs that were far longer than mine. A dark purple rolling suitcase landed next to her. It looked expensive, as classy as she seemed to be.

She turned toward the driver. I couldn't be certain, but I thought he wiped drool from the corner of his mouth. Without glancing back, she rolled her suitcase through Drew's garden gate and up the path.

The suitcase must have been heavy, as she bumped it from one stair to the next. She reached the porch and paused in front of the door. She fluffed her long mane and rang the bell.

Drew opened the door, picked her up, and twirled her around. He lifted her suitcase, and they disappeared into his house.

I hurried to my half bath and stared into the mirror. *Nope. No contest. At least not this morning.*

Jenny appeared next to me. "What are you doing?"

I jumped. "Nothing. Having coffee."

She gave me a long look. "In the bathroom?"

I brushed past her and returned to the window seat. "Your dad appears to have a visitor."

She looked out the window. "Who?"

"I don't know. What do you want for breakfast?"

"Scrambled eggs and bacon. And I wouldn't say no to one of your cinnamon rolls."

I retrieved the bacon and eggs from the refrigerator. "Would you please get two cinnamon rolls out of the freezer in the garage?"

"It's cold out there, and my feet are bare."

"Go back upstairs and get your slippers."

"Can't I borrow yours?"

I sighed and kicked them off my feet. She slipped them on.

I put the bacon in the pan.

She came back in, put the cinnamon rolls on a plate, and pressed defrost on the microwave. Then she plopped down at the counter, swinging her feet.

I gave her a stern look. "Ahem. My slippers?"

"They're so warm and toasty."

I frowned at her. She pouted, took them off, and laid them next to me on the floor.

"Thank you." I slid into them and flipped the bacon.

"So what did Dad's visitor look like?"

"A woman, tall, kind of a goddess."

Jenny's eyes widened. "Brown long hair? Looks like a model?"

"Yes. Do you know her?"

"Sounds like the woman Dad met when we went to Jamaica." Jenny gulped some orange juice. "I told you about her, Arianna Flores. She was really nice." Jenny craned her neck, looking at Drew's house.

"She's already inside. Breakfast is almost ready. Why don't you call your dad after breakfast and find out?"

Jenny sprinted through breakfast and, as the last piece of cinnamon roll disappeared, she lifted her phone to her ear. "Mom said you had a visitor. Is it Arianna?" She licked her finger and used it to pick up the crumbs from her plate. "No, Mom was not checking up on you. She just happened to see—no, you don't need to move—Dad, stop it. Okay, I'll be right over." She hung up.

I lifted my left eyebrow.

"He thought you were spying on him."

"That's silly."

"I'll be back in a little while. I want to say hi to Arianna." She ran upstairs to dress and was back in five minutes. She hopped out the back door and flew across the path to Drew's house.

How does he attract all these women?

CHAPTER 2

L ater that morning, Rob texted to say he'd arrive in fifteen minutes. I debated changing and then decided my spot on the sofa was far too comfy to move. Returning to the cozy mystery I was reading, I settled farther into the cushions.

When I woke, Rob stood over me. He bent down and gave me a kiss. "I guess we can't party like we're teenagers anymore."

I groaned. "You've got that right. That's the last time I volunteer as a chaperone."

"You didn't enjoy yourself?"

"I loved our dance."

He kissed me again. "So did I." He ambled to the living room window and pulled the curtain open. "Who's the woman with Drew?"

I immediately regretted not changing out of my rumpled sweats. I stood and tried to smooth them before I joined Rob at the window. "I'm not sure. Jenny thought it was someone Drew met in Jamaica."

Drew pulled the woman close for a hug, and kissed the top of her forehead. They meandered past my gate headed for town. Drew looked at the window, and I dropped to the floor.

Rob looked down at me, his eyebrows raised. "What's that all about?"

I gave him a rueful grin. "Lost contact?"

"You don't wear contacts." He held out his hand and pulled me up.

"Drew thought I was spying on him earlier today."

"And this doesn't look suspicious?"

Jenny burst through the back door. "Hello?"

"We're in here!"

She came around the corner. "Arianna looks so awesome, just like always. Dad's taking her for a late breakfast, and I'm going to meet them for dinner tonight."

"What about Jacob? I thought you two had a date tonight?"

She shrugged. "Dad said to bring him along." She turned and ran up the stairs to her room.

Rob nudged my foot with his. "It's probably good that she gets along with Drew's friend."

"Let's hope Arianna doesn't get murdered."

His mouth dropped. "That's a bit dramatic. You haven't even met her yet."

"I didn't mean that I was going to murder her." I sniffed. "I was merely commenting on the fact that his last two girlfriends were murdered. You have to admit his track record hasn't been great."

Rob shook his head. "I guess it's appropriate given the circumstances."

I sat next to him, and he put his arm around me. "What are your plans for today?"

"I have to wander over to Tom Butler's house to let them know JJ may have a drinking problem. Want to come?"

"Not the kind of afternoon I had in mind. I guess I could tag along, if we end up at my place later." He winked.

I wiggled my eyebrows. "And what's at your place?"

"Me. And a movie. And dinner later. And who knows? Maybe dessert before." He nuzzled my neck.

❋ ❋ ❋

Tom stood towering over his son. "My flask. I can't believe you took my flask. You're underage! Mrs. March could have turned you in! You're grounded. For a month."

JJ slunk up the steps to his room, his face mottled.

Tom's wife, Melanie, turned her gaze toward me. "Thanks for not letting Barbara know. She would have had to report it. He would have been suspended, if not worse."

Tom shook his head. "How can kids be so stupid?"

Melanie stood and put her hand in his. "We were kids once too."

"We weren't that bad."

"I seem to remember a time out at the lake—"

Tom kissed Melanie's forehead. "Enough about that. No need to bore Merry and Rob."

Rob stood. "We're not bored, but we really do need to get moving."

I got up, and we walked to the door. Tom opened it for us. "Did Jenny go with Jacob Winters to the dance?"

"Yes. He seems like a nice young man."

"His dad, Scott, was quite a fighter when he was younger, and I heard his temper led him into trouble at one of his posts. I called an old army buddy of mine to find out more about Scott when he moved into town."

"What happened?"

"I don't have all the details. He was going to look into it."

"You'll let me know what you find out?"

"Sure will." He held up the flask. "One good turn deserves another."

I strode out the door, Rob trailed behind me. I shook my head. "Jacob seems like such a nice kid. I hope his father isn't going to cause trouble."

"Until we know exactly what the trouble was, it's too soon to worry about it." He pulled me into a hug. "Now, how about wandering over to my place?"

"Sounds like a plan."

* * *

Rob's DVD collection spanned the entire wall of the guest bedroom. I ran my finger across the spines. "Are they in any particular order?"

"Of course." He pointed to the left side of the wall and moved his finger as he recited. "Comedies are in the first section, war movies are next, Romance is after that, and you can figure out the rest."

"They take up so much room. Why not just use Netflix?"

"When I started building my collection, Netflix wasn't around." He smirked. "I'm helping the environment by not pitching my DVDs."

I snickered. "Where are you hiding your Betamax?"

"Don't laugh. I still have movies in that format. Unfortunately my Betamax broke, and no one seems to know how to fix it." He lifted his chin. "It was the superior format."

I winked. "So they say. What would you suggest?"

He pulled out a DVD. "How about *Saving Private Ryan*?"

I tapped on a different one. "I think I'd prefer *French Kiss* instead. Kevin Kline is great, and I love Meg Ryan too."

"Good choice." He picked it up and strolled to the living room, stopping to place it in the Blu-ray player. "Fire on or off?"

I moved my hands up and down my arms. "On."

He flipped the switch, and I settled next to him on the sofa. Meg Ryan was wandering a vineyard when we adjourned to Rob's bedroom.

He beamed at me. "I get my wish. Dessert first."

In our robes later, we continued the movie.

His hand ran up and down my arm. "Who would you have chosen? Timothy Hutton or Kevin Kline."

"Kline, definitely Kline. I'd love to live on a French vineyard. The cheese and the bread. Oh, and I'm forgetting the wine. Definitely the wine."

"I defrosted chicken thighs. How do they, roasted potatoes, and a salad sound?"

"Sounds great. Do you use thyme on your thighs? I roast mine on high heat with the skin down. Then I turn them over for the rest of the time so the skin gets nice and crispy."

He handed me the tongs. "You are now officially in charge of the chicken."

I pulled the sash of my robe tighter and joined him at the stove. "I'm glad I left a robe here. It's more comfortable than your sweatshirt." I hugged him. "But your sweatshirt smelled like you, so that was pretty nice."

As we finished dinner the police radio squawked, then a calm voice read out some gobbledygook with numbers interspersed.

Rob leapt up. "Someone's dead. I have to go." He ran into the bedroom and threw on the clothes he had discarded on the floor.

I followed him, eyes wide. "Who died?"

"Don't know. I'll meet you back at your place if it's not too late." Grabbing his camera from a shelf, he buzzed me with a quick kiss, and hurtled out the door.

I shook my head. Lord, please don't let it be another murder.

Grabbing for my phone, I texted Jenny. "Where are you?"

My phone dinged. "Fiorella's." I let out the breath I didn't know I'd been holding.

"Everyone there?"

"Dad, Arianna, Jacob, and me."

I pulled an antacid from my purse and popped in my mouth. Then I locked up Rob's house and went home.

The cats wove around my legs as I tried to pace the length of the kitchen. Giving up, I refilled their cat bowls, and called Patty.

"Someone's dead."

She gasped. "Who?"

"I don't know."

"Then why did you call?"

"Because not knowing is driving me nuts."

Patty sighed. "Start at the beginning."

I told her about the police scanner and Rob's rapid departure. Just as I finished, the back door opened, and Rob walked in.

"Got to go." I hung up the phone. "What happened?"

My phone rang. It was Patty. "I can't believe you hung up on me."

"Sorry about that. Let me put you on speaker." I placed the phone on the counter. "Who died?"

Rob sat. "It was the florist, Jean Putty." He shook his head. "I just saw her earlier this week, when I ordered your flowers."

I moved next to him. "She wasn't that much older than us. Only fifty. Way too young."

Patty cleared her throat. "Poor Jean. She did such great flower designs. She had a pacemaker put in last year. Some kind of congenital defect. I guess it didn't work."

Rob waved his hand and shook his head.

I popped another antacid. "It wasn't her heart?"

"No."

Patty continued, "Well, she told me she had migraines. Oh my god, was it an aneurysm?"

Rob broke in. "Stop. It wasn't her heart or an aneurysm. She was strangled."

I gasped and sagged against him. "Another murder?"

"Looks that way. She was in the back of her shop. He used her lime-green grosgrain ribbon."

"He? Do they know who did it?"

Rob's brow furrowed. "I assumed it was a man, because strangling someone takes a lot of strength. The medical examiner reported it looked like she fought back. There was skin under her fingernails." He checked his notebook. "Her mother called the police late this afternoon. Apparently, they had a tradition of going out to dinner the day after Valentine's Day. She wasn't too worried when Jean didn't come home; sometimes she stayed out all night."

I tilted my head. "But if she was at the shop, why didn't anyone discover her body earlier?"

"It was closed. She never opens the day after Valentine's Day."

Patty piped in, "We'll have to take food to her mother. I'll call you tomorrow, and we can work together on it." She hung up.

"How could we have another murder in our small town?" I shivered. "I hope we all have alibis for this one."

CHAPTER 3

Jenny waltzed in the front door after her dinner with Drew and plopped next to me. "What a great dinner. You saw how beautiful Arianna is. She used to be a model. She's traveled all over the world." Jenny's eyes widened. "Mom, she's even been on the cover of *Vogue.*"

"That's nice."

"It's more than nice! It's super cool."

"I guess she has good genes."

Jenny rolled her eyes. "It's not just her looks. She's really smart. She speaks four languages. And she's so generous. She started a charity supplying books to kids in Africa."

"Sounds like the complete package."

"She is. I think you'd like her."

I coughed and reached for my glass of water. "I'm sure I will." *Great. Drew's new girlfriend is Superwoman.*

Jenny hopped off the sofa. "They want to take me skiing this weekend. Can I go?"

"How are you doing on your English paper?"

"It'll be done by Thursday."

"Then, yes, of course you can go."

She twirled in place and then danced up the stairs. "We're going to have such a great time!"

I gulped. Sure, I wanted her to like whomever Drew ended up with. But did she have to be so over the moon about her?

✳ ✳ ✳

Rob and I went to the ten-thirty Mass together. As it ended, I nudged him. "I want to ask Father Tom to follow-up with Drew." We hung back in our seats to let the crowd file out. My back-fence neighbors and good friends, Andy Perkins and his husband, Ed, spied us and stopped.

Andy nudged me. "Did you see Drew's new crush? Quite the dish. So exotic looking."

I frowned.

"Mustn't frown, Merry, you'll get wrinkles." Andy linked his arm with Ed's, and they continued down the aisle.

"It's a good thing I adore them both. Andy's humor leaves a bit to be desired."

The crowd thinned around Father Tom. "Now's our chance."

We exited the pew and made a beeline to Father Tom. "Do you have a moment?"

He shook his head. "I have an appointment in a half hour, but I have time."

"I wanted to ask if you would follow-up with Drew on the annulment paperwork."

"Why?"

I moved closer to him. "Because he hasn't filled it out yet."

"But he has, my dear. He and his friend Arianna dropped it off yesterday afternoon."

My mouth dropped. "What?"

His eyes crinkled. "I think he may want the annulment as much as you." He looked at his watch. "Good heavens. I need to get a move on. Talk to Belinda to arrange time if you have more questions."

Mouth still open, I stared at his departing back.

Rob waved his hand in front of my eyes. "This is great news, Merry. Why aren't you happy?"

I crossed my arms. "I am happy. Why would you think I'm not happy?"

He cupped my face. "Your body language, for one thing."

"It's just so fast."

Rob's face fell, as he stepped back. "You're having second thoughts."

My whole body felt hot, like the sun was beating on it. "No, not at all."

"Your words and your body aren't in sync. Why don't you call me when you figure out what you really want?" He turned on his heel and stalked out of the church.

He's right. What the heck is wrong with me?

I pulled out my phone and texted Patty. "Any time today?"

"An hour from now?"

"My place."

I stormed home. As I made my way into the kitchen, the cats gave me a wide-berth, seeming to sense my mood. I scowled as I made a peanut butter and jelly sandwich, poured a glass of milk, and sat.

Jenny pounded down the stairs and bounced into the kitchen.

"Is that all we have?"

"No. There's chicken and cheese."

She rummaged through the deli drawer, lifted the pouch of chicken, the one of cheese, grabbed the mayo, and put the lettuce container and the tomatoes on top. She started across the kitchen. The pile began to wobble, and the jar of mayo crashed to the ground, scattering glass across the floor.

I snapped, "Jenny, how many times do I have to tell you to make two trips?"

"I'll clean it up."

"Don't move. You don't have shoes on. This is why you should wear shoes."

She treated me to a major eye roll. "Fine. What do you want me to do?"

"Stay where you are." I retrieved my garden clogs from the garage and handed them to her. She slipped them on and stepped away from the mess.

"Where do you think you're going?"

"First you don't want me to clean it up, and now you do. Make up your mind."

I handed her a roll of paper towels. "Be careful. I'll get another jar of mayo from the cupboard and make you a sandwich."

Edging around the mess, I picked up the chicken from the counter and began to make her sandwich. "Cheese?"

"Yes, please. Lettuce and tomato, too, if it's not too much trouble."

Floor clean, she sat next to me at the counter and sighed. "Mom, you seem really tense lately. You need to chill. Arianna's into meditation, and she says it helps her. Maybe she can give you pointers."

"I don't need any pointers!"

"Whatever."

I stalked into the living room and paced. *What the heck is wrong with me?*

The back door opened. Jenny's voice echoed down the hallway. "Hi, Mrs. Twilliger. Be careful what you say to Mom today. She's in a bad mood. Tell her I'm leaving for the library." The door slammed shut.

Patty rounded the corner and caught me mid-turn. "What's going on?"

I sank onto the sofa and moaned, "I don't know."

She sat and put her arm around me. "Is it Drew? Did he tell Father Tom he wouldn't fill out the paperwork?"

I put my head in my hands. "It's worse. He did."

"I don't understand. He filled it out?"

"Yes."

She lifted my chin. "You are not making any sense. You should be celebrating."

I pulled a pillow to my stomach. "That's what Rob said."

Patty took a deep breath. "Talk."

"A goddess arrived yesterday to stay with Drew. She's perfect: perfect hair, perfect teeth, perfect cheekbones. And she's tall."

Patty touched my arm, interrupting my rant. "You think everyone is tall. I get it, she's beautiful. So what?"

"I know. I shouldn't care. But for some reason I do. Drew gave me a hard time Friday night. It looked like he wasn't going to complete the paperwork. Then Ms. Perfect arrives, and it's all signed, sealed, and delivered to Father Tom.

"This is going to sound silly. Maybe even childish. I don't want him back, but I don't want him to wind up with someone better than me either."

"No one could be better than you."

I gave her a wan smile and continued, "You haven't met her yet. Plus, Jenny can't stop talking about how great she is."

Patty put her feet up on the coffee table. "I think my best friend might be jealous."

"You may be right."

* * *

I tossed and turned most of the night. At five, I got out of bed and went to the kitchen to make blueberry muffins. While they were baking, I trudged to the living room and opened the door to one of the built-ins surrounding the fireplace. I pulled out a photo album and sat on the floor.

I took a deep breath, as I opened it. In the first series of pictures, we were having a picnic at the lake house. Jenny was around five, and Dad and Mom were still alive. Dad was flipping hamburgers at the grill, and Mom stood on tiptoes, giving him a kiss on the cheek. I bent to kiss the photo.

In the next snapshot, Drew was lying on his side on a wooden float fifteen yards from shore. The waves must have been bobbing it about, as the whole picture seemed tilted. A smile played on his face as Jenny was caught mid-air jumping into the lake. The next photo showed her proud doggy-paddle back to the float.

I flipped the page. Patty, Patrick, Drew and I sat in the Adirondack chairs around a roaring fire pit. Drew was kissing my hand and looking at me like I was the treasure he had waited for his whole life.

I shut the album and sobbed. I thought my life was perfect. How deluded I had been.

The alarm for the muffins rang. I straightened my shoulders and wiped my face. *He cheated on me with two different women, embezzled from our friends, and spent four years in prison.* I shoved the album back into the cupboard with a bang. Then I strode to the kitchen and took the hot muffins out of the oven, placing them on a trivet to cool.

I was applying the last bits of my makeup when Jenny poked her head around the door and gestured with the blueberry muffin. "I'm sorry about the mess yesterday. Thanks for the breakfast treat. I'll see you later."

As I left for work, I was pleased to see that the purple and green Lenten roses had started to push up around the magnolia tree. *Spring will be here soon.* Smiling, I strolled with a lighter step.

I texted Rob, "Sorry about yesterday. May I take you to dinner tonight to apologize? My treat."

"Fiorella's?"

"I'll make reservations."

The most important thing accomplished, I put my head down and dove into work. Several meetings, calls, and spreadsheets later, I left for home to freshen up before my date.

As I opened the door to the house, my phone dinged. "Dinner with Dad and Arianna. Home by nine."

I sank onto the kitchen stool. *It's a good thing that she likes her father's friend.* I sighed. *Keep repeating that mantra.* Moving into the half bath, I checked my reflection in the mirror. No changes, just regular old me. Leaning in closer, I inspected the beginnings of crow's feet at the corners of my eyes. *Maybe Botox?* I shuddered. *Nope!*

The back door opened, and Rob called out, "Anyone home?"

I made a quick swipe at my lips with lip gloss. "I'll be right there."

I joined him in the kitchen, and he gathered me into a hug. "What's going on with you?"

I spoke into his chest. "I hate to admit it, but I think I may be jealous of Drew's girlfriend."

He held me at arm's length. "Jealous because she's seeing him? You want to get back with him?"

"No, I definitely do not want to get back with him. Yuck. You know what he put me through."

"Then what?"

"It's Arianna. She's so good looking. And so accomplished. Jenny really admires her."

"Ah. It's all about the woman." He pulled me close. "I was worried it was about the man." He kissed me.

"Do you think I look old?"

"Only a day over twenty-one."

I gave him a big smile. "Let's go to dinner."

I was attacking Rob's tiramisu when my phone dinged with a text from Jenny: "When are you coming home?"

"Soon."

"Make it sooner."

"Are you okay?"

"No."

Rob's green eyes searched mine.

"It's Jenny. There's something wrong. We need to go."

Fifteen minutes later, we pulled into the drive. She barreled out the front door. "What took you so long?"

"We were over at Fiorella's. What's wrong?"

"Jacob's dad was arrested. For murder!"

CHAPTER 4

I put my arm around Jenny and steered her inside. We sat at the kitchen table. "Who is Mr. Winters supposed to have murdered?"

"The florist, Ms. Putty. Geez, Mom. How many other people have been murdered?"

I sat back. "Unfortunately, quite a few."

She rolled her eyes. "Those cases were all solved."

"How did he even know the florist?"

"I don't know. Jacob just texted me to say that his dad had been arrested for the murder. That's it. You have to help him, Mom. You and Mr. Jenson." She put her elbows on the table, hands clasped, and stared at me.

I groaned.

Rob put his hand over mine. "We'll do what we can, Jenny."

She hugged him. "I knew you'd help. I'll text Jacob." She ran out of the room.

My head drooped. "Another one. Even though I liked Jean, I was hoping we could leave this one to the police."

He rubbed my back. "Jenny would never forgive us if we didn't try to help."

I sighed. "You're right. Where should we start?"

"With Jay."

Rob stood and pressed speed dial on his phone. "Jay? What would you say to homemade chocolate chip cookies?" Rob chuckled. "Yes, Merry's making them."

I got up and pulled out my mixing bowls.

"Thirty minutes? See you then."

Rob turned to me and shrugged. "Sorry about the cookies. I felt a bribe was in order."

"That man does have a sweet tooth. You better get the coffee going."

The cookies had just been pulled from the oven when Jay opened the back door. "Something smells good in here." He pointed at the tray on the counter. "All warm and gooey, just the way I like them."

"They do have to cool for a minute or two."

"If you insist. What's up?"

"Jenny told me that you arrested Scott Winters for Jean's murder."

He picked up a cookie and tossed it from hand to hand. Then he blew on it, and took a bite. He sighed. "So good. Almost good enough for me to share information. A cup of coffee might tip me right over the edge."

Rob brought him a steaming mug.

He took a careful sip. "What's your connection to this? I understood when Drew was arrested and when Cindy was under suspicion, but why Scott Winters? He's new to town."

"His son, Jacob is dating Jenny."

"That's right. I forgot."

"So will you share information with us?" Rob held out the plate of cookies I had just assembled.

"May as well. You'll be involved no matter what I say." Jay took another cookie and pulled out his notepad. "It seems that Mr. Winters was seen arguing with Ms. Putty at her flower shop the day she was killed."

I picked up a cookie. "It's weird to think of someone new to town arguing with a florist. Didn't he like the flowers? She always did beautiful arrangements for me."

"According to a witness, the argument was not about the quality of the flowers, or her arranging abilities. It was about Desert Storm."

Rob's eyebrow rose. "Desert Storm?"

"Yes. Apparently Mr. Winters and Ms. Putty served at the same time in Kuwait. Mr. Winters was surprised to find Ms. Putty here. He'd apparently been searching for her for a long time." Jay referred back to his notes. "It gets confusing here. My witness said it was hard to hear what they were saying because she was outside the shop. Mr. Winters accused Ms. Putty of taking something. As he was leaving, he threatened her. He said, 'I could kill you for this,' and slammed the door to the shop."

I chewed slowly. "How could they have served together in Kuwait? That was back in the early nineties. I didn't think women were in combat then."

Rob said, "They were; the Government just didn't acknowledge it. I did a story on it when I was reporting in the Mideast back then."

I sighed. "I never thanked her for her service. She never marched on Veteran's Day. I would have remembered."

Rob touched my arm. "Some people want to forget."

"We celebrated the men who came back but we didn't do the same thing for her—"

Rob gave Jay a sidelong glance. "All you have on this guy is that he had an argument with Jean and threatened her?"

Jay stood. "That and the fact that he's a big guy with a history of violence."

I looked up at him. "What do you mean?"

"That's all I'm going to say on the subject. Thanks for the cookies." He nabbed one last one and sauntered out the door.

I dunked a piece of cookie into my coffee. "I think we're going to need to circle back with Tom Butler. I'll stop by his shop tomorrow."

Copying Jay, Rob snuck one last cookie on his way out. "Dinner tomorrow?"

"Sounds great. I'll cook."

I stopped by Jenny's room on my way to bed. The light from her lamp peaked from under the door. I rapped on the door. "Bedtime. Turn off your phone."

"One more minute."

I opened the door. "Now."

She groaned and put it down. I pulled up her covers and kissed her good night. "Sweet dreams. I'll see you in the morning."

I gingerly arranged myself in bed amongst the cats. My mind raced. How were we going to clear Scott Winters? Who would do such an awful thing? Will Drew's relationship with Arianna last? Courvoisier shifted into what was apparently a more comfortable position. She began to snore, and I soon followed her.

The next morning, I stopped by Tom Butler's pet store, Cuddly Companions and More. The sign above the door showed a dog and cat. The lab was on its side, and the cat was curled up against his chest. It was precious. It was a small shop, but it had a good selection. When I walked in, I could smell the cedar shavings from the hamster cages. I waggled my fingers at them as I strolled by.

Tom was helping a customer, so I perused the cat aisle looking for new treats and toys. There was a fishing pole with what looked like feathers at the end of a string. I picked it up and wiggled it, moving it up and down before putting it back on the shelf. *Don't want to train them to kill the birds in the backyard.*

I turned to one of the packages of dental treats and studied the ingredient list.

Tom joined me. "That's a good brand. It's the one I give my cat. I think Courvoisier and Drambuie would love it."

"I'll take it. Can't be too careful with tartar." I handed it to him, and we went to the register. "Did you find out anything more about Scott Winters?"

He glanced around quickly, and then motioned me closer. "Did you hear he was arrested for Jean's murder?"

I inclined my head.

"My friend got back to me and confirmed that Scott had a bad temper. It got worse after a close call with a Scud missile during Desert Storm. The combination of his headaches and heavy drinking made him a mean and scary guy to be around."

"You were in Desert Storm, weren't you?"

"I don't like to talk about it much, but yes, I was."

"Did you serve with Jean or Scott?"

"No, he was in a different platoon, but we both ended up enroute to Kuwait City at the same time. That's why I knew he was a fighter. It didn't take much to set him off back then, and when I checked with my buddy, he mentioned that when he knew him he was pretty much the same."

He shuddered. "I'll never forget all that oil being burned by the Iraqis. Strangest sight I've ever seen. The red flames and black smoke writhing along the sand. Almost as if the sand itself was on fire. It choked me." He grimaced and rubbed his nose. "And the smell. It was so acrid."

He cleared his throat and handed me the receipt. "Enough about that. Let me know what your cats think about the treats."

Halfway back to the office, I stopped in my tracks. He hadn't mentioned Jean. He also didn't seem surprised that she had been in Desert Storm.

Later that day, Rob showed up at my office, and we ambled to my house. I put my arm around his waist. "I hope you like chicken parmigiana, because that's what I defrosted."

"How big is your freezer? You always seem to have great stuff to eat."

"Thank you, but don't forget I have the one in the kitchen and the full size one in the garage. I like to binge prepare and freeze on the weekends so that my work during the week is that much less."

"That's a good idea. Healthier and more affordable than dinner or takeout."

"I'm not sure how much healthier it is, but it does keep costs down."

I tossed a salad while he set the table. Jenny joined us just as I pulled the chicken parm from the oven.

She leaned over the pan and waved the smell closer. "Yum. This looks great. Do we have any garlic bread?"

I pointed to the aluminum foil wrapped bundle on the counter. "Would you mind slicing it and putting it in that bowl?"

Jenny picked up the bundle and then dropped the bread back on the counter. She shook her hands and blew on her fingers. "This is too hot for me to slice."

Rob traded places with her and finished cutting the bread. Next, he filled wine glasses, and I poured Jenny a glass of milk.

Jenny speared a piece of chicken. "What have you found out about Mr. Winters?"

"Detective Ziebold said that he threatened Ms. Putty just before she was killed."

Jenny gulped. "That's strange. Is he sure? How did they even know each other?"

I told her about the Desert Storm connection.

"Jacob told me that his dad was pretty messed up for a long time. The last couple of years, he's been on a new miracle drug for his migraines. Jacob told me it's changed his dad's personality for the better. Plus, he gave up drinking two years ago. The couple of times I've met him, he was very nice."

"Maybe what I heard was old news. In any event, I don't want you at Jacob's house until this is resolved."

Jenny grabbed my hand. "I'll do that if you tell Detective Ziebold that he's changed. He couldn't have done this."

Rob took another piece of chicken. "He still threatened Ms. Putty."

Jenny sat back in her chair. "I know." She glanced at her phone.

"Jenny, you know the rules. No phones at the table."

She grinned. "Jacob's dad made bail. Isn't that great?"

I held my hand out for her phone.

She scowled and handed it to me. Then her face brightened. "I know. We should have them over for dinner. You need to get to know him. Once you meet him, you'll know he couldn't have done this."

"I'll think about it."

"But, Mom."

"Let's finish eating."

CHAPTER 5

At work the next morning, I straightened my desk, made sure my pencils were sharp, and lined them up. Then, sighing, I picked up the phone and dialed the number.

"Linda Winters."

"Hi, Linda, this is Merry March. I'm Jenny's mom."

"She's such a wonderful girl."

"Your son is such a nice young man. I was calling to see if you, Scott, and Jacob would be able to join us for dinner the Saturday after next." The phone was silent. "Linda?"

"I'm still here. It's just that we've been having difficulties lately and—" Her voice trailed off.

"I know your husband is out on bail. Believe it or not, I do know how difficult that is."

"Jacob told me that you have experience solving crimes."

"Just a few." I played with the pencil on my desk.

"I'm not sure."

"I think I can help."

"Do you really think so?" Her voice cracked. "We'll come."

"Great. Six o'clock."

I hung up the phone. The stuff I do for my daughter.

My stomach growled. I walked up the block to Tempting Treasures and Tasty Treats, the antiques and tea shop the neighbors behind me recently expanded. The waiting area contained an old wooden church pew, which was made more comfortable by the addition of a thick gray and black stenciled cushion. My fingers trailed over an eighteenth century writing desk. I flipped the price tag toward me and gasped. *Not in this lifetime.* The tea room's walls were covered in a beautiful, yet restrained, floral wallpaper, and the crowded room boasted a number of small café style tables that were covered in white linen. In the spring, the shaded back deck would enable them to serve twice the amount of customers.

Andy approached. "On your own today?"

I nodded.

"As you can see, we're full today. I have a spot for you over here if you don't mind sharing a table." He grinned and waved me toward him. I followed, turned the corner, and came to a complete stop. Andy gestured to Arianna Flores's table. She was perusing the menu, so I shook my head, my eyes pleading with him.

He chuckled. "Arianna, would you mind if Merry joined you?"

She looked up. "No, I don't mind." She gestured to the seat across from her.

I held out my hand as I sat. "Merry March."

She shook it. "I know. It's nice to finally meet you."

She spoke with a faint accent, which only served to enhance her exotic looks. Even more stunning close up, she wore a dark purple cable-knit turtleneck and form fitting black wool slacks. Her eyes were the color of gingerbread and her skin looked sun-kissed. Arianna wouldn't even need makeup to play a Bond girl. *Ugh.*

I put my napkin in my lap. "Where are you from originally?"

"Venezuela, but I left when I was fourteen to pursue my modeling career. I think of myself as a citizen of the world today."

I picked up the menu to scan it and put it back on the table. "Where did you meet Drew?"

"In Jamaica. I was climbing down Dunn's River Falls in Ocho Rios, and he and Jenny were climbing up." She gave a throaty chuckle. "It was a good thing too, because the rocks were a bit slippery, and I crashed right into him." She studied me. "Have you been to Jamaica?"

"Just once. It was beautiful. I remember the falls and the enormous Banyan trees at the top. Their roots looked like legs."

"You should go to Africa. The Acacia trees there reminded me of the Banyan, but upside down. Of course, the Banyan trees are much taller." She pulled out her phone and showed me a picture. "You have to imagine it without leaves."

"I see what you mean."

Andy appeared at my elbow. "Are you ready to order?"

"What's good here, Merry?" Arianna asked.

"I know it sounds like a cop out, but everything Ed makes is wonderful." I turned to Andy. "Can I get the crab cake special and chai tea? I love the remoulade, and his ciabatta bread is to die for."

"That does sound good."

Andy took down my order and turned to Arianna. "What have you decided on?"

"I'll have the same, but put the crab cake on a salad with dressing on the side. Oh, and no bread."

"To drink?"

"Spring water."

I gave her an appraising glace as Andy walked away. "I envy your will power."

Her laugh tinkled across the shop. "You think this is bad? I never ate while I was modeling." She grimaced. "It was such a stressful time for me."

"You still look terrific."

"Old habits die hard." She put her napkin in her lap. "Tell me about yourself. I know that you've done a great job raising Jenny. She's such a lovely girl. Not always with her face in her phone."

"She gets in her phone time, believe me. You must be catching her on her good days." I paused. "Drew or Jenny may have mentioned this to you, but I own a property and casualty insurance shop in town."

"Impressive. Your own business."

My face flushed with pride. "It's hard work, but I really enjoy it." I scooted my chair closer to the table. "What about you?"

"I saved my modeling money. No drinking or drugs for me." She patted her face. "I wanted to be able to keep this going as long as I could. I studied finance in my spare time to make sure I was investing well. Now most of my time is spent managing my money and giving back."

"Jenny's so impressed with your charitable foundation."

"That's sweet."

Our food arrived. I felt vaguely guilty about enjoying my sandwich while Arianna picked at her salad.

She put her fork down. "Drew and I met with Father Tom last weekend. We gave him the annulment papers."

"Father Tom mentioned it." I took another bite and chewed slowly. *Where is she going with this?*

Andy loomed over the table. "Everything okay here ladies?" He topped off our water glasses.

I snapped, "Just fine," to his retreating back.

"I'd like us to get along, Merry. We don't have to be friends, but I really like Drew. I think he could be what I've been searching for."

"Jenny is my first priority. Having a good relationship with the person in Drew's life will make everything easier."

She smoothed her slacks, stood, and held out her hand. "I'm glad we had this impromptu lunch. Thanks for joining me. It was good to meet you."

I shook her hand.

Before her seat got cold, Andy moved in. He crossed his legs and leaned toward me. "So dish. What did the exotic princess have to say?"

"She's not a princess."

"Looks like one to me."

"You sat me here on purpose."

"Oops. Got to go! That couple wants their check."

I rolled my eyes.

✳ ✳ ✳

My assistant, Cheryl, knocked on my door and poked her head in. "Got a few moments for Melanie Butler?" I nodded, and she ushered Melanie in.

"Hi, Merry. I hope you don't mind me dropping by like this, but I had something on my mind."

"Not at all. What can I help you with?"

She handed me a sample-sized bag of cat treats. "Before I forget, Tom wanted you to try these out on your cats, he's not sure if he should carry them. Let me know what your cats think." She put her purse on the chair next to her. "The reason I'm here is that I'm not sure we have enough life insurance on Tom. Jean dying so suddenly made me nervous. What if something happened to him?" She stood and paced the room. "I know it's silly, but they both served in Kuwait. It made me realize that bad things can happen when you least expect it."

I pulled a water bottle out from the small fridge under my desk and handed it to her. "It's not silly at all. I'd be happy to talk you through it. Just give me a second to pull up your file on my computer." I handed her a life insurance worksheet. "While you're waiting, you may want to give this a glance."

She sat and took a sip of water. "Thanks. Wow. This looks pretty detailed."

36

"It's important to know what your continuing expenses might look like in order to determine the amount of coverage you should have. Let's work through it together."

I led her through the worksheet, and by the end of the conversation we agreed that she might want to obtain additional insurance.

"Thanks for your help. Tom and I will take a look at this together later this week."

"Don't forget the paperwork."

She picked it up and flashed me a smile as she shut the door.

✳ ✳ ✳

Rob and I were enjoying a glass of wine before dinner when Jenny bounded in. "I heard you had lunch with Arianna today. Isn't she the best?"

"She seemed nice."

"We should have her and Dad over for dinner too."

"I'll think about it."

Her face fell. "You didn't like her."

I strode over to give her a hug. "Of course I do. I'm just not ready to socialize with both of them yet."

Jenny's eyes widened, and she hugged me back. "I'm sorry. You're right. It might be awkward. Call me when dinner's ready." She ran up the stairs.

I sat on the window seat. A loud roar startled me. Rob ran to the window. "If I'm not mistaken, that's a brand new Lamborghini Huracan."

"That's a hot looking car. And it's the color it should be; fire-engine red. I wonder who owns it."

Drew clambered out of the driver's seat and Arianna out of the passenger side. My mouth dropped open. "What does a car like that go for?"

"Starts at two hundred thousand."

I raised an eyebrow.

He put up his hand as if to stop me. "Not that I ever looked at one. Not seriously, anyway."

"Do you think Arianna—oh. His inheritance from his murdered girlfriend must have paid out." I sat back down and buried my face in my hands.

Rob rubbed my back, continuing to stare out the window. "It's a beauty."

"I'm sure it is. How long do you think it will take to be the talk of the town?"

My phone dinged. Patty's text read: "Lamborghini? Really?"

CHAPTER 6

The next morning came far too early. I stretched and rubbed my still-closed eyes. They shot open. A Lamborghini? Please tell me I dreamt that part. I slipped out from under the covers and padded over to my bathroom window. *Nope. No dream.* It looked even better this morning. I yawned. *Guess it's going to be an exciting day.*

I pulled on slacks and a turtleneck. Wandering downstairs, I turned on the coffee and then ambled to the window seat. Ed and Andy were circling the car, grins splitting their faces. Drew walked out his back door and beeped the doors open. He joined them as they leaned into the car. The interior was sumptuous black leather.

Jenny came up behind me. "What are you looking at?"

"Your dad's new car."

She squealed. "It's beautiful." She threw on her shoes and pulled her coat over her pajamas.

"Jenny, get dressed first."

"I'll only be a minute." The door banged shut, and within seconds she joined the rest of the people ogling the car.

It looks fast. I wonder what it would feel like to drive it.

The cats claimed my attention, demanding food. I complied and poured myself a cup of coffee. When I returned, they were studying the engine in the rear of the car. Rob had joined the gaggle of onlookers. Jenny was sitting in the driver's seat pretending to turn the wheel. I had a flashback of her sitting on her dad's lap in our old Ford pickup as he slowly drove down the road.

Smiling, I turned to get breakfast ready. My phone dinged. Patty texted: "Patrick wants to see the car."

"Rob's already out there."

Jenny swept back in. "It's cold."

"Maybe if you had something on, other than PJs, it might help."

She rolled her eyes. "Dad promised he'd take me for a spin later."

I walked back to the window. The hood was propped open, and Drew was pointing out something to Rob and Patrick. *Wow. Doesn't look like you could stow much more than a briefcase in there.*

I turned back to Jenny. "Scrambled eggs and bacon okay?"

"I'll set places at the counter."

"Better set one for Rob. I have a feeling he'll be hungry."

There was a quick knock, the back door opened, and Rob sailed in. "That car is fantastic."

"Didn't look like it had much storage space."

Rob patted my arm. "You don't buy a Lamborghini for the storage space."

I cracked the eggs. "Did you have breakfast yet?"

He looked sheepish. "No. I heard that everyone was looking at the car so I hurried over."

Jenny beamed. "It's the best. I'm going for a drive with Dad later."

I put plates in front of Rob and Jenny, and then came around the counter to sit. "It's not going to take people too long to put together that Drew got his inheritance." I gave Rob a measured glance. "I really don't want to have to relive that."

"They won't blame you. Who knows? They may think Arianna bought it for him."

"One can only hope."

Jenny finished eating and put her plate in the sink. "Good breakfast, Mom."

She left the room, and Rob began filling the dishwasher. "The Home and Garden Show is today, feel like going? I want to get some shots for the paper."

"Sounds like fun. It'll get me in the mood for spring." We walked outside to his Audi and slid in.

Rob sighed, looking at Drew's car. "I used to love this car."

"This car is great." I stroked the seats. "Nice and comfy."

"His car is sexy, and my car is comfy. Is that supposed to make me feel good?"

I stroked his arm. "I think you're sexy. With or without your car."

He laughed and put the car in drive.

As we waited in line for tickets, three different people came up to me and asked how Drew could afford the car he bought. I told them that they'd have to ask him.

Jay and Barbara joined the end of the line. Jay waved. "Wait for us if you want to go through the show together."

Rob bought the tickets, and we moved to the side to wait. I sniffed. "I can smell the hyacinths from here." Craning my neck, I spied flowering pink dogwoods paired with deep burgundy azaleas, light pink cyclamens, and white hyacinths. They bordered a meandering path. "So pretty."

Jay put his change in his wallet. Barbara grinned. "It smells like spring."

I pulled on Rob's hand. "Let's go. I can't wait to see everything."

We wandered the paths. One of the exhibits featured a pergola heavy with wisteria blooms. My eyes widened. "How do they do that?"

Barbara strode forward to touch it. "Magic."

Rob and Barbara moved ahead to look at the tiny house display. Jay asked, "Could you live in three hundred square feet?"

"I'm ashamed to tell you that I couldn't. Give me my excessive eighteen hundred any day. Plus, I like toilets that flush."

"I heard about Drew's car." His eyes narrowed.

I stared at him.

"People are going to be upset once they realize how he paid for it. A lot of people think it was money he shouldn't have gotten."

"But his girlfriend left him it to him."

Jay leaned forward. "People aren't stupid. She didn't have that kind of money. They're going to figure out he gave it to her to hold for him, just like you did." He sighed. "I was hoping that Drew would play it low key."

"He's never been one to play it safe. How bad do you think it will get?"

He shifted his weight from one foot to another. "If you talk to him, you might want to pass along my warning."

Rob poked his head out of the tiny house. "Merry, you need to see this bathroom. It has a full size tub."

"Now we're talking." I grabbed Rob's outstretched hand and walked into the house.

* * *

Drew pulled out of the driveway with Jenny. Arianna waved to them. I hesitated and then strode over to her. "Flashy car."

"It's a dream to ride in."

I cleared my throat. "Normally this would be none of my business, but it's important. Did Drew tell you about his time in prison?"

"Yes. We don't have secrets from each other. He's changed. He told me that prison reformed him. Why are you bringing this up now?"

I stared straight at her. "To warn you. This is a small town and emotions run high. Especially as it relates to Drew. The people here feel Drew betrayed them."

"He paid everyone back."

I snorted. "I paid everyone back from the money Drew had left in his accounts. But there wasn't enough to pay the gains he promised. There was only enough to cover their investment."

"I'm confused. He used an inheritance from his girlfriend to pay for the car. It wasn't the town's money.

"That would make sense if she had money to leave him. But everyone knew she didn't. It won't take them long to figure out she hid it for him. I can't prove it, but I think the money she left him was the profits the town never saw."

She looked thoughtful. "And the car is rubbing it in their faces?"

"Yes."

"I'll talk to him." She turned on her heel and went back into Drew's house.

The Lamborghini screeched into the driveway. Drew and Jenny laughed as they climbed out.

I tapped my foot. "I'd appreciate it if you didn't drive like that when Jenny's in the car."

"He was just showing me what it could do," Jenny protested.

"Whatever." I walked back inside.

Jenny followed me. "Mom, relax. You're so tense."

"I'm not tense."

"Yes, you are." She ran up the stairs.

Courvoisier jumped up next to me. I petted her. "You'd be tense too if you lived next to your lying, cheating ex-husband."

She purred and butted my hand with her head. "All you want is more pets, don't you."

I could have sworn she smirked.

I picked up my phone and texted Patty. "Free time this afternoon?"

"Three-thirty? My place?"

"Works."

I tossed a load of wash in and turned on the machine. Then I settled on the sofa with my book. I jumped when my phone alarm buzzed. It was time to leave.

While I sauntered over to Patty's house, I enjoyed the brisk air. Not too cold. *Spring is definitely around the corner.* I bounded up her back stairs and let myself into the kitchen. She was mixing a pitcher of lemonade. "Want some?"

"Would love some. Rob and I went to the Home and Garden Show today, and it really put me in the mood for spring."

She handed me a glass, and I took a sip. "You know, for a mix, this isn't too bad."

"Thank you for that back-handed compliment. Some of us prefer to spend our time on important things, not squeezing lemons. Let's go to the living room."

I sank into the couch and put my glass on a coaster. "Have you seen the car yet?"

"Not up close. It was a blur as he came roaring down the street. He ought to be more careful or he's going to get a ticket. I bet the police are just chomping at the bit to give him one, if only to get a closer look."

"I've always heard that people with red cars get more tickets."

"If that's true, I'm sure that the stats for an expensive red car are even worse."

"Have you heard any talk about where he got the money?"

"Half of the town is saying it was his ill-gotten gains from swindling them. The other half is insisting that Arianna is his new sugar mama."

"Let's hope they believe the latter." I stood and walked to the fireplace. I lifted a picture of Patty's family. Her youngest son was on the tire swing, and the rest of the family posed around him. "Is this new?"

"The photographer took it last fall. It's taken me this long to get a frame for it."

"It's nice."

"We like it. You should get a new one taken of you and Jenny."

I put the photo down and sat.

"My sources say you had lunch with Arianna yesterday."

"I did."

"And?"

"She's nice. Even more beautiful up close, if you can believe it."

"Did she invite you to lunch?"

"No. Andy thought it would be funny to seat us together. They were slammed, but I could have waited."

She shook her head. "That man has a warped sense of humor."

"He does."

"You look tense."

"That's what Jenny keeps on telling me." I sipped my lemonade. "She may be right. Her solution is for me to go all 'new age' and meditate like Arianna."

"Lots of people meditate. It's a big business now. There are quite a number of books and apps devoted to mindful living."

"It's just that I hate to have Drew's new girlfriend be held up as a shining beacon."

Patty raised one eyebrow. "I repeat. I do believe you are jealous."

My eyes slid from hers. "Perhaps."

"And tense."

"Definitely tense."

She reached into her purse. "Lucky for you, I have a solution. I got a flyer in the mail for a new spa that opened up in the city." She held it up. "Ten percent off, and their massages get good ratings."

I held up my hand to stop her. "I don't want one of those deep tissue ones. I'm a wimp."

"Okay. I'll book both of us Swedish massages and tell them to go easy on you. We'll have lunch afterward. I've been looking for an excuse to pamper myself."

"Now that's settled can we talk about what I wanted to talk about?"

"Yes, of course."

"Was there anyone else in town who served in Desert Storm?"

"Why?"

I plumped the throw pillow and put it behind me. Settling back, I continued, "I'm not sure. Jean served, and she was there. Scott's accused of killing her, and he was there. I just want to identify who all the players are."

She leaned back in the chair and tapped her pencil on her chin. "Let me think. The only other person I can think of is John Little."

CHAPTER 7

J enny placed cheese and crackers on the counter, along with wine glasses, assorted sodas, and iced tea. I put an ice bucket nearby and checked the freezer to make sure the ice bin was full. As Jenny turned her attention to setting the dining room table, I hurried down the hall toward her. "Don't forget to get out the candles."

She rolled her eyes, waved the candles, and stuck them into the holders. "I have set the table before."

I hugged her for a minute, and then she broke away. "Let me finish. They're going to be here any minute."

The back door opened. "Anyone home?" Rob stuck his head around the corner and held out a cake box.

"Oh good, you remembered. Did you get the strawberry cream?"

"Yes. I'll put it in the fridge."

I followed him back to the kitchen. "Better let me. It's kind of full." I opened the door and shook my head. "Too full. You'll need to put it in the garage." He took it from me.

He walked back in. "What's the plan for tonight?"

"Get as much information from the Winters as they are willing to share."

The doorbell rang. Rob looked toward the living room. "You can tell they're new to town; they didn't come to the back door."

I playfully shoved his shoulder. "Be nice."

He gave me a quick kiss on the lips, and we joined the Winters in the living room. My eyes widened. *That is one big man. His hands. So large.*

Jenny took their coats, and Rob asked, "What would everyone like to drink?"

Jacob piped in with, "Root beer."

Scott agreed. "The same for me."

A small glass of white wine, if you have it," murmured Linda.

Rob retreated with Jenny to the kitchen.

Linda glanced around. "Your home is so beautiful."

I smiled. "Thanks, we love it. Have a seat."

Jenny returned with the cheese and crackers and deposited the tray on the coffee table. She perched on the arm of Jacob's chair. Rob came in with the drinks. He raised his glass, "To new friends."

We toasted. I said, "I hope everyone likes chicken."

"Love it." Scott leaned forward to put cheese on a cracker. His sweater inched up his arm, exposing a deep scratch that was just beginning to scab.

I gasped. "That looks like it hurt."

He tugged his sweater back down. "I was stacking boxes in the basement and put the last one a little too high. There was a nail sticking down from the rafter, and it really got me."

"I hope your arm doesn't get infected."

"No worries. Linda made me clean it, and my tetanus shot is up to date."

We moved into the dining room. Jenny and Jacob helped bring everything out. Dinner breezed along as we got to know each other better. Once the cake was cut, Jenny turned to Scott. "I told Jacob that my mom and Mr. Jenson have solved a few mysteries. I asked, and they've agreed to help you."

Scott leaned back in his chair. "I appreciate it Jenny, but I'm sure that the police will find the guilty person."

Linda touched his arm. "How can you be so sure? I'm scared."

I passed Scott a piece of cake. "We have had some experience. My ex-husband was suspected of murder last year, and we uncovered the guilty party. And prior to that my best friend's daughter was accused. We found who really committed that crime too." I leaned forward. "I don't want to be blunt, but I've found the police do a great job until they settle on a suspect. Once they do they quit looking. Unfortunately, in this case, that suspect is you."

Linda paled. "It's a nightmare. I don't know how they could believe Scott would be capable of such a thing."

Scott squeezed Linda's hand. "I'm not, and I appreciate your support." He turned to me. "I guess if you're willing to help, I'm willing to listen."

Rob cleared his throat. "We're going to have to ask you some questions. They might be uncomfortable."

"Bring them."

"We heard that you have quite a temper."

Jenny inhaled. "Mr. Jenson. That's a bit rough. You're supposed to help."

Scott twisted his napkin. "It's okay. It's no secret that I was a hot head when I was younger. I thought everything could be settled with these." He raised his fists. "But then I met Linda, and we had Jacob. I was happier than I'd ever been. I knew that, unless I changed, I'd lose everything that was dear to me." He lifted Linda's hand to his lips and kissed it.

"So I enrolled in anger management classes. They gave me the tools I needed to dial back my temper in tough situations. Then Desert Storm happened. We were on the march to Kuwait City, and a Scud missile landed way too close to our vehicle. I was the lucky one. I only had a brain injury. Everyone else died." He took a sip of his root beer. "It gave me headaches. Nothing the V.A. did seemed to help. That's when I started drinking. When I was drunk, all the lessons I learned disappeared."

Linda moved her hand in small circles on his back. "It's okay. That's not who you are now."

He smiled at her. "That's right. Luckily, they found a drug that helped. It was like a miracle. My headaches went away. I stopped drinking. I've been sober for two years."

Rob leaned forward. "That's a big accomplishment."

"It is. I don't take it for granted. I'm determined not to slip up."

I poured tea into Scott's cup. "How did you know Jean?"

He groaned. "Our platoons bivouacked together with the support group she was in on the way to Kuwait City. She had an affair with Jim Jefferson, one of my buddies." He rubbed his eyes. "He was one of the people killed in the Scud attack. He had a girl back home he wanted to marry. We were scared, all those fires. It wasn't right, but he found comfort in Jean's arms. He thought they both knew it was a temporary thing. He showed me the ring he was going to give to the girl back home. He carried it all the way to Kuwait with him to remind him what he was fighting for. His family came from money, and it was a large sparkler.

"I woke up in the hospital in Germany. When I got back stateside, I asked my Sergeant if his girlfriend got the ring. He told me they didn't find it on Jim. I figured Jean took it. I ran into her a year later when I was stationed in Texas and asked her about it. She denied having the ring. I threatened her, and that's when I ended up in the stockade. She was transferred out, and I never saw her again until the other week when I shopped for flowers for Linda. I just saw red. Everything came flooding back. So, yes, I threatened her."

He looked me straight in the eye. "It just burns me that Jim's girl never got to have that ring. She should have gotten it. I don't know, maybe it would have given her comfort. His girl was nice enough to write me when I was convalescing. I felt so bad for her; she was devastated by his death."

Linda took his hand. "Hopefully time helped her heal. I think Jim would be happy if she was able to move on with her life."

He gripped her hand tightly. "What if it had been me? Could you have moved on? Would you have been able to be happy?"

"Jim, that hurts." He dropped her hand. "I would have missed you terribly. But hopefully, with time, I would have learned that missing you didn't mean the end of my life. I'm so blessed you survived." She touched his face. "I love you."

Jacob shifted in his seat. "Dad, maybe it's time to go."

"You're right. Merry, thanks for the wonderful meal."

Rob, Jenny, and I made short work of ferrying everything to the kitchen. Rob loaded the dishwasher, and Jenny put the tablecloth and napkins in the washing machine. She leaned into the kitchen. "What did you think?"

I toweled a wine glass dry. "I thought it was a sad story. He suffered a lot. But he admitted he used to have an anger management issue. And I didn't like his reaction at the end. He hurt Linda's hand. I don't want you to go over there until this whole things resolved."

Jenny wheedled, "Jacob needs my support."

"He can have it. Just not at his house."

"Okay. Need anything else?"

"Thanks for your help today."

She ran in and kissed me. "Thanks for doing this." She turned and bounded up the stairs.

I stopped putting the leftovers in the fridge. "You've been awfully quiet. What do you think?"

Rob wiped the counter. "That was quite a scratch on his arm. Don't forget what was in the medical examiner's report. Jean fought back."

I shuddered. "It did look bad. Jacob is such a sweet kid. It's hard to believe his father is a murderer. Plus, why would Scott kill for a ring that didn't even belong to him?"

"I'm not sure why he was so positive Jean took the ring to begin with. If it was that large a stone, plenty of men might have taken it."

I lifted my shoulders. "I guess he just thought it was more likely that a woman took it. Especially one who was sleeping with Jim." I closed the refrigerator door. "Jean's mother was so broken up at the funeral. Patty and I should pay her a call."

* * *

The closed heavy drapes made the house seem somber. When Martha opened the door, a faint haze of dust mites danced about her. The air seemed stale, and the house was hot. She looked skeletal; her clothes hung off her like they were three sizes too large. I gulped. "We stopped by to see how you were doing."

Martha extended her arm toward the living room. "You never expect to outlive your child. I was so worried when she went to Kuwait. I thought I might lose her then." She sighed and pulled her sweater close. "It's hard to believe that she died here, in Hopeful. I guess I should feel blessed that I had her for as long as I did. It just hurts so much." She dabbed the corner of her eyes with a tissue.

"I can't even imagine the pain you must be going through."

Patty held out a coffee cake. "We thought you might like something sweet."

Her half smile quivered as she sat. "I made tea."

"May I?" I poured.

She put a spoonful of sugar in hers and stirred it. "It's been lonely. I don't feel up to going out yet, so I do appreciate it when people visit."

Patty cut a large piece of the coffee cake and put it on a plate. She offered it to Martha. "I know that apple and cinnamon is your favorite."

"It is, dear. I haven't been eating much lately, but that looks tempting." She took the plate and ate a forkful. "This is good."

I put my plate down. "I used to love visiting Jean's shop. She had such lovely flowers. Her arrangements were always so distinctive."

"They were."

Patty expanded on the theme. "She did my friend Becky's wedding flowers. She had the loveliest bouquet I'd ever seen. It was a riot of white roses, stephanotis, and sweet pea. So fragrant and so beautiful."

"She had so much talent."

I broke off another piece of the coffee cake with my fork. "My earliest memory of Jean is from when she owned the shop. Was she ever married?"

Martha waved her hand. "Oh, no. She was way too independent for that. She was always strong willed, and being in the Army just further honed her edges. I always hoped that she'd change her mind. I would have loved grandchildren." She dabbed her eye again.

"So there was never anyone special?"

"She had beaus, sure, but none that she was serious about."

Patty poured more tea. "I'm sorry she never fell in love."

"She had a full life with many friends. I'm happy for that."

I stood. "We don't want to tire you." I motioned to Patty with my eyes.

Patty rose. "We're so sorry for your loss, Martha. We'll be back soon to visit." We hugged her, and then strolled toward Patty's house.

"It was so warm in there."

"And depressing. We need to go back. It's not good for her to be alone."

"Those drapes. They didn't let in one iota of light." I shuddered. "I don't know what I'd do if I lost Jenny."

"I know what you mean. If I lost any of my kids, I wouldn't survive it."

We walked into Patty's kitchen. She opened the fridge. "Soda?"

I filled two glasses with ice. We sat at the counter. "If Jean took the ring, Martha never saw it."

"She's been living with her mom since she left the service five years ago. Maybe she sold it?"

"Jean just didn't seem to be that kind of person. I know I've been fooled before, but I can't see her taking the ring. If she did, I can't see her selling it."

"And I can't see her taking it out of spite."

* * *

Rob and I sat in my living room after dinner. The fire was lit, and his arm was around me. I sighed. "This feels so cozy."

He kissed my forehead. "It does."

"What did you think about what Jean told Patty and me?"

"Unless she hid the ring somewhere in her room, I think her mom would have known about it. Plus, why take it if you're not going to create a story around it?"

I shifted away from him to look in his eyes. "What do you mean?"

"She could have kept it and worn it. When she came back here her narrative could have been that her fiancé was killed. Everyone would have sympathized with her."

My eyes narrowed. "But she didn't. Plus, even if she had wanted to she wouldn't have taken the chance that John or Tom would recognize it."

He shrugged. "It could have happened. But it didn't in this case."

I leaned back against his chest. "She just didn't seem like the kind of person who would steal anything."

"She seemed pretty nice to me too." He caressed my arm. "What's next?"

"Three things. First, talk to John Little, since Patty told me he also served in Desert Storm. Second, follow-up with Tom Butler because I think he purposely didn't tell me that he knew Jean. And third—" I shuddered. "Offer to help Martha go through Jean's things."

"How can I help?"

"Patty and I will handle the third one. I'll work on the second, since I had the conversation with Tom. Will you see what you can get out of John?"

"Happy to help. I was thinking about calling him anyway. He wants to get publicity around the grand reopening of the VFW hall. They've apparently done it up right."

CHAPTER 8

Patty picked me up for our trip into the city. I slid into the passenger seat. "I don't have time for this. I don't know why I let you talk me into going to the spa. It's expensive and time consuming."

She chortled. "You're in the car. We're going. Why don't you lean your seat back and try to relax. The way you're protesting just proves how much you need this visit."

"Did you request a female masseuse?"

"Yes."

I reclined the seat. "Good."

Patty shook my shoulder. "Wake up, sleepy head. You really did relax. If you were any more relaxed you'd be comatose."

We changed into robes and met in the cozy tearoom. The centerpiece of the room was a rock studded wall with water dancing down it. I sat on the off-white chaise lounge facing the wall and crossed my feet. "This is peaceful. I love the sound of water."

Patty slid onto the chair next to mine. "Did you notice that the sandals massaged your feet when you walk?"

I giggled. "The best."

An attendant walked in. "May I bring you something to drink?"

Patty piped up, "We'll both have a mimosa."

My mouth dropped. "It's not even eleven."

"So? A mimosa is officially a brunch drink, which means it's acceptable to drink before noon."

The attendant tilted her head. I shrugged. "She's the boss. Make it two mimosas."

Patty's eyes crinkled. "I knew you'd see things my way."

The attendant returned with two full champagne glasses. Patty lifted hers. "To less tension."

"I'll drink to that."

The door to the tearoom opened, and Arianna walked in. The muscles in my neck clenched.

She strode to my chair. "You must have gotten one of those advertisements too."

"Patty did."

The attendant stood waiting. Arianna turned. "I'll have water with two cucumber slices." She gestured to the chair next to Patty. "May I join you?"

I groaned, under my breath, and then forced a smile. "Of course."

Patty looked Arianna up and down. "You look like you've been here a while."

She stretched in her chair, yawning. "My massage was at eight, and I've had my toes and fingernails done." She displayed her purple bedecked toenails.

"How pretty. Are you done?"

"I still have some maintenance work scheduled." She gestured at fine lines in her brow.

Patty leaned closer. "I don't see anything."

Arianna glowed. "That's because I keep on top of things. I get my injections every four months like clockwork." She eyed the glasses in our hands. "Alcohol is very drying. And caloric." She held up her ice water. "This is so much better for you." Arianna sunk farther into her chair. "If this doctor does a good job on my face, I'll give both of you his name. It's better to get started early."

Patty flinched. "If you had four kids you'd know that I earned every one of these wrinkles. I prefer to think of them as badges of honor."

The attendant came to retrieve Arianna. She rose. "Ladies, there is no shame in correcting nature. I've already had these lifted." She pointed to her chest. "It's important not to let things go." She followed the attendant out the door.

I drained my mimosa and laughed.

Patty shoved my knee. "What's so funny?"

"When I thought everything about her was natural, I was so envious. Now that I know it's not, I don't care."

The attendants called our names, and I followed mine to my room. The massage was just what I needed. After a quick shower to remove the oil, I rejoined Patty. "You look relaxed."

"You don't look so bad yourself."

"Lunch?"

She stood. "I thought you'd never ask. Do you mind if we go back to Hopeful? I have some things I need to do this afternoon."

She drove us back, and we walked into the Golden Skillet. The waitress sat us in one of the high-back red pleather booths and handed us menus.

The special was shrimp and grits. I pointed to the listing. "I know what I'm getting."

Patty donned her cheaters and read the description. "Oh. It has andouille sausage. Nice and spicy, just the way I like it. I'm going to join you." We placed our order, and caught up on the antics of our children.

A voice rose from the booth behind me. "I don't know why you aren't worried. Now that Jean's gone, they could be next." My eyes widened. I gestured toward the booth. Patty leaned forward.

"There's no reason why someone would want to kill Tom or John."

"Tom's been so distracted lately. I know that they weren't exactly poster children in the army. What if their past misdeeds caught up with them?"

"No one is going to care about pranks thirty years later. For goodness sakes, do you even remember what you were doing that long ago?"

I strained, lifting in my seat, trying to see over the back of the booth, but it was too tall.

"Back in the day, they were all close. I'm scared. Why did that Scott Winters have to come to town? Everything was fine before he arrived."

"Melanie, there's no reason to be afraid."

"I can't lose Tom. But if I do I'm going to be protected. I've already spoken with Merry about additional life insurance. You should do the same. Before it's too late."

I shuddered. The voices moved away. I peered around the booth. Melanie Butler and Nancy Little strode out the door. I turned back to Patty. "They've left."

Patty's eyes widened. "Was that Melanie and Nancy?"

"It was."

"What kind of pranks could Tom and John have done that would get them killed almost thirty years later?"

CHAPTER 9

"Surprised to see you back so soon." Tom Butler arranged leashes on a display. "Out of food already?"

"The cats have been behaving themselves lately, so I thought I might give them a treat. They liked the sample you sent over. Should I go with that again?"

"You could. Some new ones just came in that are liver and salmon flavored." He gestured to a shelf behind him.

I grimaced. "Liver doesn't sound like much of a treat to me, but my cats do like it. I'll give it a try." I took the package down and handed it to him.

He rang it up. "Need anything else?"

I shook my head. "There's something I've been meaning to ask you. The last time I was in the store, you mentioned that you met Scott on the way to Kuwait City. He met Jean on the same mission. Did you run into Jean there?"

Tom rolled and unrolled a leash before placing it on the display. "Jean was with the support group that traveled with our platoons." He shuddered. "I don't like to talk about those days. I don't even visit the beach. I had enough sand to last a lifetime."

"Were you close?"

"I guess. Our group wasn't that large. You had to be able to trust people with your life. I wasn't as close to her as others though."

"Did you stay in touch once you got back stateside?"

He picked up another leash and shrugged. "She didn't come right back here. She was posted down in Texas and then some other places. Plus, life happens. We spoke some, sure, but time passed. I was married; we had JJ. Jean and I were always friendly."

A customer walked in the store.

"Good talking to you. Hope the cats like the treats."

I ambled back to my office. Why didn't he mention Jean the first time we spoke? Was he hiding something?

Focusing on work made the day pass quickly. I finished last minute items, and Rob appeared in my door. "Feel like eating out tonight?"

"Out would be great. Jenny is with her dad and Arianna again. How about the Golden Skillet? I could use some down home cooking right about now."

The hostess sat us, and we chatted about the day. Dinner orders given, I told him about my conversation with Tom.

"You're right. It does seem suspicious that he didn't mention his connection with Jean the first time you spoke with him. On the other hand, maybe Tom was just distracted after telling you about Scott."

I studied the restaurant's metal rooster collection. "You could be right." I caressed his hand. "It's also interesting that he didn't mention anything about John Little. Maybe that's because I know they're friends. He could have thought that I already knew they served together."

"It just seems so long ago; it's been almost thirty years. It's hard for me to believe that anyone could keep a grudge that long."

"I was only nine years old then."

"I was twelve. I bet you were a cute kid." He smiled at me.

"My front two teeth probably reappeared by then."

Rob kissed my cheek. "That must have been fun."

"It made eating corn a challenge."

He chuckled. "I bet. I'm meeting John tomorrow at three. He's going to show me around the VFW remodel."

"Ooh. Take pictures so I can see them later."

"That was the plan. I'll also see what I can get him to divulge about his time in the military."

"Dessert?"

He raised an eyebrow. "What about dessert at my place? It's still early."

I smiled. "An even better idea."

* * *

Figuring penance was in order, I rose early the next morning to go to Mass. Father Tom's homily centered on gaining a deeper understanding of our neighbors. He pointed out that our lives have become so busy we accept what people tell us at face value. He urged that we delve deeper. Through his counseling work, he knew that families were struggling. *Do I do that? Guilty.*

I made my way to Father Tom after the Mass. "I appreciated your homily. What kinds of things can I do to make sure I'm more present in my interactions?"

His kind brown eyes twinkled. "Ask deeper questions. Seek to be of service. And don't look at your phone."

"Got it."

"I've been meaning to call you. I visited with Martha Putty the other day. Her spirit is still so low. She mentioned that you and Patty stopped by. It was the only time I saw a spark come to her eyes. Do you think you could find time to visit with her again? Maybe even help her transition Jean's things out of the house so that she doesn't have that weighing on her?"

"I'd be happy to help, and I know that Patty would too." I was careful not to smile as I walked away.

After taking care of a few urgent items at the office, I texted Patty: "Free for a few hours on Saturday to help Martha?"

"Of course."

I tapped Martha's number into my phone. "Patty and I were wondering if you'd like us to come over on Saturday to help you go through Jean's things."

Martha was silent.

"If it's too soon, we certainly understand. When you're ready, we'd like to help."

Her voice sounded heavy, and she spoke softly. "That's so nice. It would take such a burden off me not to face it alone. Saturday is fine."

"We'll be there around two."

I met with several clients and worked my call list. At five, Rob poked his head in the door. "Dinner?"

"Sounds great. I put stew in the crockpot this morning. Jenny's going to be home. Between Jacob and Drew, she hasn't been around much lately."

"Ready?"

I shoved paperwork into my folio and grabbed my coat. "What did John Little say when you saw him this afternoon?"

"Patty was right; he was in Desert Storm. In Jean's supply unit. Of course, he knew Tom Butler, since they were both from here. And he remembered Scott, though their paths crossed only briefly. He mentioned that if we wanted to know more about Jean we should reach out to Wendy Tucker. She and Jean were tight during the war. She only lives about an hour away."

"I'll give her a call. Are you free on Sunday if she's available?"

He gave me a hug. "That can be arranged."

"Patty and I are going to help Martha with Jean's things on Saturday."

His eyes narrowed. "How did you arrange that?"

"It was Father Tom's idea."

He shook his head. "Small towns. I love the feel of them, but I don't think I'll ever understand them."

I was up early on Saturday. Humming and doing my stretches, I gave the cats a few errant pets. When I lifted my light weights, the cats scattered, having seen me drop one once. "It was just that one time," I called to their retreating figures.

Workout finished, I flipped on the coffee machine and made my way to the laundry room to put a load of wash in. Task accomplished, I grabbed a coffee mug, filled it, and sat on the window seat. I took a sip. My eyes widened. Someone had keyed Drew's car. A large scratch ran from front to back. The coffee went down the wrong way, and I coughed.

Should I call and tell Drew? *Nope. Though I hope I'm looking when he finds out.* People without garages shouldn't buy such expensive cars. Especially not when they've pissed off most of the town.

With a spring in my step, I mixed pancake batter and heated milk for hot chocolate. The back door burst open. Drew stood there, veins in his neck bulging. "Did you do that?"

"Do what?"

"Key my car."

I waggled my index finger. "I'm a grown woman. I have never keyed anyone's car. There's only one lawbreaker in this family."

He sneered. "As you like to point out, we are no longer a family." He slammed the door.

Jenny popped into the kitchen, still in her pajamas. She yawned. "Who's making so much noise?"

"Your dad."

"Why was he here?"

"Someone keyed his car last night."

She ran to the window. "That's terrible! Can it be fixed?"

"I don't know. It will probably never look quite right."

64

She slumped on one of the stools at the counter. "What are you making?"

"Pancakes."

"Blueberry?"

I sighed. "If you get them out of the freezer in the garage I'll add them."

She bounded into the garage. Racing back in, she put the blueberries in a colander and rinsed them. "One thing I don't understand."

"What's that?"

"Why would Dad come over here to tell you about his car?"

I groaned. "He thought I might have done it."

She gasped. "You didn't, did you?"

"Of course not. Why would you even ask that?"

I floured the blueberries, and then folded them into the batter. The back door opened. Rob asked, "Did you see Drew's car? Someone really went to town on it. That's going to cost a pretty penny to fix." He grinned. "Blueberry pancakes. My favorite."

I handed him a mug of coffee and set another place at the counter. "What's on your list today?"

"There's a meeting of the school board. I thought I'd cover it for the paper. They're talking about increasing the fees for after school sports, as well as lab classes to cover the higher equipment costs."

My eyes widened as I passed pancakes around. "It seems like they're getting money from both sides. They raise the tax levies for the schools, and then they increase the costs to parents via fees. How can people of limited means afford all this?"

"They're proposing that kids on the assisted lunch program pay only half."

"Half is still a lot. I'd hate to see kids steered away from science classes or not be able to participate in after school activities because of money. Doesn't seem right."

"Costs are going up everywhere."

"I guess." I picked up the plates from the counter and put them in the sink. "Patty and I are going to head out to Martha's around two." I gave Jenny a quick hug. "What are your plans today?"

"Cindy and I are going to work on a report that's due next week. We're meeting Jacob and Michael at the library."

I hugged her. "That doesn't sound like a lot of fun either. Tell you what, why don't we all meet back here for dinner to commiserate? I'll pick up steaks and make twice baked potatoes."

Jenny wheedled. "Pie?"

"And pie. I'll see what they have."

Patty picked me up in her car. "I put boxes in the trunk. I figured they'd be better for donating things or if she wants to store anything." She shivered. "I'm not looking forward to this."

"Me either, but if we can help bring her closure, I'm happy to do it."

"I picked up another coffee cake for her. She looked so thin when we last were here."

Martha welcomed us when we arrived. "Thank you so much for doing this. I just haven't been able to face it. I made tea." She blinked. "That is if you have time. I feel so guilty for imposing."

Patty sat on the sofa. "I'd love tea. Fair warning, I brought another coffee cake to tempt you. I know you like apple and cinnamon, but a little bird told me you like apricot as well."

Martha inclined her head. "I do."

I walked to the large picture window and pulled the heavy drapes open. "Let's have a bit of natural light in here, shall we?"

Martha tensed and held her hand up to block the light.

"Is the sun too much for you?"

"No. I guess it's time to rejoin the living." Her eyes widened. "My, it's dusty in here. I'll have to call the cleaning people. I used to do it myself, but Jean arranged for a cleaning team when she moved back in. She was always so thoughtful." She pulled a tissue from her long sleeve and wiped her eyes. "To tell the truth, dusting is not my favorite job." She opened the pastry box. "This looks yummy. Let me get plates and forks." Returning to the living room, she cut large slices and handed them around.

I took a bite. "This is great. I can really taste the butter, and the apricot filling is luscious."

Martha took a bite. "It is lovely. Thank you both for bringing it. I'm happy Delightful Bites opened up."

"Merry and I are taking a series of cooking classes there soon. The owner, Gary Johnson, is going to teach us how to make pasta."

"Sounds complicated."

"Hopefully it won't be more than we can handle."

A photo on the built in shelves caught my eye. I strode over and picked it up. "Such a nice picture of Jean. Who is this with her? They could almost be twins."

She joined me. "That's Wendy Tucker. She was Jean's best friend in the service." She picked up another silver-framed photo. "Here's one of Wendy with her husband at their wedding. Jean was her maid of honor."

Patty looked over her shoulder. "I remember them from the wake. I thought they looked like they had stepped off the pages of a magazine. She was so striking, tall with long blond hair, just like Jean. But her eyes were mocha colored, and Jean's were cornflower blue."

Martha nudged Patty. "Her husband is quite an eyeful as well."

I took the picture from her. "I must have left before they got there."

"Wendy and Jean were like sisters. They grew close during their deployment. There were so few women at that time. More now though."

I put the picture down and my teacup on the coffee table. "I guess we should get started. We thought it might be easier for you if we sorted her things into three stacks: items you may want to keep, items to donate, and items to discard."

Martha wiped tears from her eyes. "I don't mean to cry. It's wonderful of you both to do this for me. It's just tough." She straightened her shoulders. "That sounds like a wonderful plan. Jean's room is the second one on the left. Let me know if you have any questions."

I climbed the stairs; Patty trailed behind me. I sighed as I opened the door. "This is going to be difficult. She was such a nice woman." I shuddered. "I hate to think of someone having to do this for me."

Patty punched my shoulder. "It would probably be me, so you better live a long and healthy life, or I'll throw out your Santa collection."

"You wouldn't dare!"

"Just try me. Now, let's get started here."

Working steadily, we soon separated her clothes, jewelry, and keepsakes into piles. I sighed. "Well if she took the ring, it's certainly not here now. We would have found it. I'll call Martha."

She made her way slowly up the stairs, grasping the handrail. Wiping her face, she trudged into Jean's room. "I can't believe how quickly you were able to do this."

Patty hugged her. "It's easier for us. We don't have all the memories you do." She ran down to retrieve a glass of water for Martha, and I explained the piles on the bed and chair.

Martha caressed a dark green tea dress on the bed. It was embroidered with delicate satin leaves and white roses. "This was Jean's graduation dress. I was so proud of her."

"Would you like me to move that to the keep pile?"

Her smile quivered. "I'd like to think of someone else enjoying it as much as she did."

I picked it up. "It really is a beautiful dress. Someone is going to be very lucky."

Martha paused here and there, but made her way fairly quickly through the stacks. Her hand hesitated over a turquoise pendant with silver chain. "Wendy gave Jean this for her birthday when they were stationed in Texas. Maybe she would like it back, as a reminder of Jean." She turned to me. "I'm still not ready to go out yet, and I can't bear the thought of mailing it to her. I guess I'll just wait on this." She laid it down gently on the dresser.

"Does she live far from here?"

"About an hour south."

"Rob's been looking for an excuse to take a Sunday drive. Why don't we bring it to her."

"That's too much to ask. It can wait."

Patty picked up the necklace and put it into an envelope. "Merry will take it." She ran down to her car.

Martha stared at her retreating back. "No dithering for her."

I rolled my eyes. "You have no idea."

Patty returned with the empty boxes. We packed the items being given away and the items that Martha wanted to keep. She took a few framed photos for her bedroom. We stored the rest of the keepsakes in her attic.

Patty and I loaded the boxes marked for donation into the car. We both gave Martha a hug as we left. I promised, "I'll be back to visit you soon."

After dropping the boxes off, I asked Patty, "Do you mind if we stop by the store? I promised steaks to Rob and Jenny."

She shrugged. "No problem. I always need stuff at the store."

Making my way to the meat counter, I ran into Scott Winters. "Patty and I just came from helping Martha Putty clean out Jean's things. We didn't find the ring. And we were pretty thorough."

He stroked his beard. "You didn't? Maybe she gave it to someone else or sold it."

"Isn't it more likely that she didn't take it?"

CHAPTER 10

After Mass, Rob and I drove to Wendy Tucker's house. It was a brilliantly sunny day that felt deceptively warm in the heated car. I stretched in my seat and purred, "Don't you just love days like these?"

"I like it better when it is warm versus just seeming like it's warm. I can't wait to turn my heat off."

"Me too. I love opening my windows and hearing the sounds of nature." I tilted my head. "Although the birds are pretty loud at sunrise."

"What did you say to Wendy on the phone?"

"I told her that Martha wanted me to stop by and give her a necklace that Jean always loved." I pulled it from the envelope in my purse and dangled it. The shiny silver teardrop shaped pendant shimmered in the light. At its center was a round blue-green piece of turquoise that rivaled the color of the Caribbean Sea. "It really is beautiful. I'm sure Wendy will appreciate it."

The house was set back from the road, at the end of a white-picket fence lined drive. Tall, stately evergreens framed the house and provided a windbreak from the pasture surrounding it. Chickens scurried past. "Watch out!"

"I see them. Aren't they supposed to be in a pen?"

"Maybe these are free range."

He chuckled.

The white farmhouse was adorned with black shutters and a wide front porch that looked fit for a tall glass of lemonade. Wicker furniture stood at the ready, waiting for the cushions that would signal spring.

A woman who looked just like Jean strode through the front door. As she neared, I noticed her eyes were a sparkly brown, not Jean's blue, and she was taller than Jean. I climbed out of the car. "It's lovely here."

Her hand extended. "Wendy Tucker."

"You look so much like Jean."

"We got that a lot." We shook hands. "My husband Ray should be here shortly. He had to fix the chicken fence."

Rob grinned. "That explains the chickens we encountered."

"Yes, having them loose is like ringing a dinner bell for the foxes and coyotes." She rubbed her arms. "Let's go inside, and I'll fix some tea."

We bundled in after her. I halted when I saw the massive mahogany staircase. "That's gorgeous. And these floors! I don't think I've ever seen planks that wide. They're so well preserved."

"They are. This house is well over a hundred years old. Ray's parents lived here and his grandparents before them. It takes upkeep, but it is lovely. Come into the parlor."

Rob and I sat on the low-slung sofa. Logs stood at the ready in the large stone fireplace. The walls were covered in a light green grass cloth. A quarter-sawn mahogany coffee table was in front of us. I caressed the top of it.

Wendy stood near the fireplace. "Anyone still chilly?"

"Me."

She lit the fire.

I stood, walked to the corner of the room, and touched the upright piano. "Do you play?"

"A little bit." She poured the tea.

Rob sipped it. "How long have you been here?"

"We moved in about six years ago. It was nice to be near Jean again. She'd come up some weekends, and we'd ride the horses."

"You have chickens and horses?"

She chuckled. "Plus, cows, pigs, goats, and a stray cat or two. This is a working farm."

My eyes widened. "Did you always want to be a farmer?"

"My husband did. I love him, so here I am."

"It's still impressive. And hard work." I handed her the envelope containing the necklace. "Martha thought you might want to have this as a remembrance of Jean."

Wendy paled as she lifted the pendant. "I still can't believe she's gone. She was always the most vibrant person in the room."

Wendy put the necklace around her neck and clutched the pendant. "I remember when I gave her this. It was for her twenty-fifth birthday. We were stationed in Texas. I went to an open air market in September and knew it would be perfect." She caressed the turquoise. "Her birthday was in December, so it was her birthstone." She picked up a tissue and wiped her eyes. "I cried for days when I found out she'd been killed. I thought I was past that now. Thank goodness they arrested the man who did it."

"Scott Winters."

"That's right. He's the guy who roughed her up in Texas. We were leaving a roadhouse, and he grabbed her. He spouted all kinds of nonsense about her stealing a ring when we were traveling to Kuwait."

"And did she? Take the ring?"

Wendy crossed her legs. "That's not the kind of person she was. I thought you knew her."

"I did. She was always nice to me."

"She was always nice to everyone." She chuckled. "Of course that's not to say that she didn't have a wicked sense of humor. The pranks she pulled." She sipped her tea. "Anyway, that idiot, Scott, got it in his head that she took the ring from Jim Jefferson just because she slept with him once. Ridiculous. It didn't mean any more to her that it did to Jim. They joked about it afterward. I could see her taking the ring as a joke, but she would have given it right back. She wouldn't have held onto it."

Wendy seemed mesmerized by the dancing flames. "Luckily, Jean's transfer came through, and she was able to leave town. Too bad they didn't lock Scott up for good. Then Jean would still be alive." She stared at her tea.

"Do you have any idea who took the ring?"

She shrugged. "Could have been anyone. Jim certainly flashed it around enough. It was a mighty big ring."

A large man came in from the back of the house. He looked like he could be the cowboy hero of a steamy romance novel. His jeans were dusty and his hands scratched. He brushed his chestnut colored hair back from his brow. "I finally got the fence put back together. Oh, sorry. I didn't realize we had company."

Wendy introduced us.

Rob and I rose. "We were just about to leave."

She protested, "You don't need to leave yet."

"Honey, we need to get after those chickens if we want them back in the pen before dark."

She stood. "It was kind of you to come all the way out here." She put the envelope down. "Jean had gotten quite close to a fellow in the last few months—darn. What was his name? Oh well, it will come to me later. He was in the service too." She tapped her chin. "She didn't talk about him a lot. If you ask me, he might have been married. Come to think of it, it's strange that he didn't introduce himself at the funeral, of course it was so crowded he could have been there. Hmm."

I slid into the car and turned to Rob. "Who do you suppose she was talking about?"

"Not that many people in town served in the First Gulf War. Scott Winters, John Little, and Tom Butler. Those are the ones we know of so far. That's just in our town." He made a note on his phone. "I think I'll drop by and see John. Our VFW serves quite a few towns around here. He should know of other veterans."

"How are you going to approach him?"

"Easy. He wanted to take a look at the VFW pictures for the newsletter."

"Sounds like a plan."

"Wendy seemed pretty certain that Jean didn't have the ring."

"Too bad she didn't help us narrow down who took it."

I sighed. "What's our task? Is it to find out who took a ring from thirty years ago, or to find out who killed Jean?"

"The latter."

"Okay. Let's agree that the ring is an interesting side note, but unless Scott killed Jean she wasn't killed for it. So why was she killed?"

"Maybe she figured out who took the ring."

I put my hand on his shoulder. "Stop with the ring. She wasn't looking for the ring, so how would she have figured out who took it?"

"Maybe she saw it again and recognized it. From what everyone described, it was a memorable ring."

I reclined the car seat. "Looking at all those chickens made me hungry. Wake me when we get near, and I'll run into the supermarket."

He pouted. "You're going to sleep? Who's going to keep me company?"

"You're such a baby. Listen to the radio."

"I'd rather listen to you."

I closed my eyes.

* * *

On Monday, I called Martha. "Rob and I were wondering if you felt well enough to go out to dinner with us Thursday night." Silence greeted me. "Or, I could cook, if you'd rather not go out in public yet. I just thought it would be nice for you to get out of the house."

"That's so sweet of you." She paused. "I think I would like to go out. The house is starting to close in on me."

"We'll pick you up at six."

On Thursday, Rob helped Martha into the car. "I hope you like the Golden Skillet."

"I love their fried chicken. They soak it in buttermilk, just like my mother did."

The hostess seated us at a table midway through the restaurant. I was touched when so many people stopped by the table to wish Martha well and to tell her how glad they were to see her out and about. One woman asked if she was going to play bridge the following Wednesday, and I was heartened to hear her reply in the affirmative.

Our meals came. Martha murmured, "I'm so sorry for all of the interruptions."

I assured her, "Everyone's so happy to see you out again."

Her smile trembled. "It was time. Jean would have hated me staying home all alone." She took a bite of the chicken. "This is so good. The mashed potatoes are wonderful. I'll have to watch what I eat for a week to make up for this."

"Speaking of chickens, we had a good visit with Wendy. She asked us to give you her best."

"Thank you for going all the way out there. I appreciated it."

Rob told her the chicken story.

"My husband and I raised chickens back in the day. It was tough to keep all the critters away from them."

I took a roll and passed her the basket. "I hope you don't mind me asking, but Wendy seemed to think that Jean had a special someone she was seeing."

Martha froze in the middle of placing a roll on her bread plate. "I didn't know that." She sliced a piece of butter. "Of course, Wendy was Jean's best friend. Jean did spend a few weekends out of town, but she was either visiting Wendy or attending flower arranging classes." She put her knife down. "Jean always wanted to be the best at what she did."

"She always went out on Wednesday nights. That's my bridge night, you know." She clutched her napkin. "I wonder who it could have been. If he was important to her, why didn't she tell me about him? And why didn't he come to the funeral?" She started crying.

I grabbed a tissue from my purse and handed it to her. "Maybe Wendy was wrong. She couldn't remember the guy's name. I'm sorry. I shouldn't have mentioned it."

"That's all right, dear. I'm sure there are other things I didn't know. Jean was fiercely independent." She sagged in her chair. "He was probably married. That way she wouldn't have to worry about him getting too close. I hope you don't mind, but I'd like to leave now. I'm quite tired."

Rob signaled for the check.

We dropped Jean off at her house. On the way back, the windshield wipers slid back and forth, wiping the driving rain away with extraordinary precision. I turned off the radio. "I feel so guilty."

Rob concentrated on the road ahead. "Me too."

"I thought she might have known something. I made her cry. She'll probably never want to see us again."

The wipers continued their relentless routine as we turned into my driveway. I gave Rob a quick kiss. "I'll talk to you tomorrow."

I sprinted into the house. Drambuie wound her way around my feet. I picked her up, petted her, and asked, "Am I a bad person?"

Patty declared, "Nope. You're just nuts. You're talking to the cat."

I jumped and gave her a dirty look. "What are you doing here?"

"The kids were in bed, and my husband was watching Sports Channel, so I wandered over in the off chance you'd be home. You weren't, but luckily you had an open bottle of wine on your counter." She gestured to me with her wine glass. "Want some? It's pretty good."

"I know. I had some last night. No need to bestir yourself, I can pour my own glass."

She arched a brow. "Not much of a good night kiss. You do know I live vicariously through you, right?"

I groaned and sank onto the seat next to her. "Wait till you hear what's been going on." I told her.

Her eyes widened. "So Jean was seeing someone?"

"That's what Wendy told us. Not sure who though. I wish she'd been able to remember his name."

"I'm sure she will."

"Hopefully Rob will have better luck when he talks to John Little."

CHAPTER 11

The next morning, I sipped my coffee while peering out the window at the driveway next door. The Lamborghini was gone, and a taupe, older model Camry sat in its place. *Some come down.* I snickered, put my phone in my purse, and left for work.

My first appointment was with Tom and Melanie Butler. "You're doing the right thing. With the goals you have, you need additional life insurance." I handed Tom the application. "Just sign where I've indicated. I've arranged for a telephone interview tomorrow where they'll take your medical history. Once that's completed we'll know exactly how much the extra coverage will cost, and we can finalize everything."

Tom signed the application. As they were leaving, Melanie turned back to me. "Thanks. I'll sleep much easier once this is taken care of."

It was busy, so the rest of the day whizzed by. Rob popped in right on time at five thirty. He sat down. "How was your day?"

"Good. I'm close on a life insurance sale. I always feel so much better when people get the coverage they need."

"Who bought it?"

I came around the desk and tweaked his nose. "Confidentiality. I can't tell you."

He pulled me onto his lap. "What do you feel like doing tonight?"

"Jenny's got a basketball game. Drew and Arianna are going to be there, but I'd like to show our support too."

"I'm always up for a good bball game."

It was noisy when we walked into the gym. The opposite team was one of the Roughriders' big rivals, so the stands were packed. Rob picked out Patty and Patrick in the crowd. We wove through to sit by them. I pulled on my ear. "It's so loud in here."

She shrugged. "Just wait till they start playing."

A whistle signaled the opening tip-off, and the game was underway. It was physical and before five minutes were up, Jenny took an elbow to the jaw. I stood. She shook it off and went to the foul line for her free throws. She made both.

Patty pulled me back down. "You're going to embarrass her. Sit down."

"That had to hurt." I leaned forward to see if she was bruising.

Patty put her arm around my shoulders. "She'll be fine. She's a trooper."

The team ran up and down the court. Even though the score was close, my eyes wandered to the crowd. Drew and Arianna were seated across the gym five rows up from the benches. They were deep in conversation. *It would be nice if they actually glanced at the game from time to time.* Her head was bent towards his, her long hair gleaming. His hand rested on her well-toned leg.

My eyes moved right a few sections and landed on John Little and Tom Butler. Instead of watching the game, they seemed fixated on something on our side of the gym. I tried to follow their stares but couldn't see over Patrick. I elbowed Patty. "Ask Patrick to lean back for a moment."

She whispered to Patrick. His eyebrows rose, but he complied. John and Tom seemed to be staring toward where Scott Winters and his family sat.

Rob elbowed me. "What are you looking at? Why aren't you watching the game?"

"Look at John and Tom. They're about five rows up across the gym."

"So?"

"They seem to be staring at Scott Winters." The crowd roared. Jenny had scored a three-pointer. "I can't believe I missed that."

"I can't believe you made me miss that. Let's focus on the game, shall we?"

Hanging my head, my eyes returned to the court. Cindy made a two-pointer, and we stood to applaud.

The Roughriders won by six. Jenny bounded up. "Did you see my three-pointer?"

"I saw your foul shots." I turned her head to look for any bruising.

Jenny twisted away. "Mom, I'm fine."

Jacob ran towards us, picked up Jenny, and twirled her around. "Nice game!"

She rested her head on his shoulder. "Thanks."

Scott and Linda caught up with him. They both congratulated Jenny on the win. Tom Butler and John Little strode past, their eyes never leaving Scott's face.

I gestured to Scott. "Why have John and Tom been staring at you all night?"

He turned his head toward their retreating backs and shrugged. "I have no idea." He pulled on Jacob's arm. "It's late. We need to be getting home."

Jacob gave Jenny one last hug. "I'll see you tomorrow."

Rob put his arm around my shoulders. "What was that all about?"

"Who knows? Jenny, let's get you home and put ice on your chin."

As soon as we returned home, I strode to the freezer and pulled out an ice pack.

Jenny groaned as handed it to her. "It's fine. I don't know why I need to do this." She grabbed a banana from the fruit bowl and ran up the stairs.

Rob sat on the sofa. I joined him. "What are the chances she's actually going to use the ice?"

He tilted his head. "I'd say it's somewhere between nil and maybe."

"I don't know why I even try."

He put his arm around me. "You try because you have to. You're a mom."

I snuggled closer. "Why do you think John and Tom were staring at Scott?"

He shrugged. "I don't know. I didn't get a chance to tell you earlier, but I took the VFW photos over to John this morning."

I sat up. "What did he say?"

"First, he told me the photos were amazing. Want to see?" He showed me his phone. We scrolled through.

"These are good." I elbowed him. "You know that wasn't what I was talking about. What did he have to say about Jean?"

Rob chuckled. "You're so impatient." He paused. "Apparently, over the past few months, he'd seen Jean pretty regularly at the VFW. And she wasn't alone."

"Finally. Who was she with?"

He patted my shoulder. "Don't freak out, but he couldn't remember the guy's name."

I groaned. "What is it about this guy?"

"He's from two towns over."

"That's helpful, but a name would be better." I rubbed my forehead.

"The guy usually shows up on Wednesdays. He hasn't seen him in the last few weeks though."

"Can we get into the VFW?"

He shook his head. "Neither of us qualifies. We can only go as someone's guest."

I waited.

"I told John I wouldn't charge him for the photos if he took us next Wednesday."

* * *

John pulled into the VFW parking lot in front of us and waited by the door. I climbed out of Rob's car. "I hope this guy shows up tonight."

"What the worst that could happen? He doesn't show up, and we have a good time with John?"

I pouted. "I'm just frustrated. Why is it no one remembers this guy's name?"

John held the door open. "After you."

Strolling in, my breath caught, and I stopped in my tracks. The walls were a creamy white and the window trim a pastel blue. "Wow. What a change. It's even better than the photos Rob took. I love how you've lightened everything up."

"Everyone agreed the wood paneling had to go. It was cozy, but we wanted to attract more wedding business. The charity fashion show last year really opened our eyes to the potential." He stared at the ground. "Of course, the clean up after that was pretty bad. It also showed that we needed to provide security for larger events."

I cleared my throat. "Well, it looks terrific now."

We walked through the hall to the bar. John gestured toward a table. "This work?"

I slid onto a seat. Rob and John retrieved drinks. Rob handed me a glass of wine. "Thanks." John sat and took a swig of beer. I asked him, "Did you see the guy Jean was dating?"

His eyes roamed the bar. "No, not yet, but it's early. If he's coming, he probably won't be here for another half hour or so. Are you in a hurry?"

I sighed. "Just curious." I sipped my wine. "Rob told me that you were in the same supply unit as Jean."

"I was. Such a shame about her death. My wife loved her flowers. Nancy's birthday is coming up; I'm going to have to find a different florist." He blanched. "I guess that sounded bad. I liked Jean for more than her flower arranging."

I touched his shoulder. "I understand. I liked her flowers too."

"She always knew her mind. Quite a few guys were interested in her over the years, but she wasn't looking to get serious."

"Did you keep in touch after the service?"

"Some. I moved back here and married Nancy. Jean bounced around, and then ended up here. We went out as a group a few times, but I don't think we were ever again as close as we were in Kuwait."

"When did she start seeing the mystery man?"

He stared into the distance. "I don't know exactly, but if I had to guess, sometime last October, just before my son was kicked out of college. The last few months they would meet here, have a drink, and leave together."

Rob was just about to ask a question when a tall, well-built, man walked in the bar. He looked like he was in his late forties. He had sandy blond hair speckled with gray, steel-blue eyes and a noticeable limp. Rob raised his eyebrow at John.

He nodded. "That's him."

Rob asked, "The limp?"

"Shrapnel from a Scud missile."

I shivered.

John stood. "I'll ask him to join us."

The man waited at the bar for his drink. John talked to him, and the man's eyes flicked in our direction. He gave a curt nod, and they made their way to the table.

Rob stood and extended his hand. "Rob Jenson." He gestured toward me. "Merry March."

The man smiled at me. "Pete Vassal."

I shook his hand. "It's good to finally meet you."

His eyes narrowed. "You've been looking for me?"

My gaze slipped to his hand. He had a wedding band on his ring finger. "Did you know Jean Putty?"

His eyes teared up. "Of course I did. It'd be pretty stupid to deny it in here. This is where we used to meet." His arm swept the room. "Everyone knew we were in love. This is my first time back here since she died. I wouldn't have come, but I had a job on the next street and figured it was time." He took a sip of his beer, cleared his throat, and put it down. "Why are you asking?"

"It's a long story. We knew Jean from town. She was an acquaintance, and I feel a little guilty that I didn't know her better." I sipped my wine.

He swigged down the rest of his beer. "If we are going to discuss Jean, I'm going to need another one of these." He stood and motioned to the bartender. He grabbed the proffered beer, returned to the table, and sat. "Finding Jean was such a revelation. She had such a zest for life. And hoo boy did she travel her own road. It took me a month just to get her to say that she liked me. She didn't want to be beholden to anyone. She wanted to live her life on her own terms.

"That's probably what attracted me to her first. It seemed like a relationship with her would be simple." He shook his head. "It sure didn't end up being what I thought it would."

I pointed toward his left hand. "I noticed your ring. How did your wife feel about all this?" Rob kicked my foot. I waved him off.

Pete rubbed the back of his neck. "She didn't know." He looked toward the ceiling, "At least I think she didn't."

I waited.

"I've been a good husband. My wife was sick. Cancer. I've taken her to appointments, made sure she ate, and kept track of her medications. Before she got sick, my life rose and set on her. She was ill for such a long time. It changes you." He retrieved another beer. "When I met Jean, she was so alive. I was drawn to her. She was kind. She let me babble on about my wife." He looked me straight in the eye. "Being a caretaker is hard. I think you only know how hard it is when you experience it.

"Anyway, on Wednesday nights I would slip away from my wife and come here. Jean and I would have a drink or two, and then go to that motel down the road. It's kind of a dump, but Jean never seemed to mind. She insisted that being together was the important part." Tears ran down his cheeks. He pulled out a bandana and wiped his face. "Enough of that."

"If you and Jean were so close, why didn't you go to her funeral?"

"Couldn't chance it. No one's going to talk here. We keep each other's secrets. Out there I'd have to explain my presence to too many people. I didn't want my wife to know that I was cheating on her. " He guzzled more beer. "Is that what you wanted to know?"

I felt myself flush. "It gives us a better idea of who Jean was. I know it was painful for you, so thanks for sharing your story with us." I touched his arm. "Do you have any idea who would want to kill Jean?"

He drew back. "Scott Winters killed her. He's been charged. How did you not know that?"

"I did know. I'm just not convinced that Scott was involved in this."

"She told me he threatened her over a ring in Texas."

"I heard that."

"She also called me the day she died. She left me a voice mail telling me that Scott had threatened her that morning. She was so shocked to see him standing in the shop. He 'claimed' that it was a coincidence he had ended up there. He was looking for flowers for his wife."

"Did you tell the police?"

"I didn't want them to upset my wife, and besides they arrested him anyway."

Rob put down his beer. "I can see why you would want to stay out of this. However, you have a civic duty to report it. We have a friend in the police department. He's pretty closed mouthed, and if your secret is not germane to the investigation, he'll keep it."

He scowled. "Let me think about it."

CHAPTER 12

Gary Johnson greeted us as we filed in to Delightful Bites. Patty elbowed me. "I'm still not sure why you signed us up for these cooking classes. We both know how to cook. I'd rather go to a bar if you want a bonding experience."

"Don't worry. Gary told me that, since he was doing night classes, he'd include wine as an option. I already paid the upcharge for us."

We grabbed aprons and moved to a station near the front. "I don't see any wine."

"Look to Gary's left."

"Oh. You're right." Her shoulders loosened. "I'd hate to think I was wasting my time without the kids."

The other class participants filled in around us. Gary pointed to various workstations. "If you don't have a partner, you can fill in anywhere that there is an open spot." He started pouring wine and handing out glasses. Then he moved to the front of the room. "Thanks for signing up for Springtime in Italy, our first class. Tonight we'll be making wide noodle pasta with spring peas and mushrooms. What are some of your favorite mushrooms?"

Someone answered, "Button." Another person blurted, "Shitake." A Spanish-accented voice piped in, "Morels."

I turned around in surprise. Arianna stood at the station behind me, paired with Barbara Ziebold. Both gave me a quick wave. Gary continued, "All good choices." He beamed at Arianna. "Morels are the best, of course. Too bad they're only available for a few weeks in the spring. Tonight we'll be using portobellos. But, first, we'll make the pasta." He held up the recipe sheet. "Everyone should have this at their station."

Patty and I picked our copy up. She measured the flour and put it on the counter, making a well. I cracked in the eggs, and she mixed the dough. Gary stopped by. "That looks like the right consistency. Don't be afraid of over kneading it. You want it pliable."

He returned to the front of the room. "All teams have a pasta roller in front of them. Make sure it's at the widest setting and then fold your dough so that it will fit in the roller." He demonstrated. "Remember to sprinkle the dough with flour; you don't want it to stick."

I folded the dough, and Patty carefully fed it into the roller, turning the crank. Conversations swirled around us. Most centered on the workout we were getting with the manual crank of the roller. As I floured and folded the dough again, I picked out Arianna's accent.

"I love Drew. I'm just not sure that this town is the best place for us to live. He has so much history here."

Barbara asked, "Where would you move?"

My dough was getting longer, and I forgot to flour it. It stuck to the table. Patty's face flushed. "Pay attention. I'd like to have something to eat tonight."

"Sorry." I pried it off the table and floured again. Making the setting smaller, I fed the dough into the roller, as Patty cranked.

Arianna said, "We'll have to work with Merry on visitation. Drew doesn't really want to leave while Jenny's finishing her junior year of school, but we need to think of ourselves too." She laughed. "It can't be all about what Merry wants."

My mouth dropped. I missed where they'd be moving. *Drat.* Patty took the stretched dough and used a pizza cutter and ruler to make the noodles. "This makes it much easier."

I sipped the wine. "You're much more precise than I am. Mine would be in tatters."

"Good thing you have many other talents."

Dish finished, we dug in. I groaned. "This is so good. All that butter and cream. The pasta is so rich." I checked the calorie count. "Won't be making this too often." I finished everything, as did Patty."

We moved to the front of the kitchen to drop off our plates. Arianna scraped most of her meal into the garbage. My mouth dropped. "Didn't you like it?"

"I loved it. But I can't afford the calories." She put her plate into the sink.

Patty rolled her eyes.

Arianna asked, "Can I walk home with you?"

"Of course." Patty waved goodbye to Gary.

"Are desserts next? I think I'd do better at them than pasta." I tilted my head. "Although it was kind of fun to see that we could make it from scratch."

Patty cradled her arm. "Easy for you to say. You weren't the one who was cranking."

Arianna dropped back behind us to avoid running into the fire hydrant. "I have a pasta attachment for my mixer. It does all the rolling for me. It's much easier than using the manual one."

My eyes widened. "That sounds far better. How was it partnering with Barbara?"

"She seems like a nice woman. But I don't think we have a lot in common."

"I couldn't help but overhear that you and Drew are thinking of moving." My stomach churned.

She blanched. "We haven't made a decision yet, and I know it's something Drew wanted to talk to you about in person. He won't be happy if he knows I've been talking out of turn."

"Where are you thinking of moving?" I strolled slightly ahead of her.

"Again, we just started talking about it. I have a house in Miami that I love. It's right on the inland waterway. You can see the dolphins playing as the sun dances on the current." She looked up at the sky, then shifted her gaze to the street in front of her. "It's warm. Plus, it's more cosmopolitan. This is a nice town, but it's small. I don't know that I could be happy here."

Patty chimed in, "It grows on you. Of course, we haven't led the exotic existence you have."

Arianna's laugh tinkled across the brisk night. "It's probably not half as privileged as you might think. The modeling world is glamorous, but it's also cutthroat." She stopped in front of my gate. "Please don't let Drew know I mentioned it. He loves Jenny, and this decision is going to be hard for him."

I made my way inside. Does Drew moving make my life easier, or harder? Ugh.

Jenny was sprawled on the sofa, phone in hand. "How was your cooking class?"

I shook my head. "I don't think pasta making is my thing. Not when you can just buy a box in the supermarket. Although if I had one of those automatic rollers Arianna was talking about—"

"Arianna was there? What was she wearing?"

I shrugged. "I don't know. Clothes. We had aprons on."

"Mom, you are hopeless. If Arianna and I worked with you on your wardrobe you would look fabulous."

"My wardrobe is just fine."

Jenny rose to hug me. "You can believe that if you want to Mom." She ran lightly up the stairs.

I looked down at my jeans and teal turtleneck. My eye caught the hall mirror as I plucked dried flour from the ends of my sleeves. With the exception of a few errant white streaks, I looked pretty good. I stuck my tongue out and ran up the stairs to get ready for bed.

The next morning I finally had time to google Pete Vassal. It showed links to his military career, as well as reports of his marriage to Karen Vassal. The society page detailed her bout with cancer and her fundraising efforts. I zoomed in on her photo. She had spikey blond hair and blue eyes. She was in street clothes being supported by friends at a finish line somewhere, and she looked tired. My eyes widened. Either all the people around her were very short, or she was extremely tall. I checked the date. It had been taken over a year ago. No telling how she was now. I read further. She used to be a pro-basketball player. *Tall, really tall.*

I strolled to work, enjoying the spring-like weather. When I got to the office, I was glad to see that Tom Butler's life insurance requirements had been completed, and there was an offer from the insurance company. I phoned Melanie and made arrangements to deliver the policy and collect the premium that evening.

Patty texted me to meet her at Delicious Bites for lunch. As I opened the door, I was almost sad they didn't have their outside furniture in place. A stray breeze made it down the back of my neck. I shivered. *Nope, not quite warm enough yet.*

I ordered the lunch special and took an empty cup over to their coffee station. I filled it with a Chilean blend and sat at one of the tables. Patty bustled in and waved. After ordering and getting her coffee, she joined me. "Glad you could make it."

I gestured with my cup. "Me too. This coffee hit the spot."

"Have you heard anything more from Drew?"

My left eyebrow rose. "On the impending move? No. And I didn't mention anything to Jenny. I don't want her to be upset if there's still a chance he might not be leaving."

She leaned closer to me. "How would you feel if he did move?"

I shrugged. "I'm trying to avoid thinking about it. As much as I hated him moving next door, it made things simpler. Jenny stayed in her own room and popped over to see him whenever she wanted. I didn't have to worry about alternating weekdays or weekends and remembering where she is supposed to be from one day to the next."

"She'll be a senior next year, and then moving away to college."

"I know. I thought I wouldn't have to deal with any of this until then. If he moves somewhere far, she won't just be gone for dinner, or a quick weekend, she may be gone for a month." I sagged in my chair. "On the plus side, I won't have to worry about Drew being around every corner with Ms. Enhanced Perfection."

Patty waggled her finger at me. "That's not nice. Arianna seems like a good influence on him and a good role model for your daughter."

I sighed. "I know. I can't believe I'm going to say this, but I actually like her. It just bugs me how much Jenny idolizes her."

"Be glad she's enamored of the whole package: brains, money, and charitable foundation; not just the fact that she was a model."

I picked at my food. "Just as long as she doesn't pick up on her Botox habit. But you're right. He could have ended up with someone much worse. Who knows? With his track record he still may."

"What's going on with his car?"

"It's in the shop. They're trying to buff out the scratches. They looked pretty deep to me, so I'm not sure how successful they'll be." I tittered. "I know it's wrong, but it makes me happy knowing he's tooling around town in a Camry. It's such a come down."

Patty gave me a playful punch on my shoulder. "What would Father Tom say?"

I laughed. "He'd understand."

At five-thirty, I ambled over to Tom and Melanie's with their paperwork. They made quick work of signing everything and gave me a check for the first premium. Just as I walked to my door, Rob pulled up at the curb. Halfway out of the car, he asked, "We eating out or in?"

"Out." I shoved my folio inside the front door and locked it. I hurried to Rob's car and slid in. "Let's go to the Screaming Pigeon. We haven't been there in a while."

The host showed us to our table. Rob paged through the menu. "What's new with you?"

"Drew may be moving."

"What?"

"Arianna was behind me at class last night. She didn't realize I could hear her and Barbara chatting. I almost ruined our pasta."

He took my hand. "Wouldn't it be better if they did move?"

"I guess. If it weren't for Jenny, I'd be dancing. They haven't made a decision yet."

"Change is always hard. Especially when it involves your daughter. But it sounds like it's too early to worry about, either way, at this point."

"I guess."

He kissed my cheek. "I researched Pete and Karen Vassal."

"And?"

"Good news. Apparently she's in remission."

"That is good news." I paused. "It's strange that Pete didn't mention it."

Rob held out his phone. A tall woman stood there, looking really buff. She was flexing her muscular right arm. My eyes widened. "That's his wife?"

"Yes. Their local paper just published an article on how she battled cancer and is now hyper-fit."

I scrolled on my phone for the picture I found earlier in the day. I held it out to Rob. He whistled. "Wow. That's some change."

"It is. I would think that Pete would be overjoyed that she was in remission."

Rob stroked my hand. "If it were you, I'd be shouting it from the rooftop."

I drank my coffee. "It's a major change though. He was used to being her caretaker and now—" I gestured toward Rob's phone. "That woman doesn't look like she needs anyone to help her. She looks like she could bench press him."

"It makes you wonder. She had to have been recovering when he met Jean."

"If she was on the mend, why would he take up with Jean?"

"That is the question."

"Did you find out anything else?"

"I got confirmation that Pete also served in Desert Storm and was in Kuwait at the same time as Jean, Tom, John, and Scott."

"That's a lot of people from this area."

"It is."

Rob dropped me off at the house with a quick kiss goodbye. I made my way into the kitchen and kicked off my shoes. There was a knock at the back door, and Drew stuck his head in. "Good, you're home. Where's Jenny?"

"Upstairs, I think. Do you want me to get her?"

"No. I wanted to talk to you."

I motioned toward the table. "What's up?"

"Do you have any wine?"

I poured him a glass and sat across from him.

He lifted the glass. "Aren't you going to join me?"

"I'm good. Get to the point Drew. What do you want?"

"Arianna and I have been talking about leaving here."

I tried to look surprised. "Where would you go?"

He swirled his wine. "We haven't decided yet. We may go abroad, or to Miami, where Arianna has a house. It's no secret that I haven't been able to get a job around here."

I rolled my eyes. "That's an understatement. When were you planning on leaving?"

"We're still working through the details. We thought we might wait another month or so, that way it would be closer to when Jenny gets out of school."

My stomach clenched. "And?"

"That way there wouldn't be such a gap till I saw her again. She could come and live with Arianna and me for the summer."

"I was planning on taking her to look at colleges this summer."

"Why doesn't Jenny make a list of schools she's interested in, and then I'll take her?"

My eyes started to tear. I swallowed, trying to hold them back. "It's just that I thought this would be a special time for me and Jenny. Plus we go on vacation in the summer."

He sipped his wine and just stared at me.

"This is a lot to take in. You're going to have to give me time. When were you planning on telling Jenny?"

"Not till we decide where we want to live. I think we'll have that figured out by the end of the month."

I stood. "Thanks for letting me know. When you figure out what you're doing, let's talk. I want to make sure we are in agreement on everything before you talk to her."

"Will do, Ms. Control Freak."

Tapping my foot, I motioned towards the door. "Was there something else we needed to discuss?"

He shook his head and stood. Jenny careened around the corner. "Dad, what are you doing here? Where's Arianna?"

"I was talking to your mother. Arianna is home reading a book."

"Are we still on for Fiorella's tomorrow?"

"You bet." He kissed her on the forehead. "See you then, smart stuff." He shut the door.

Jenny crossed her arms and leaned against it, one eyebrow raised. "Why was Dad here?"

I picked up Drew's wine glass and put it in the dishwasher. "He wanted to talk to me."

"About what?"

"Adult stuff."

"Mom, I'm seventeen."

I sighed. "And you are a very adult seventeen too. Sit down." She sat, and I took the seat next to her. "Your dad and Arianna are thinking about moving."

She jumped up. "He doesn't want to be near me anymore?"

"Listen to me, Jenny. Sit down." I pulled her onto the chair. "Of course he wants to see you. You know that this is a difficult town for him to live in. No one will give him a job."

"Why does he need a job? He got all that money from his old girlfriend. Isn't that enough for him to live on?"

"It was a lot of money. But your dad is not a saver; he's a spender. He's also a people person who likes to be doing something. It may be better for him if he goes somewhere else and gets a fresh start."

She glared at me. "You wanted him to move, and now he is."

"It's true that I didn't want him to move back here when he got out of prison. However, I know how happy it's made you to have him close. If I had to choose, I'd choose for him to stay here and be close to you."

She slumped in her chair. "Where are they moving?"

"They don't know yet."

"When are they going?"

I mussed her hair. "When they figure out where they're going. It's early days yet. Your dad just wanted to give me a heads-up."

She stood. "I hate change." She ran up the stairs.

I bent over to pet Drambuie. "Me too."

CHAPTER 13

The second load of laundry was in the dryer when the phone rang. I picked it up. "Merry March."

"Merry? It's Wendy, Jean's friend."

"How are you? Did you and Ray get all of the chickens back in the pen?"

"Barely. Listen, I just wanted to tell you that I remembered that fellow's name."

"Pete Vassal?" The phone went silent.

"How did you know his name?"

"It's a long story. He told us he was in love with Jean."

She sniffled. "I'm sorry. It still makes me sad. If he was so in love with her, why didn't he come to the funeral? Why didn't he pay his respects to her mother?"

"Your suspicions were on point. He is married. And his wife had cancer."

She cleared her throat. "So he was cheating on his cancer-stricken wife?"

"We think she might have been in remission. Any way you cut it, it seems pretty ugly. He was afraid of exposure if he went to the funeral."

"Do you think he really cared for Jean?"

"I do. When he talked about her, he got emotional."

"I guess that's some solace. Do you think he'd talk to me? It would mean a lot to share stories with someone else who loved her."

I picked up my phone and googled him. "I've found his work number. It looks like he's a contractor." I read it to her. "Good luck. Let me know if anything else occurs to you."

I took the clothes from the dryer and folded them. Then I squared my shoulders and put on a jacket. I hurried over to Drew's. Arianna answered my knock. "Merry, come in."

She looked like she had just stepped off the runway. She was wearing a fuchsia and lime green form-fitting dress. I looked down at my sweatpants and inwardly groaned. "Thanks. Is Drew around?"

"He's at the library. Is there something I can help with?"

I sank onto a chair. "I told Jenny you might be moving."

Her eyes narrowed. "I thought you and Drew agreed we would all discuss it once we'd made our decision on where to relocate."

I crossed my arms. "That was our agreement."

"Then why did you tell her? We still don't know where we are going, or if we even are going."

I held up my hands. "She caught Drew and me talking last night. She wanted to know what was going on. She's a smart kid."

Arianna paced the floor. "We're having dinner with her tonight."

"I know. That's why I wanted to give you a heads up."

She pushed her gleaming hair back over her shoulder with a practiced motion. "Drew's not going to be happy."

I stood. "I know. I figured it'd be worse if I didn't tell him, and he found out from Jenny tonight."

"You're right. I'm not happy you told her with so much in the air, but I do appreciate you giving us a heads up. I'll let Drew know."

"Thanks." I slunk out.

* * *

Jenny bounded in the back door at nine o'clock. Rob and I were in the living room. She strolled in, talking a mile a minute. "I don't know why you were trying to get me all upset. I talked to Dad and Arianna, and they aren't even sure they are going to move." She kissed the top of my head. "I brought you two cannolis. They're in the fridge. I'll be upstairs facetiming with Jacob." She sped up the stairs.

"What was that about?"

"Jenny caught me talking to Drew last night. I had to tell her they were thinking about moving."

"Ah. Did you tell Drew you already knew about it?"

"I didn't want to get Arianna in trouble."

"That makes sense. What kind of cannoli do you think she brought?"

I stood. "Knowing her it's chocolate. Do you want one?"

He rose. "What do you think?"

"Two chocolate cannoli coming up."

I put the cannoli on plates and Rob put coffee on. He filled mugs, and we sat at the counter. I took a sip. "Wendy called me."

"What did she have to say?"

"She wanted to tell me that Jean was dating Pete. I think she was a little disappointed we already knew."

Powdered sugar floated back onto the plate, as Rob took a bite of his cannoli. "This cannoli is good. I may have to get this instead of the tiramisu next time."

I wiped a bit of the cream from the side of his mouth with my napkin.

He gave me a quick kiss. "Thanks. Did you tell her what we found out?"

"I didn't tell her about Scott. But I did give her Pete's number. I think she's looking to reminisce with other people who miss Jean."

"I still don't understand why Pete was cheating on his wife It seems really scuzzy. But then again, I read that fifty percent of married people who get cancer get divorced." He sipped his coffee. "I guess being faced with mortality forces people to examine their life and priorities."

I shivered. "It just seems so awful."

* * *

The next day I was at the office putting together a presentation on the advantages of pet insurance. I dragged pictures of my cats into the PowerPoint. There was a cute one of Courvoisier attacking a ball of yarn. I chuckled as I put it in place. There was a sharp rap on the door, and Cheryl rushed in. "Tom Butler's dead."

My hand went to my mouth. "That's terrible. What happened?"

"A customer walked into his store and found him hanging from dog leashes."

My eyes widened. "Was it suicide? Or did someone kill him?"

"I don't know."

"Oh my God. Poor Melanie." I shook my head. "They just bought more life insurance. I'll need to let the insurance company know. Thank goodness I delivered the policy and collected the check on Friday. They're covered." I stood. "Unless it was suicide. Then they wouldn't pay."

I texted Rob: "Did you hear about Tom?"

"There now."

"Suicide?"

"Unclear. Talk later."

My eyes lifted to find Cheryl studying me. "Rob's at the pet store. He doesn't know what happened yet. Better connect me to the insurance company's underwriter."

* * *

I was chewing my fourth antacid of the day when Rob appeared at my door. I stood and ran to him. "I can't believe it. I was just talking to Tom the other day. I loved his pet store. He was such a nice man."

He pulled me to him for a long hug.

"What did you find out?"

"The medical examiner's just finishing up, so I'm not sure what her findings are. I talked to Jay—you may want to sit for this part." He guided me to a chair, and I sat. "Three leashes were tied together and looped over one of the rafters. There was a ladder nearby, so he may have used that to climb up."

I shivered. "Why would he have killed himself? He didn't seem depressed." I gasped. "Jean was strangled in her store. The similarities can't be a coincidence."

"It is disturbing. We'll just have to wait and see what the medical examiner says." He stood. "Have you had lunch yet?"

I groaned. "How can you eat?"

"Let's walk over to Delightful Bites. You'll feel better with fresh air."

I donned my coat, and we strolled to the restaurant. The day had turned gray and dank. "I just can't believe it."

"Why don't you have a seat, and I'll order something for you?" I took a coffee mug and filled my cup. Rob joined me a few minutes later. "Feeling better?"

"A little."

"I ordered you a cup of soup and a half an egg salad sandwich. I know how much you like their egg salad."

I gave him a half smile. "Thanks. I'm still not sure how much I'm going to be able to eat."

Patty walked in the door. I waved her over. "Sit with us. We'll move to a bigger table." I picked up my coffee and moved to a four-top. Rob joined me. "I guess I should have asked if it was okay for Patty to join us."

"It's fine."

Patty sat down with her coffee. "Did you hear about Tom?"

"It's so sad."

"I have a turkey tetrazzini casserole in my freezer. Do you want to take it over to Melanie with me tonight?"

"Yes. I have frozen homemade rolls. We can bring those too." Our food arrived. "What did you hear?"

"I heard he might have committed suicide. It's so strange. He was such a positive person."

"I think he was murdered. If it turns out to be suicide, I'll be surprised. Plus, I'll feel even worse about Melanie. It's bad enough when someone dies, but suicide?" I shuddered.

Rob rubbed my back. "Let's not get ahead of ourselves. We don't know that it was suicide."

* * *

Melanie's mother, Pam, opened the door and ushered us in. "Melanie's resting right now." She took the casserole and rolls. "It's so kind of you to bring these. Would you like to sit?" She gestured to the living room. "Let me put these in the kitchen."

Barbara Ziebold was in the living room. She waved as we came in. "Would you like tea?" We nodded, and she poured two more cups. "It's so sad about Tom. He was such a nice guy."

Patty took a cup from her. "Thanks. Were you able to see Melanie?"

"I arrived only a few minutes before you."

Pam rejoined us. "It's so lovely that you ladies stopped by. I know Melanie will appreciate it."

I leaned forward. "How is she doing?"

Pam shook her head. "Not well, I'm afraid. It's been such a shock for her." She lowered her voice, "And suicide. It's so awful."

Barbara touched Pam's arm. "Now, Pam, we don't know that it was suicide."

Pam's eyes narrowed. "What else could it be? There was a ladder there. He used his own leashes. What kind of man leaves his wife and child behind?" Her eyes teared. "His parents will be here tomorrow. I'm not sure what to say to them."

I turned to Barbara. "Does Jay know when the medical examiner will release her findings?"

She shook her head. "He knows better than to push for a date. She can get a bit ornery." Barbara patted Pam's hand. "Hopefully it will be soon."

Melanie drifted down the stairs. Pam leapt from the sofa. "Honey, you shouldn't be out of bed."

"I heard voices."

I stood. "Melanie, we're so sorry for your loss."

Her eyes didn't quite focus. "It's so kind of you to stop by." She jerked, as she realized Barbara and Patty were there too. She gestured vaguely with her arm. "And, the rest of you—" Her voice trailed off.

Pam took her arm, and led her back upstairs.

Patty said, "Wow. She seems really out of it." Barbara and I exchanged glances.

Pam returned and sighed as she sat. "She was hysterical when the police told her, so her doctor gave her a shot of something. You'll have to excuse her. As you can tell, she's in a fog."

Barbara touched her arm. "How's JJ taking it? My son Bobby wanted to come with me, but I thought it was too soon."

"He's upstairs. When I last checked, he was playing a video game. Hopefully that will take his mind off things."

I sipped my tea. "Do you know when the wake will be?"

She shook her head. "The police haven't said when they will release the body."

Patty elbowed me and stood. "Please let us know if there is anything else we can do. We'd love to help."

I rose. "Anything at all."

We walked silently back to Patty's house. As we turned down her path, I muttered, "How awful for JJ. He's only 17. I'm glad he has good friends to see him through."

Patty opened the door. "Glass of wine?"

"I thought you'd never ask." The house seemed silent. "Where is everyone?"

"Probably watching a movie in the den. If we're quiet, maybe they won't know I'm back."

I punched her shoulder. "Do you know how bad that sounds?"

She poured two glasses of wine. "I love my brood, but sometimes mama needs grown-up time." She clinked her glass with mine.

"To grown-up time."

"Amen."

We sat at the counter. "Do you think it's odd that two people in town have been strangled in the last month?"

She grimaced. "When you put it that way, it does sound strange. And scary."

"Let's not forget that both of them served in Desert Storm. They knew each other."

Patty tapped my arm. "Stop it. Are you trying to say that there's a Desert Storm serial killer?"

"I don't know that I would go so far as to say a serial killer, but this seems to be a big coincidence." I drummed my fingers on the quartz countertop. "You know how I feel about coincidences."

"Mom's home!" What seemed like a thousand small feet pattered into the kitchen.

Patty's youngest climbed up on her lap. "I missed you, Mommy."

She kissed his forehead. "I missed you too, sweetheart." She mouthed, "Later," to me.

CHAPTER 14

John Little seemed to be aimlessly pushing his cart at the grocery store the next day. He looked shell-shocked. I stopped him as he wandered by. "John?"

"Oh, Merry. I didn't see you there."

"Are you okay?"

He tried to nod, but failed. "I guess I'm not."

I touched his arm. "Losing Tom is tough."

He sighed. "I knew him for thirty-seven years. We served together. We were like brothers. I can't understand why he would kill himself. I talked to him just the other day. We had plans to go to the Blues, Brews, and Stews Winterfest this weekend. I always looked forward to that." His whole body seemed to sag. "I thought he did too."

"Have the police ruled that it was a suicide?"

"What else could it be? I heard there was a ladder and everything." He ducked his chin.

"Did he seem depressed to you lately?"

"He seemed normal. I can't believe it. First Jean was killed, and now Tom is dead. It's almost like there is a curse on us." He shook his head and walked away mumbling.

I stared after him. A hand clasped my shoulder, and I jumped.

Drew scolded. "Merry, you're so twitchy."

I glared at him. "You scared me."

"Whatever. I owed you that for telling Jenny we were moving."

"She saw us talking; I had to tell her something."

"You're right. She's a smart girl. I would have told her too."

I put my hand on my hip. "Have you and Arianna made a decision?"

"Nope. Not yet. We'll keep you posted though." He chuckled as he strode away.

I felt my face flush. *That man.*

Another hand clasped my shoulder. I swatted it away. Rob's eyes widened. I sighed as I hugged him. "Sorry, I just had a run in with Drew."

He kissed the top of my head. "Apology accepted. Have they made a decision?"

"He's going to draw it out as long as possible just to drive me nuts." I glared at the grocery cart.

He inspected it. "Dinner in tonight?"

"Yes. Scallops were on sale, and the broccoli looked good too. How about that sautéed with garlic and butter?"

"Sounds scrumptious. I'll wander over to the baking aisle and pick out a dessert. Meet you back at your place in twenty?"

I gave him a peck on the cheek. "Sounds great."

The broccoli was rinsed, and the wine poured when Rob walked in the back door. "Better mood?"

I kissed him. "Somewhat. Before Drew surprised me, I had a grueling conversation with John Little."

"What did John have to say?"

"He feels the cadre who served in Desert Storm is cursed."

"It does seem suspicious that two of them have died recently. And both from strangulation."

"That's what I told Patty. I think we need to find out more."

"What would you suggest?"

I heated the pan for the scallops. "We should find out more about Karen Vassal and her relationship with Pete."

"What about Scott?"

I put a tablespoon of oil in the hot pan and dropped in the scallops. "What about him?"

"I don't think he's telling us everything. He should be on our contact list too."

Flipping over the scallops, I gave Rob a long look. "Any other loose ends right now?"

"Probably, but why don't we start there?"

I put the broccoli in a serving dish and loaded the scallops onto a plate. "Would you mind texting Jenny and telling her we're ready?"

✳ ✳ ✳

Karen Vassal owned a bookstore. I smiled. *I love books. Time to do some shopping.* I picked up my phone and pressed speed dial for Patty.

"What?"

"Is that any way to answer the phone?"

"It's perfectly acceptable when you've had the morning I've had."

"What happened?"

"I won't bore you with all the details. Suffice it to say that it involved spilled milk, yelling, and two changes of clothing."

"Sorry you had such a stressful morning, but do you want to go book shopping with me tomorrow? I heard about a new place in Washington Township that sounds good. It's called The Pearl Within. I'll even treat you to lunch afterward."

"What's wrong with the bookstore here?"

"The Pearl Within is owned by Karen Vassal, Pete Vassal's wife."

"Desert Storm Pete? The guy who cheated on his cancer-stricken wife?"

"The same."

She sighed. "I should have known there was more to this than just a trip to a new store. What are we trying to find out?"

"Anything we can. Pick you up at ten."

A light snow was falling when I woke the next morning. The flakes seemed to float in the air. I asked Alexa for the weather forecast, and she opined that, after a brief squall, it would be sunny the rest of the day.

The cats were fed, and I turned the coffee maker on. While it brewed, I checked Facebook. There were quite a few tributes to Tom. I poured myself coffee and sat at the counter to read them.

"Such a great guy." "A real family man." "Kind to animals." He really was a good guy. I blew on my coffee and took a sip. "I know what he did. Guess who's next." My mug landed with a bang. *Whoa? What? Who posted that?* I scrolled up, and the post disappeared. What happened? It was just there—I scrolled all the way up and all the way down. I didn't see it. *Did I imagine it?* A shiver rolled down my spine.

I pulled into Patty's drive. She ran out and hopped in the car. "Thank goodness you were on time. Step on it."

My eyebrow rose.

"I'm running away from home."

"Anything in particular?"

"Syrup and sticky hands."

"Yuck." I backed out of the drive. "The strangest thing happened. I was on Facebook reading all the nice tributes to Tom and there was one that read, 'I know what he did. Guess who's next.'"

"Who wrote it?"

"That's what's so maddening. I was scrolling up to see who posted it, and the post just disappeared."

She poked my arm. "Are you sure you didn't imagine it?"

"I don't think so. Maybe Rob can figure it out." I parallel parked a few spots away from the building.

Patty clapped. "I'm impressed you can still do that."

I grinned. We sauntered to the store. It had an old fashioned sign hanging from a long black peg above the door. It was a carved rendering of a book opening with a shimmering pearl peeking out. "Nice sign."

"I like the name too." She opened the door. A bell rang somewhere farther in the shop.

A voice called out, "Good morning. I'll be with you in just a minute."

Patty went left, and I went right, perusing the selections. The store was really quaint. There was a small gathering spot near the window that included four burgundy leather club chairs as well as a small round table in the middle. I pushed my hand against the upholstery. *Feels cushy. Must be comfortable.* A good book and a cup of coffee, and I'd be set.

"Are you finding what you were looking for?" I turned to find Karen Vassal towering over me, the top of her head tilted slightly to the right.

Wow. She's even larger in person. She must be six foot three.

She cleared her throat.

"I'm sorry for staring. It's just that you're so tall."

She sighed. "It's okay, I'm used to it. I used to play pro-ball."

"I wish I were taller."

"Trust me, you wouldn't on a plane. Was there something I could help you find?"

"It's such a pretty store. This is my first time in."

"It's a small shop, but let me give you the quick tour." She strode over to the area I had just been admiring. "This section is for folks who appreciate curling up with a good book."

"The chairs look really comfy."

"They are. Feel free to try one out later." She escorted me to the rear of the shop. A small selection of coffee urns lined a breakfront. Mugs emblazoned with the store's logo hung from pegs. "This is our coffee station. Would you like some?"

"Yes." I poured myself a cup.

"The mystery section is over here." Patty sat at the end of the row of books in a dark green wing chair. She seemed mesmerized by what she was reading. Karen glanced at her as we ambled by. "Children's books and non-fiction are up the spiral staircase, travel's down that corridor there, and cooking is up by the registers."

"It seems like you have all the bases covered."

"I try to stock a variety." She held out her hand. "Karen Vassal."

I shook it. "Merry March."

"Are you from town? I don't remember seeing you before."

"It's our first time here. My friend and I are from Hopeful. I saw a flyer for your shop, and I liked the name. I'm always looking to discover new bookstores."

"My husband's a veteran. His favorite watering hole is in Hopeful." She shrugged. "Playing pool and listening to war stories isn't really my thing, so I let him go solo."

"You look really fit."

"Thanks. I'm a cancer survivor. When I was going through chemo, I made a vow to get back in shape. I bulked up and started lifting weights again." She displayed her impressive right bicep and laughed. "I'm sorry. I know I shouldn't do that, but it's so much fun."

"If I had those guns, I'd be showing them off too."

"I suppose I should get back to work. Let me know if you have any questions or need a suggestion on a good book." She strode to the back of the store.

I wandered across the store to Patty. She was ensconced on the same chair. The only difference was that she had apparently settled in farther, and both legs were now over one of the chair arms. I swatted one of her feet.

"Ow. What did you do that for?"

"Are you enjoying yourself?"

" Comfy chair, a good book, what's not to like?"

I gestured with my eyes toward the back of the store.

"Are we tag teaming?"

"I didn't get a lot from her, and you are known for your charm."

She groaned, got to her feet, and placed her book on the chair seat. "I feel flattered, but you should know I plan to come back to this seat later."

I lifted the book and plopped down on the recently vacated chair. Opening the book, I started to read. I heard the rise and fall of voices in the next aisle as they drew closer.

Patty asked, "How long have you been married?"

"Fifteen years. My husband was such a blessing when I was diagnosed. He took excellent care of me. I don't know what I would have done without him."

"He sounds like a good man."

"He is." There was a pause. "I know this is going to sound weird but it's almost like our marriage was at its best when he was taking care of me. He became more distant when I went into remission." She gave a short laugh. "I don't know why I'm telling you all this."

I silently moved the chair a little, and then stretched my head back. Patty reached up to touch Karen's shoulder. "It's okay. Sometimes we just need to talk."

"I feel guilty wanting more. He was so good to take care of me when I was sick. We seemed so in tune. Now it's like we're on different stations." She sighed. "It was getting worse, and then, a few weeks ago, there seemed to be a turning point. He started to stay home more." She reshelved one of the books in her hand with a thud. "I'd do anything to save my marriage. Anything." She took a deep breath. "I don't know how we got off on that tangent. The book I was talking to you about is right here." She plucked a book from the shelf and handed it to Patty. "Let me know if you have any other questions."

We took our purchases to the register. While Karen checked us out, I pointed to an old photo near the register. It looked like it was a prom picture of a much younger Karen with her date. He was scrawny and had an unfortunate case of acne. I lifted the photo. "Is this from your prom?"

She took it from me. "Yes, that's me and my husband, Pete. He hates this photo. We met as freshmen in high school." She traced Pete's face with her finger. "He was so skinny then. And shorter than me. He was always getting picked on. He told me that he spent half his high school years with either a wedgie or his head being pushed into the toilet." She shook her head. "Young boys can be so vicious."

"That's surprising. He's so big now."

She stared at the photo. "He is. He had a growth spurt senior year. He also started bulking up, and lifting weights. He vowed he was never going to be picked on again. He was right about that. For a while." She started to put the photo down. "Look at me rambling on. Enjoy your books." She handed me the receipt, and her eyes narrowed. "Wait a minute. How do you know how tall my husband is now? Do you know him?" Her gaze traveled from my face to my ringless fingers and pointedly lingered there.

I shivered. "I met him when I was with my boyfriend at the VFW."

Patty chimed in. "Yep, Merry and Rob have quite the relationship. Almost inseparable. Surprised he isn't here with us now. Got to go." She backed out the door, pulling me with her.

"Almost inseparable?"

"Hey, don't quibble. I got us out of there in one piece. Did you see the look on her face? That's one jealous woman."

I sat in the car. "That was tense."

"It was and awkward situations make me hungry. Feed me."

Stopping at a place I found on Yelp, we ordered lunch. I handed the menus to the server. "It's fun to try a new place."

"It is."

"Explain to me how you got Karen to tell you all about her relationship with Pete."

"A talent I have. You should try it some time. It's called empathy."

"I softened her up for you."

"Whatever. You certainly caused enough of a commotion just before we left." She lifted the bulging bag at her feet. "At least I got cool new books to read."

"She was facing away from me when you were in the stacks. Do you think she knew her husband was cheating on her?"

Patty shuddered. "I don't know. I certainly wouldn't rule it out. Her face turned red, and she seemed pretty vehement when she stated that she would do anything to save her marriage. That plus the frigid atmosphere when we left means that she's not a woman I'd like to cross."

✳ ✳ ✳

Jenny glided through the kitchen on her way out the door. "Going over to Dad's. I'll be back in time for dinner."

Rob reflected, "She's spending a lot of time over there."

"She's making up for lost time. Plus, she really likes Arianna. To be honest, I'm not sure who the main attraction is between the two of them."

"Does it bother you?"

I kissed his cheek. "A little. It could be worse. Drew could have picked another loser."

He placed a sweet kiss on my mouth. "Tough talk."

"And true."

Before I knew it I was on his lap, and we were necking like hormonal teens. I pushed myself up. "This roast takes an hour or so to cook. I better get it in the oven, or Jenny will return and nothing will be ready."

Rob kissed me again. "Wouldn't be the worst thing in the world."

I put the roast in the oven.

"What happened at the bookstore today?"

I lifted the bulging bag sitting on the chair next to him and handed it to him.

He browsed through it. "Looks like you got some good books." He pointed to one. "I'd like to read this one when you're done."

"I have quite a selection. You can read that one first and return it to me."

"Thanks. I will." He picked up his gloves and put the book under them "What was Karen like? Did you find out anything?" I gave him a synopsis of our visit.

"So she's strong, huh."

"Buff, really buff, and big. Almost made me want to work out more."

"We could go to the gym together."

"My emphasis was on almost." I shuddered. "She made me a little nervous. She's very protective of her relationship with her husband."

"What happened?"

"Nothing really. I made the mistake of letting her know I had seen her husband. She didn't take it well. Then Patty talked fast and told her all about the perfect relationship I have with you."

"It is perfect, at least as far as I'm concerned." He hugged me. "Oh, before I forget. I called John Little today and told him that we'd like to go to the Blues, Brews, and Stews Winterfest with him tomorrow in remembrance of Tom."

"Good idea. If we drive, we might be able to get a few brews in him to loosen his tongue."

CHAPTER 15

The Blues, Brews, and Stews Festival was rocking when we passed through the gate. Someone was playing a haunting rendition of *The Thrill is Gone*. I moved to the side and closed my eyes, appreciating the sound. The band stopped. I grinned. "That was great. This is going to be a fun evening."

John grimaced. "I don't know if this was a good idea. It's too soon."

Rob asked, "What was your favorite part of the Festival when you used to come with Tom?"

He gestured with his head toward the white canvas draped brew tent. "The craft beers. They have so many. Last year, they had a chocolate cherry one in honor of Valentine's Day."

Rob grimaced.

"I know what you're thinking, but it wasn't sweet. It was slightly bitter with just a hint of cherry." His chin lifted. "If they have it this year, I'm going to get it again."

We meandered toward the beer tent. Food stalls lined the way. The air was fragrant with the smell of cumin and chili peppers. I observed, "Yum. It isn't just stews; there's definitely chili to be had. Look! We get to vote for the ones we like best." Each of the stations had a small cauldron for patrons to drop tickets in.

John noted, "You can vote for the best beer too."

As we walked into the beer tent, I was happy to see they had space heaters strategically placed throughout. I pointed to them. "Looks like they thought of everything."

Rob held the door for me. "What are you going to try?"

I studied the elaborately scripted board. There must have been thirty different beers, all including a brief description. John's eyes lit up. He pointed to the cherry chocolate lager on the board. "I know what I'm going to start with."

Rob ordered a Russian wheat beer, and I went with the India pale ale. We made our way to one of the tall tables near a heater. Rob waved me in so that I could take the position closest to it. I gave him a grateful smile.

John took a sip of his beer, and the smile on his face widened. "It's just like I remember it. So good." He gestured with his glass to me. "Want a taste?"

I sipped it. "This is good, but it's a lot stronger than mine."

I tried to hand it to Rob. He held up his hand. "I'm good."

"It's tasty."

"I'll take your word for it. I want to enjoy this wheat beer."

The woeful sound of a saxophone pierced the tent. "At some point I want to see who's playing."

John assured me, "Don't worry, we'll do that. Let's have another beer, and then we'll taste the food samples." His glass was empty, Rob's was halfway finished, and mine was still three-quarters full.

Rob gestured with his glass. "Get a refill. I need to pace myself because I'm driving."

John wandered back to the makeshift bar. My eyes widened. "He downed that pretty fast."

"I know. We're going to need to make a food run soon or he's going to feel it in the morning."

John returned. "I'm trying apple cider ale now." He took a sip, and his mouth puckered. "That's tart. May have to go back to the chocolate cherry."

He tried to hand me the glass. I waved my hand. "I think I'll pass."

Rob shook his head.

John shrugged. "To each his own." He chugged a good portion of the beer.

I eyed Rob. "I'm starving. Why don't we check out the food and come back here?"

It had gotten fairly crowded in the tent, so Rob volunteered, "I'll hold onto the table. Bring me back what you think I'd like."

John and I perused the "stews." I picked up a tray and loaded it down with a portobello mushroom stew, a venison chili, and a five-alarm fire chili. John picked up a few others for us to try. He gasped as we passed one of the vendors. They had a meatball stew. "I have to get this one; I was hoping they'd be here this year. It was Tom's favorite."

We made our way back to Rob and set the trays on the table. Rob's eyes widened. "That's a lot of food." He pointed. "Is that corn bread?" He broke off a piece. "I love corn bread."

John lifted his empty glass and pointed toward the bar. He walked in that direction.

I explained what was in the various bowls. Looking up, I whistled as I saw John coming back with another beer. "If we want to get anything meaningful out of John we better do it pretty quickly."

Rob picked up the bowl of meatball stew. He dipped his spoon in and ate. "This is delicious. I can see why it was Tom's favorite."

John raised his glass. "To Tom."

Rob and I raised ours. "Tom."

I sipped my beer. "We knew Tom from the store and from the chamber meetings, but you knew him far longer. What was he really like?"

"He was great. Back when he was young, before he got married, he was always full of mischief." Tom looked up at the ceiling. "When we were in the army, he was always getting us into trouble. I can't tell you how many latrines we scrubbed because of him." He tipped his glass back. "I didn't mind. The fun was always worth the punishment." His eyes narrowed. "Not everyone felt that way. Like Scott Winters. He thought we went a little too far."

"Scott?" I put my bowl back on the table.

"Yes, Scott. He was always kind of straight-laced. Never one for a good gag. He sure liked his beer though. Got kind of ornery when he got drunk, and then he'd pass out." He shook his head. "Anyways, there was this one time when that happened and Tom, Jim Jefferson, and I painted half his face red." He chuckled. "Course it wasn't water based paint. It took him months to get that red tinge off. We pulled some other good ones."

I leaned forward. "Do tell."

He blushed and turned away. "Some I can't mention in mixed company. That Tom was a real firecracker. And Jean. When you got the two of them together, whoo boy, you had to watch out!" He raised his beer. "To Tom and Jean, gone far too soon." We echoed him. He drained his beer. "Time for another."

I elbowed Rob. "I wonder how often Scott was the brunt of their practical jokes."

Rob took the napkin out from under his beer and folded it into a small square. "Could explain the animosity. Of course, this makes things look worse for Scott. It gives him a stronger motive, if he was always the odd man out."

I raised my forefinger. "Give me a minute." I texted Scott and asked if he'd meet me for coffee on Monday.

My phone dinged. "Fine."

✳ ✳ ✳

Arriving early for breakfast, I ordered a scone and coffee and made my way to a table. A few minutes later, Scott strode in and waved. He bought a latte and a cherry cheese Danish and sank down next to me. "I love this place." He patted his stomach. "I think it shows."

"I hope I didn't get you up too early."

"Nope. I'm an early bird." He popped a piece of the Danish into his mouth.

"We're still trying to help you with your case."

"I don't think there's much you can do, but I am appreciative."

"Rob and I went to the Blues, Brews, and Stews festival on Saturday."

"And?"

"John Little went with us. Apparently, it was an annual thing for him and Tom."

Scott groaned. "Those two. Always together. Always in trouble."

I stirred more sugar into my coffee. "John mentioned that they had a reputation for practical jokes. He told us about the time they painted half your face red."

His hand touched the right side of his face. "I can't tell you how much scrubbing it took to get that paint off. It would have been one thing if they used water-soluble paint. But, no, they had to use whatever was available. They made my life miserable."

"Were you normally the butt of their practical jokes?"

He appeared to study the restaurant's menu board. "Not always. Their target changed based on whoever wandered into their sights."

"John mentioned that Jean was quite a prankster too."

Scott shook his head. "That she was. That's how she and Jim Jefferson got close. She, Jim, John, and Tom played a really bad prank on a guy in Kuwait." His eyes narrowed. "I think even they thought they went too far with that one."

"What did they do?"

He turned red and coughed. "I'd rather not say. It was embarrassing. Suffice it to say the guy had difficulty walking for a few weeks till the chemical burn went away."

I gasped. "That sounds serious."

"At first they thought it was hilarious. That's the kind of people they were." He touched his face again. "It wasn't like painting my face. Thank goodness that happened earlier on, before their pranks escalated. I have to say, though, after the chemical burn prank they toned it way down."

"Having your face painted must have made you mad."

"You have no idea. But after I came home, I kind of understood. We were all so young back then and scared. Everyone had different ways of dealing with it. Mine was drinking to excess. Theirs was practical jokes. It's up to God to determine which was worse." He finished his Danish and stood. "I need to get going. Was there anything else you wanted to know?" We walked out together.

"Who was the guy with the chemical burns?"

He stopped in his tracks and seemed to study the street sign for a moment. "Pete—Pete Vassal."

I hurried to my office, texting Rob as I walked. "Pete Vassal target of practical jokers."

"Wonder if he has sense of humor. Talk later."

The insurance company underwriter followed up with me to see if the medical examiner's report on Tom had been released. I told him that I hadn't heard yet, but would keep him apprised of developments. I lifted my phone and punched in Jay's number.

"What?"

"You need to work on your answering skills."

"I'm busy. What do you want?"

"Melanie and Tom bought a life insurance policy just before he died. I'm getting a lot of pressure from the insurance company to find out if it will be ruled suicide or murder. Melanie's got a lot of bills coming in. I'd like to get them to cut her a check."

"I followed up with the ME today. She'll have something for me before the end of the week."

I sent a note to the insurance company underwriter to update him and started on my sales calls.

At day's end, Rob poked his head around my door. "Dinner?"

"If you're okay with pizza. Jenny's going to be home, and that was her request." I gathered what I needed to take home.

"Sounds good." He took the heavy briefcase from my hand. "What was your text about earlier?"

I kissed his cheek as I walked past him out the door. "Glass of wine first."

We bundled in my back door. Jenny was studying at the table. She looked up. "Good, you're home. I'm hungry."

I ordered the pizza. "Pie will be here in 30 minutes. Will you please clear off the table?"

She groaned and gathered her papers together. With full arms, she ran up to her room.

Rob poured me a glass of wine. "Now do you want to explain your text? "

"Yes. Would you set the table while I put together a salad?" He got to work. I put the greens in a bowl and cut a tomato. "Apparently Pete Vassal was the object of one of the group's more vicious practical jokes. Scott wouldn't tell me exactly what happened, but he implied that Pete was having difficulty walking for a bit, and there were chemical burns involved."

Rob winced. "Sounds painful."

I put the salad bowl on the table. Returning to the counter, I sipped my wine. "The part that I don't understand is why Pete would get involved with Jean. According to Scott, she was one of the people involved in the practical joke."

"That is strange."

The pizza arrived, and we sat down to dinner. Jenny asked, "What's new with Jacob's dad?"

Rob took a big bite of his pizza and gestured that his mouth was full. I gave him a dirty look. "We're still trying to figure out what happened. There are a lot of people involved."

"Jacob's worried, because his mom has to pay a lot for the lawyer."

I rubbed her shoulder. "I know it's hard, honey, but this is going to take a bit of time."

"Is there something Jacob or I could do to help?"

Shaking my head, I started to gather the dishes. "Not right now. Let Jacob know we are working on it. I saw his dad this morning."

"What did he have to say?" She handed me her empty milk glass.

"Not a lot. Apparently a few people in this town used to be practical jokers."

"Those people are the worst." She ran up the stairs.

I sank down next to Rob. "Thanks for the help."

He hugged me. "I knew you had it."

"I just wish we were further along."

There was a sharp rap at the back door, and Jay stuck his head in. "Good. You're done with dinner." He walked in and took off his coat, placing it on the kitchen stool. "Any coffee?"

Rob stood. "For you, always." He made the coffee. I pulled out the cookie jar and set it on the table.

Jay sat down and turned the jar this way and that. "What kind are these?"

"Oatmeal, cranberry, and raisin."

His eyebrow lifted.

"I had cranberries left over from Thanksgiving that I was tired of seeing in the freezer."

Jay unscrewed the jar, pulled out a cookie, and took a bite. "Good."

Rob set two mugs of coffee down on the kitchen table and then returned with his. "To what do we owe this unexpected pleasure?"

"The medical examiner's report came in early."

Rob pulled out his notebook. "What did she say?"

"He was murdered."

I gasped. "That's horrible."

Rob asked, "How could she tell?"

"He had bruising and scrapes that were consistent with defending himself. He also had someone else's skin under his fingernails."

"That means the killer was scratched."

"Yes." Jay took another cookie, dunked it in his coffee, and ate it.

Rob pulled the cookie jar closer to him. "Are you thinking that the same person murdered both Jean and Tom?"

"They both served in Desert Storm, and they were both strangled. I think it's a safe bet that they were murdered by the same person. My gut tells me that person is the strong Scott Winters. We still have his DNA from the last time he was arrested. Too bad the lab is backed up for a few months."

I sighed. "I guess it's time for us to bring you up to date." I told him what we uncovered.

"It sounds like Scott had a motive for killing Tom: revenge for the practical jokes they played on him."

Rob took another cookie. "It's hard for me to believe that he would have waited over thirty years to get back at someone for paint on his face. It seems like really old news."

I broke in, "When I brought it up with Scott this morning he didn't seem angry."

Jay stood. "Maybe that's because he already killed off the jokers."

"What about Pete Vassal? It sounds like he had a better motive."

"I'll check him out." He shut the door after him.

I lowered my head to the counter. Rob said, "What's wrong?"

"We just made things worse for Jacob's dad."

CHAPTER 16

The next day, I was in my kitchen reviewing my calendar and making notes, when someone rapped at the back door. I called out, "It's open."

Arianna strolled in. "I know it's early, but I wanted to catch you before you went to work."

"Would you like coffee?"

She nodded.

"Cream and sugar?"

"A teaspoon of cream, no sugar." She ambled to the window seat. "You have such a pretty kitchen. I love window seats. And your cushion is so cheery." She stroked the blue and red flower pattern.

I handed her a mug. Arianna's makeup was artfully applied, and she was wearing a tight wool winter-white dress that complemented her complexion and her figure. *Why does she always look so perfect?*

"Thanks." She took a sip and sighed. "I do like coffee."

"Would you like to sit?"

"Yes." She perched on a chair. "I have a favor to ask."

My eyebrow rose.

"Drew's car comes back from the shop today. They did a great job. You really have to look for the scratch and, even then, you can only see a slight imperfection."

I sipped my coffee.

"We don't have a garage. It would be terrible to leave it in the driveway and have it scratched again."

I groaned under my breath. I knew where this was going.

Jenny pounded down the stairs, screeching to a halt when she saw Arianna. "What are you doing here so early?"

Arianna stood to give her a hug. "I wanted to ask your mom if she'd let Drew and I park his car in her garage for a little while."

"That's a great idea. That way Dad doesn't have to worry about his car getting scratched again. We have an extra door opener." Jenny paused.

"Jenny, it's a one car garage."

"So?"

"Where am I going to park?"

"Your car's old. It doesn't have to be in a garage." She turned to Arianna. "It's just for a little while right?"

"Just till we figure out what we're doing. It'd mean so much to us."

I stood. "Two weeks. I'll let him use the garage for two weeks. That should give you enough time to either come to a decision, or to make other arrangements. Jenny, grab the extra garage door opener for Arianna. I need to get to work."

Arianna stood. "Thank you."

I walked out the door, shaking my head. How do I let myself get talked into these things?

I texted Patty as I pounded the pavement to work. "You will not believe what I just agreed to."

"Sounds like a story. Lunch?"

"Meet you at Delightful Bites at noon."

Cheryl handed me my call list. "Don't forget you have that meeting at ten."

"Come in for a minute and shut the door."

She sat, pen and pad at the ready. "What's up?"

"I spoke with Jay last night. Tom was murdered."

"Oh no." Her hand went to her mouth. "Strangled, just like poor Jean. Who would do such a thing?"

"I intend to find out."

She leaned forward. "You don't think Melanie did it, do you?"

My eyes widened. "What would make you think that?"

"The insurance money. You have to admit it's suspicious. She applied for the policy so recently."

"Why would Melanie kill Jean?"

She sat back in her chair. Her pen tapped her pad. "I know! Jean and Tom were having an affair. Melanie killed Jean, applied for the insurance, and then took out Tom."

I shook my head. "It would have taken a lot of strength to lift Tom up to hang him. I don't think Melanie is that strong. Plus, she's not that tall."

"Tom wasn't that big. He was only five-seven and maybe a hundred and eighty pounds." Her voice softened. "Okay, he might have been too big for Melanie to handle." She perked up again. "Maybe she was having an affair, and she convinced her lover to do it for her."

I groaned. "So what you're saying is they were both cheating on each other? And we never heard a word about it? How likely is that in this town?"

Her shoulders sagged. "It's just a theory."

"I know. You didn't see her the other night. She was a wreck. I think she really loved Tom." I pushed my hair behind my ear. "I do appreciate you sharing your suspicions with me. But let's keep them that way. Just between you and me."

She stood. "You got it boss. What do you want me to do?"

I sat back in my chair. "Call the insurance company underwriter. Give him a heads up that the death was not suicide, and we'll be filing a claim once we receive the death certificate."

She stood. "Anything else?"

"That's it for now."

* * *

Patty was at the counter ordering when I walked into Delightful Bites a few hours later. "What are you getting?"

"I debated between a salad or a Reuben. The Reuben won." She took her coffee mug and went to select her brew.

I joined her by the dispensers, after putting in my lunch order. "Just hot water for me today." I dangled my tea bag.

"Tea instead of coffee." She pulled the tea bag closer. She gasped. "Decaf?"

"Trying to turn over a new leaf. I'm hoping that less caffeine leads to a less stressful life."

She chuckled. "Good luck. I need my high-test to keep up with the kids." We sat in one of the booths. "So what did you agree to now?"

"Before we get to that, I'd like to ask you a strange question."

"Okay."

"Did you ever hear any rumors about Melanie and another man?"

Her mouth dropped. "What did you hear?"

I shook my head. "It's silly. Something Cheryl mentioned. I'm sure there's nothing to it."

She tipped sugar into her coffee and stirred it. "What was your text about?"

"I told Arianna that Drew could park his car in my garage."

Her eyes widened. "Why on earth would you do that?" She slapped her hand on the table. "And they have some nerve even asking you."

I cringed. "It would have been easier if Drew asked me, but he sent Arianna. Then Jenny came in the middle of it. She didn't think it was such a big deal."

"She's not the one parking in the driveway when it's cold out." Patty fixed me with her mom glare. "You are going to park in the driveway right? He's not making you park in the street so he can get his car in and out more easily?"

I hung my head. "We didn't talk about that. I told Arianna I'd give her two weeks to figure out what they were going to do."

"You're a better person than I am." She chuckled. "I would have keyed his car."

"It's such an expensive car. I'm sure it cost a fortune to get it fixed."

"I know. You are such a patsy. You gave them two weeks." She pulled out her phone and made a note. "I'm going to hold you to that."

I popped another antacid when I returned to the office. *When will I be rid of Drew?* I picked up the phone and called Father Tom. "I wanted to follow up with you on the annulment."

"I haven't heard anything yet. Merry, you need to prepare yourself; this can be a long process."

I put my head down on my desk. "Thanks, Father."

My phone dinged. "Eating with Dad and Arianna tonight. Back by nine."

I texted Rob. "Dinner at your place tonight? Takeout?"

"Great idea. Busy till six. Let yourself in."

Rob walked in the door at a minute past six. I handed him a glass of wine. He kissed me. "I could get used to this treatment." I unbuttoned his shirt. His hand stopped me. "Whoa. Don't you think we should order dinner first?" I shook my head no, took his hand, and led him into the bedroom.

As we cuddled afterward, I kissed him. "Thanks, I needed that."

"Are you hungry?"

"Starved."

He got out of bed and retrieved a folder of menus. Climbing back in, he pulled me close. "What are you in the mood for?"

I looked through the menus. "I'd love some moo shu pork."

"Chinese it is. I'm in the mood for General Tso's chicken." He punched in the number and ordered, then turned back to me. "Dinner will be here in thirty minutes." He propped himself up on one elbow. "Whatever should we do until then?" He lowered his face to mine for another kiss.

I was in the shower when the doorbell rang. Quickly drying off, I dressed and joined Rob in the kitchen. "Yum crab rangoons." I pulled one apart and ate half, covering my mouth. "So good."

"I guess you worked up an appetite."

I kissed him on the nose. "I did. Let's eat."

He sipped his wine. "How was your day?"

I groaned mid-bite. "Let me give you the short version. I agreed to let Drew house his uber-expensive car in my garage for two weeks, and Father Tom hasn't heard anything about my annulment yet."

His eyes widened. "Let's take the second one first. We knew that this was going to take time. Why are you so down?"

"I just want it to be over with."

He patted my back. "It will be. Now let's talk about the first thing. What on earth were you thinking?"

I finished my wine. "I know."

I pulled my car up to the house and left it in the street. *The least amount of interaction with Drew the better.* I scurried to the front door. Jenny was lying on the sofa, seemingly enthralled by her phone. She looked up. "You're home late."

"It's not late. It's only ten."

"Whatever. Why did you come through the front door?" She stood and looked out the window. "And why is your car in the street?"

"So I don't have to move it all the time."

She hugged me. "I love you, Mom. I'm sorry I asked you to let them use your garage. I guess we should have talked about it first."

I hugged her back. "It's two weeks. I'll survive, and you're worth it."

* * *

Rob texted me: "John wants company at the VFW tonight. He'll spring for dinner. Want to join us?"

"Sure."

"Pick you up at six."

I slid into Rob's car. "Why did John want us to join him tonight?"

"He had fun at the festival last Saturday. I think he misses Tom. His wife's coming too."

"It will be good to speak with Nancy. I haven't seen her in a while."

Rob pulled into the VFW parking lot. John and Nancy were walking into the hall. They waited for us in the vestibule.

I pointed to the ornate ropes on the walls. "What are those for?"

John caressed a blue one. This is an Army Shoulder Cord. It's worn with a dress uniform.

I touched a gold one. "What's this?"

"It's called an aiguillette. That one's worn by military aides to big wigs. These are actually longer than they're supposed to be. Our decorator thought they would look better in the design."

"They really are lovely."

"Our wedding bookings have skyrocketed since we redecorated."

"I guess it was worth it then."

"It was." John pointed toward the bar. "I hope you don't mind. They're only serving in there tonight."

Rob led the way. "No problem. I looked at the menu last time, and it seemed like they had a pretty good selection." We sat.

I opened the menu. "What's good here?"

John put his menu to the side. "Pretty much everything. Their specialty is burgers. They grind their own meat and do a blend of short rib and chuck. They serve the burgers on grilled buns slathered with garlic butter."

I put my menu down. "Talked me into it. I'm getting the one with blue cheese and mushrooms."

We ordered. John sipped his beer. "Not near as good as the chocolate cherry lager."

Nancy put her napkin in her lap. "When John got home, all he could talk about was that beer. I'm sorry I wasn't able to go."

The burgers arrived, and we dug in. I wiped my face with my napkin. "Going to need more of these." The waiter handed me a small stack. I passed some to Nancy. "Just in case."

The door opened, and Pete and Wendy walked in. I poked Rob and pointed. "Guess she reached out to him."

Nancy turned. "Who is he?"

John stated, "One of the guys who served in Kuwait."

Her eyes widened. "Which one? Not the guy who was cheating on his wife?"

"Yes, him."

She turned again as they sat in a booth against the wall. "The woman he's with—she looks just like Jean."

I shook my head. "That she does. She was Jean's friend. She told me she wanted to reach out to him."

"Is she married?"

"Wendy's married. And her husband is quite a looker." I winked at her.

Rob elbowed me.

"Hey." I gave him a peck on the cheek. "Not nearly as good looking as you, needless to say."

He sat back in his chair, a broad smile on his face.

As the discussion continued at our table, Wendy and Pete were deep in conversation, their heads almost touching. The door to the bar swung open with a bang, and Karen strode in. Wendy and Pete didn't even look up, they were so engrossed. My eyes widened. Karen stopped directly in front of them, eyes blazing. She pointed at Wendy.

"Would you like to tell me who this is?" She sneered, "Is she your new flavor of the month?"

All eyes in the VFW turned to the scene unfolding in front of them. Pete stood and grabbed his wife's arm. He whispered in her ear.

"I won't be silent. I'm not going to stand for this again." She yanked Wendy out of her seat. "He's mine." She slapped her across the face and looked like she was winding up again.

Wendy's hand flew up to block the next slap. "Stop it. I'm not having an affair with your husband."

Ray walked in. He strode to his wife. "Sorry I'm late." His eyes widened. "What happened to your face?" He closed the distance to Pete. "Did you hit my wife?" His fist drew back.

Wendy put her hand on his arm. "He didn't hit me; she did." She pointed at Karen.

The bartender approached the group. "Folks, you're going to have to settle this outside. We don't allow fighting here."

Pete flushed and threw money on the table. "Sorry." He grabbed his wife's arm and hissed, "We're leaving." She glared at him, but allowed herself to be led from the bar.

The bartender pointed toward Ray. "You'll need to leave too."

Ray touched Wendy's face gently. "You okay?"

"Yes. Let's go." She swiveled and walked out of the bar; he followed close on her heels.

The decibel level rose as everyone started talking at once. I turned to Rob. "What on earth do you suppose that was about?"

He looked pensive. "I guess it looked compromising, in view of his history."

John agreed, "It's going to be tough for Pete to explain how he knew Wendy."

Nancy touched my arm. "You were right. Wendy's husband is one fine looking man. So tall."

＊ ＊ ＊

By midmorning the next day, my curiosity was killing me. I called Wendy. "Hi. I just wanted to see how you were doing this morning."

"I'm fine. Why do you ask?"

"I was at the VFW last night." Dead silence. "Are you still there?"

"The whole thing was so embarrassing. I made plans for Ray and me to meet Pete to talk about Jean. Ray was late; one of the cows had her calf. I was catching up with Pete, and his wife walked in. You saw it. She thought he was cheating on her with me."

"How's your face? It looked like she gave you quite a blow."

"She did. That's one strong woman. I've been icing it, so the swelling's gone down."

"Was it helpful to talk to Pete?"

"It was. At least before his wife showed up. You were right. He really cared for Jean. He told me about the time they had, and then we reminisced about being in the service. I forgot that he was one of the guys we ran into in Kuwait." She paused. "It's such a small world. I wouldn't mind seeing him again, but Ray's pretty upset."

"I could see why. Are you and he free Saturday night? Rob and I would like to have you over for dinner. We could make it early, since you have a bit of a drive."

"I think we could make it. Let me touch base with Ray and I'll get back to you."

＊ ＊ ＊

Rob set the table. "Remind me again why we're having dinner with Wendy and Ray?" He pulled me close. "Are you succumbing to his charms?"

I kissed him. "No, silly. I think the key to what's happening stems from Kuwait. It can't be a coincidence that all the major players have Desert Storm in their background." I placed the napkins and cheeseboard on the coffee table. "Wendy has more to tell us. I just know it."

The doorbell rang. We greeted them. Rob poured wine and handed Wendy a glass. Ray put his hand out. "Not for me. It's a long drive home."

"Merry has non-alcoholic beer, if you'd like that instead."

"That sounds good."

Rob returned with the beer and poured it into a pilsner glass. "Here you go."

I toasted. "To new friends."

Rob spread a cracker with Boursin cheese. "Merry told me you got all the chickens back safely in the coop."

Wendy shook her head. "It took us a while, but we managed to have them all back in by nightfall. We're monitoring the fencing more carefully now to keep on top of any repairs. It was an exercise I'd rather not repeat."

I took the cracker Rob handed me and bit into it. "I love this cheese."

Ray put two pieces of dill Havarti on a cracker. "This is my favorite. It's so nice of you to invite us to dinner."

"You lead such interesting lives. I was curious to learn more. How did you two meet?"

Wendy chortled. "He pursued me relentlessly."

Ray touched her shoulder. "It was actually the other way around."

"Guilty." Wendy winked at us. "I mean, look at him." She gestured to her husband. "What woman wouldn't go for that?" She chuckled. "I was at a bar in Texas with my girlfriends. Ray walked in, and I couldn't take my eyes off him. I decided right there and then that he was the man for me. I walked up to him and asked him to dance." She shrugged. "What can I say. The man has a mean two step."

"You're not so bad yourself."

"That was his last single night. We didn't get married for another two years, but the only time we spent apart was when I deployed." She sipped her wine. "Ray's mom died when he was young, and his dad started to go downhill. We moved back here to be with him. He died a few years ago, and we took over the farm."

I said, "Farming seems like a lot of work."

"It is. I had no idea how hard it would be. It's rewarding though."

I stood. "Everyone ready to eat?"

We moved into the dining room, and Rob and I ferried the food in from the kitchen. I put the platter down. "I hope you like chicken. It's cooked with mushrooms and port wine." I pointed to another covered dish. "This is wild rice." Then I gestured to the dish Rob put down. "That's broccoli. Let's dig in."

Dishes were passed, and everyone filled their plates. "I hope you don't mind me asking, but it looked like you and Pete were having a pretty intense conversation the other night."

Wendy tore off a piece of roll and buttered it. "We were. We started talking about Jean, and somehow that led to us talking about Desert Storm." She popped the piece of roll into her mouth and sipped her wine. "Some things disappeared when we were there. At first we thought it was a prank, that they'd get returned. Then we realized it wasn't a prank. Someone was stealing." She picked up her knife and fork again. "It takes a really bad person to steal from their brothers."

"Is this about the ring?"

"Not just the ring. The ring was big, but it came later. Before the ring disappeared, other things went missing: one guy's pocket watch, someone else's Swiss army knife, a pair of earrings. That kind of thing."

"Did you ever figure out who was doing it?"

She moved her food around on the plate. "We had our suspicions."

I put my fork down. "Who?"

"I hate to speak ill of the dead, but we always thought it was Tom. Him and John. We never proved anything, but they always seemed to be around when things went missing."

CHAPTER 17

Rob waved as I hurried up the church steps the next day. He gave me a quick hug and put his arm around me. We strolled in and sat midway up the aisle. Rob touched my elbow. "Do you want to head back to my place after Mass?"

I nodded as Father Tom began. Patty sat a few rows in front of us. She turned and gestured with her eyes toward the back of the church. I elbowed Rob. "Looks like Patty wants to talk to us."

The Mass ended, and Patty waited for us at the rear of the church. As I joined her, she pulled on my arm and whispered, "I can't believe you didn't tell me about Tom. He didn't commit suicide?"

I felt my face flush. "Sorry. It slipped my mind."

"We talked about where Drew is going to park. How is that more important than a person being killed?"

"My bad."

She backed up, and her voice adopted a more normal level. "It certainly was. Are you going to the wake on Tuesday?"

"Yep. We're going."

"Then I'll see you there. Is there anything else you 'forgot' to tell me?" Her fingers emphasized the quotation marks.

I rolled my eyes, and walked out of the church. Rob and I strolled to his house. "She gets so worked up over the smallest thing."

"A murder is inconsequential?"

I pushed his shoulder. "You know what I mean."

He hugged me. "I do." He opened the door.

I followed him in. "Brr. It was cold out there."

"I'll put the fire on."

I turned on the coffee maker and retrieved two mugs. "What did you think about Tom and John being thieves?"

"They don't seem the type. I checked them out, and they don't have any kind of record." He blew steam from his cup. "It was a long time ago. We don't know what they were like when they were younger."

✳ ✳ ✳

Rob picked Jenny and me up on Tuesday night for the wake. The old wooden floors creaked as we entered the vestibule. It smelled musty, like the indoor-outdoor carpets in the viewing rooms were no longer able to be truly cleaned. Overstuffed floral sofas and chairs were stationed at a discrete distance from the casket.

Jenny peeled off to join the young crowd around Tom's son, JJ. Rob and I ambled toward the casket. Tom looked like he was sleeping. The makeup was not overdone, and his shirt collar and tie were high enough to mask any bruising on his throat. We knelt to say a quick prayer. Then we waited in the receiving line. It inched along. Melanie wore a plain, high-necked black dress. It was accessorized with a beautiful necklace. The pendant was a large round-cut emerald encircled by diamonds. My eyes widened. The whole thing had to be at least two carats.

I hugged Melanie when we reached her. "I'm so sorry for your loss."

She dabbed her eyes. "I'm sorry I wasn't fit to receive you the other day. It's been tough."

"Don't worry about it. It's perfectly understandable." I patted her shoulder. "Your necklace is beautiful."

Her smile trembled. "It was the first thing Tom gave me. He didn't want me to wear it out much." She looked down at it. "He thought I might get mugged. I don't know why he'd give me such a fancy thing if he didn't want me to wear it. I've only worn it one other time this year." She sniffed and wiped her eyes. "He was such a good dancer." Her gaze went to the next person in line. We moved on.

Patty and Patrick were watching a tribute video when we came up beside them. Patty turned to me. "Nice necklace." She lowered her voice. "A bit sparkly for the occasion."

I poked her shoulder. "It was one of the first things Tom gave her."

She held up her hands. "Just saying."

John and Nancy made their way through the line. He appeared to flinch when he approached Melanie. Nancy hugged Melanie as John watched. It seemed like he couldn't take his eyes from Melanie. He embraced her next and shook his head as he walked away.

I moved in front of him. "Something wrong?"

His mouth dropped. "My best friend died, so, yes, I would say something is very wrong."

I gasped. "I meant other than that."

He glared and pushed past me. Nancy touched my shoulder as she went by. "He's just upset."

Rob came up behind me. "What just happened?"

"I'm not sure. I think he was upset that she was wearing the necklace."

Rob stared after John and Nancy. "Why would he care?"

I sighed. Jenny gave me a small wave. "I think Jenny wants to leave. Are you ready?"

Rob drove us back home. I asked Jenny, "How's JJ?"

"He's okay. He never shows a lot of emotion." She shivered. "I'd be a wreck if Dad died."

"Your dad will be around for a long time." I hugged her. "Everyone has different ways of dealing with death."

"I have a paper due next week. I better get to it." She ran up the stairs.

I turned to Rob. "Something to drink?"

"I'll get it. Why don't you get comfortable near the fire. Do you want a glass?"

I nodded and turned on the fire. Sitting on the couch, I reached over to open the side table drawer, take out a notepad, and retrieve colored pencils. I sketched quickly. I drew a large round green center stone completely encircled by clear smaller stones. I held it at arms-length, pleased with my effort.

Rob handed me a glass. He toasted. "To you and happier times." I drank. He picked up the pad. "What's this? If you added a chain, it would look just like Melanie's necklace."

"Good. That means I got it right."

He raised his eyebrow.

"I had the strangest thought when I was looking at it."

"And?"

"I thought how big, yet beautiful, the necklace would be as a ring."

He sank farther into the sofa, pulling me with him. "Ah."

It must have sleeted overnight. *Too slippery to walk.* I cursed as I slipped and slid my way to the car. I beeped the trunk open and grabbed the ice scraper. Then I tried to open the door locks with the remote. Nothing. I beeped them again and groaned. The locks were frozen. I pulled out my key and worked it back and forth. Finally the driver door opened. I started the car and turned the front and rear defrosters on high. *Why on earth do I have a garage? I should be charging him rent.*

A car pulled up behind me and the horn gave a short blast. Jacob jumped out. "Let me do that for you, Ms. March. Jenny texted that she wanted a ride to school."

I handed him the ice scraper and retreated to the driver seat. Jenny stared at me as she slid by on the sidewalk waving her arms and mouthing, "I'm sorry." She carefully climbed into Jacob's car.

I pushed the down window button. "Drive carefully, Jacob. There may be slick spots."

He grinned through the windshield. "No problemo. I'm a careful driver."

I pulled antacids from my purse and chewed two. *Thank heavens the roads have been salted.*

Jacob gestured for me to open the trunk. I complied, and he put the scraper back. I pulled carefully away from the curb, and my wheels gained traction on the salted road. I slowly made my way to the office. After parking the car, I extended my arm out, touching the brick storefronts for handholds in case I should slip. I almost made it to the door when my feet slid out from under me. Grumbling, I gripped the door handle and pulled myself up. I edged around the door and into the office. I grabbed the bag of ice melt, opened it, pulled out the scoop, and tossed a few handfuls out the door onto the sidewalk. I brushed off my coat and slacks.

Cheryl's eyes widened. "Did you fall?" I grimaced. She followed me back to my office. "Are you okay?"

"I'm fine. Would you please send out that flyer on the importance of clearing your sidewalks?" I paused. "Oh, and dig out that one on washing your dog's paws to take the salt off. You can send them out together to my client list. Let's call the people who are supposed to be taking care of our sidewalk. They should have salted it by now." I rubbed my hip. "That smarted."

After my conference calls, I punched in Scott's number. "I wondered if you might have time to stop by my office this afternoon. I have a few questions." We agreed on four o'clock.

My stomach growled. I pulled up the shades. The sidewalk in front of my building looked good, but farther down looked like a high-gloss rink. *Still slippery.* I opened the small refrigerator under my desk, reached for a yogurt, and dug in. After lunch, I worked my call list and met with a few associates.

At four, Cheryl knocked on my door and stuck her head in. "Scott's here."

I rose to shake his hand. "Thanks for coming."

He sat. "The roads aren't too bad, but the sidewalks are dicey."

"Your son was kind enough to scrape off my car windows this morning."

He tilted his head. "I thought you had a garage?"

I took a sip of water. "I do, but it's otherwise occupied at the moment."

"I know how that feels. We still have boxes from the move clogging our garage, so our cars have been outside too."

"I wish that was my problem." I tapped the pencil on the desk. "I heard some things recently and wanted to see if you had heard anything similar."

He sat back in his chair. "Like what?"

"Rumors that someone was stealing things while you were in Kuwait."

"I already told you about the ring."

"I know, but I heard it wasn't just the ring. That other things were taken."

He scratched his head. "I don't remember—wait, there were a few things. One of my buddies reported that someone took his Swiss army knife. To be honest, I always just thought he lost it." He shrugged. "He was that kind of guy. Then someone lost the pocket watch his granddad gave him. Boy was he pissed off." He squirmed in his seat. "Huh. So someone could have been taking things all along."

Reaching behind me, I took a blank sheet of paper from my printer. I handed it to Scott. "Do you remember what Jim's ring looked like?"

"Of course."

"Could you draw it?"

He picked up a pen from my desk. "I'm not an artist but I'll try." He sketched for a few minutes. The drawing, though not in color, looked remarkably like the one I did the night before. He handed it to me.

"Was it all diamonds?"

"No." He pointed to the center of the ring he drew. "See that big stone there?" I nodded. "That was an emerald. That stone alone had to be at least a carat, carat and a quarter."

"Thanks for coming by. I heard so much about the ring, but I realized the other day that I had no idea what it looked like. I appreciate you sketching it for me."

Rob arrived at five-thirty. I handed him the sketch. He asked, "Why did you draw it again?" He moved it closer and then farther away. "The one you did last night was better."

"I didn't draw this one; Scott did."

"It's time to loop Jay in. It's clearly the ring put on a necklace." Rob texted Jay: "Meet at Merry's at eight?"

"Better have cookies."

✳ ✳ ✳

The last dish went into the dishwasher when the back door opened. Jay walked in. Rob handed him a mug full of coffee, and I took cookies out of a bag and put them on a plate. Jay stopped in his tracks. "Store bought?"

I shrugged. "What can I say? I didn't have time to bake."

He sat at the kitchen table, picked up a cookie, and dunked it in the coffee. He bit into it and sighed. "Not the same." He fixed Rob with a stare. "Why am I here?"

"We wanted to tell you a story." Rob and I took turns, telling him what we learned. I placed the drawing I made next to the one Scott drew.

Jay leaned forward. "What you are telling me is that Tom stole a ring from someone nearly thirty years ago and had it made into a necklace for his wife? What on earth am I supposed to do with that?"

"It might have been reported stolen to the Military Police."

"From what you told me, the guy who owned it is dead. And we know that the guy who supposedly stole it is dead. Seems like a waste of time." He stood and gathered his things. "I have a friend who used to be a MP. I'll check with him, and we'll take it from there." He paused. "Merry, I saw your car in the street. Why don't you put it in the garage? With the ice we had last night, you're lucky no one plowed into you."

I groaned and put my head on the table. Rob massaged my shoulders. "Where are your keys? I'll pull the car into the driveway on my way out." I pointed to my purse. He kissed me goodbye.

I wandered upstairs and put on my pajamas. I picked up my book and slid into bed. Someone banged on the back door. I pulled on my robe, went downstairs, and opened it. Drew stood there blowing on his hands. "The door was locked."

"I wasn't expecting any visitors."

"Your car's in the driveway."

"I know."

"How do you expect me to get my car in the garage?"

I groaned and pulled on my boots. I grabbed my keys, started the car, and backed out. Drew pulled his car in past me and shut the garage door. I pulled back into the driveway. Muttering, I stomped back into the house, kicked my boots off, and clomped up the stairs.

Jenny stuck her head out her door. "Why are you making so much noise? I'm trying to study."

I glared at her. "Moving the car. Again."

"Oops." She withdrew into her room and carefully shut the door.

The next morning, tiny prisms of ice looked as if they were creeping their way up the storm window. I shivered. *Will this winter never end?* I carefully lifted the covers so that I could get my legs out of bed without disturbing Drambuie. She gave me a disdainful look, stood, circled, and settled back down. "Sorry." I showered and dressed quickly.

While the coffee brewed, I texted Scott: "Would anyone in the military have a record of the ring?"

"If Jim filled out a Personal Property Record, the DCSPER should have it."

"?"

"Deputy Chief of Staff for Personnel."

I sent him a thumbs-up emoji and texted Jay with the information. I opened the front door and bent over to retrieve the paper. The headline read: "Murder, not suicide." My stomach clenched as I kicked the door shut. *Poor Tom.*

I poured a bowl of cereal, sat at the counter, and began to read. Jenny flew through the kitchen on her way to school. "I'm late. Love you." The door banged shut.

I texted her: "Promise me you'll eat something at school." No reply. I sighed, put my dishes in the dishwasher, and left for work.

I texted Patty: "The Pearl Within again on Saturday?"

"Pick me up at ten; I need to be home by two."

Rob met me at Jenny's basketball game that evening. We watched the team move up and down the court. Jenny hit a two-pointer and three-pointer within five minutes, and my hands hurt from clapping. During halftime I told Rob about my plan to revisit The Pearl Within.

"What do you hope to find out?"

I squirmed. "I'm not sure. I need to know more about Karen and Pete. There's something there."

He caressed my back. "I trust your instincts."

I leaned against his shoulder. "We also have to figure out if John is involved in all this."

"Let me think about how to approach him." The game started back up, and Jenny's team pulled ahead.

✳ ✳ ✳

Patty slid into the car. "At least it's warmer today."

"Any day over forty degrees is a gift. And look, the sun is even out."

"Not that I object to an outing, but I still have quite a few books to read from our last trip."

I poked her shoulder. "Isn't Patrick's birthday coming up?"

"It is. But he has his heart set on a new video game he wants to play with the kids."

"Books improve the mind."

"Video games improve eye-hand coordination."

My eyes widened. "Are you really defending video games?"

"You know me. I prefer books. What's your plan of attack?"

"Hold on a minute." I executed a perfect parallel parking job two spots down from the store.

"Rock star parking."

I grinned. "My plan is to ask about her VFW trip last week." The store's old-fashioned bell tinkled as I opened the door.

Karen was checking out a customer. She looked up. "Back for more books?"

Patty said, "Yes." And we began browsing.

The bell tinkled again, and Karen joined us. "Are you looking for anything in particular?"

"My husband's birthday is in a few weeks. I thought he might like a book. He loves mysteries." We walked back to the mystery section.

She lifted a book. "This one just came in. It's gripping, a real whodunit." Her hand brushed the spines of the books as she strolled

146

on. Stopping, she pulled out another one. "This is also a good one." She handed it to Patty.

As Patty read the descriptions, I asked. "What happened at the VFW last week? You seemed upset."

She gasped. "You were there? It was so embarrassing."

"We were dining with friends."

"Let's have a seat over here." She led us to the burgundy club chairs, and we sat. "It was like déjà vu. It was a Wednesday night, Pete made a flimsy excuse and left. I tried to focus on working out, but I got madder and madder. I figured he was at the VFW. He was. And he was inches away from that woman. What else was I supposed to think?"

Patty leaned forward. "Has this happened before?"

Her mouth trembled. "Maybe. I think so." She stood, walked to the coffee station, and held up a mug. "Anyone want some?" Patty and I raised our hands, so she poured three cups. "I can't believe I'm telling you all this. I'd tell my friends, but I don't think they'd ever forgive him." She gave us a wry smile. "You know how that is.

"Anyway, it's difficult to explain. I finished chemo, was feeling much better, and started working out. Things were good between us." She moved her hands up and down her arms. "Really good. For about two months. Then I noticed that he was out every Wednesday. He told me he was working late. This went on for a few months. I decided to surprise him one Wednesday evening. I brought dinner to his office. It was locked."

Her brown eyes searched mine. "Do you know how bad that felt?"

"I have some idea."

"The next Wednesday, I waited in the far corner of his parking lot. When he left, I followed him. I made sure I stayed a few cars away from him. He never noticed me. He went into the VFW. I relaxed. He was just going to be with his buddies. I waited for a few minutes and decided I was being silly. I started the car and was about to pull out when I saw Pete and a blonde exit the VFW. They had their arms around each other. He opened his car door for her, and she got in. He joined her. Once they were in the car, they couldn't keep their hands off each other." She slammed her hand on the arm of the chair. "Their windows fogged. I was just about to go over and bang on the door when the car left. I followed it. They went to that cheap hotel down the road. I felt sick to my stomach. Instead of confronting them, I went home." She seemed to sag in the chair. "I was a coward. I went home and pretended that I hadn't seen anything. I did that for a few weeks. Then, all of a sudden, Pete started to stay home again.

"That's why I reacted so badly to Pete being with another woman. When we got home after the scene at the VFW last Wednesday, he explained everything to me."

My eyebrow arched.

"It turns out that the woman Pete met with served with him in Kuwait. She heard that Pete was a contractor. She and her husband inherited a farm, and they are thinking about remodeling it." She sighed. "I guess he won't get the job now, since I smacked her face."

Patty shook her head. "You don't know that. Maybe she'll understand."

"Not likely. Did you see how mad her husband was when he found out I hit her?" She put her head in her hands. The bell tinkled, and she jumped. Standing, she looked over her shoulder, speaking to the hovering customer, "I'll be right with you."

She pointed to the books in Patty's hand. "Did you decide which one you wanted?"

"I'll take both."

Patty and I slid into my car. I started it and pulled away from the curb. She turned to me. "I just have one question."

"And that is?"

"If she just saw Jean from a distance, how did she know Wendy wasn't the woman Pete had been seeing? They looked very similar.

CHAPTER 18

M y phone rang; it was Linda Winters. "It's Jacob's birthday this week. I was calling to see if you, Rob, and Jenny would be able to join us for dinner on Thursday night. I'm almost embarrassed to tell you this after the scrumptious dinner you prepared, but we'll be going out."

"We'd love to join you. Where should we meet?"

"Fiorella's at seven."

I hung up the phone and made a note. *Need to pick up gift.*

We bundled into Fiorella's right on time. We ordered, and then Jacob opened his gifts. Jenny got him a video game he wanted, and Rob and I presented him with a gift certificate to the LEGO store.

Our meals came, and we enjoyed our dinner. Rob insisted on sharing his veal saltimbocca with me. I closed my eyes and savored it. "You're right. This really does melt in your mouth." Returning the favor, I gave him one of my scallops. As I put the scallop on his plate, I noticed that Melanie Butler sat a few tables away with John and Nancy Little. She was wearing all black. I sighed.

Rob nudged me. "What's wrong?"

I gestured with my head. "Melanie. It's nice that she's getting out. I feel so bad for her though."

Scott glanced at their table. With a bellow, he stood and strode to it. "Jim's ring! Where did you get it?" He grabbed the necklace with his meaty hand and pulled. It popped off, and an angry red line bloomed on Melanie's neck. He shook the necklace in her face. "Where did you get it?"

A waiter held up his cell phone. "I'm calling 911!" He put it to his ear.

Melanie's mouth dropped, and she clutched her blouse, where her pendant used to lay. "It's my necklace. My husband, Tom, gave it to me years ago." She began to sob.

John stood. "Give it back."

Scott towered over him. He shook his head. "It doesn't belong to her. It belongs to Jim's girl. I can't believe I thought it was Jean all this time."

A policeman hurried in. "Okay folks, what seems to be the problem?"

John pointed at Scott. "This maniac took her necklace."

"You're going to need to come with me, sir." The policeman took the necklace from Scott and attempted to hand it back to Melanie.

Scott protested, "It doesn't belong to her. It was stolen."

The policeman's eyebrow rose. I broke in, "You may want to check with Detective Ziebold in Hopeful. He's been working on this."

Tom turned ashen. "What do you mean?"

"When I saw the necklace at the wake, I thought it might be the ring that was stolen from Jim Jefferson almost thirty years ago."

Melanie cried out, "My husband was not a thief!"

The policeman held up his handcuffs. "I'll hold onto the necklace and call Jay, but, sir," he pointed at Scott, "you'll still need to come with me. You assaulted that woman." He led Scott away.

The room began to buzz. John and Nancy led the sobbing Melanie from the room. We sat. Linda's eyes were huge. "What just happened? I haven't seen Scott like that in years."

Rob leaned toward her. "Do you want to leave? I could drive you back."

She moved the silverware on the table. "But we haven't had dessert yet. Jacob's cake. I special ordered it."

Jacob slid into the seat his father had vacated. "It's okay. We'll get it to go and have it when Dad comes home."

"Who knows when he'll be released? I can't take this anymore." She started to cry.

Rob signaled for the check. He paid it and helped Linda up. "I'll take Linda and Jacob home. Merry, would you get the cake and drive my car to their house?" He handed me the keys.

Rob and Jacob escorted Linda out of the restaurant. Jenny and I retrieved the now boxed cake and hurried to the car. Jenny slid in, carefully holding the cake. "What do you think is going to happen to Mr. Winters?"

"I don't know. We'll call Detective Ziebold when we get home."

We dropped off the cake. Linda mouthed that she was on the phone with Scott's lawyer. Waving distractedly, she continued pacing. Jacob followed us out. "How bad do you think this is going to be for my dad?"

Rob put his hand on Jacob's shoulder. "I'm sure that your dad's lawyer will get over there tonight and work something out."

Jenny gave Jacob a quick hug. "I'm sorry your birthday turned out to be so bad. I'll take you to a movie when your Dad gets out. See you tomorrow." Jacob went back in the house.

I handed Rob the keys and climbed into the passenger seat. "I hope they let Scott out tonight. I hate to think of him having to spend the night in jail."

Rob parked in the street behind Drew's car, and we walked in the front door. Within two minutes, Drew was at the back door. "Where have you been?"

"Out."

"Why did you leave your car in the driveway?" He shook his head. "It wasn't very considerate."

I felt the blood rushing to my face. Jenny's eyes widened. "Mom's been really nice letting you park the car in her garage. You shouldn't talk to her like that."

I touched Jenny's shoulder. "I've got this."

Drew sputtered, "I had to park on the street. My car's worth a lot."

Jenny's eyes flashed. "So what? You knew you didn't have a garage when you bought it. Mom's had to deal with the ice and everything. Maybe you should think of someone other than yourself every once in a while." She pulled on her coat. "I'll move the car so you can get yours in tonight. But you better figure out something for tomorrow. Mom needs her garage back." She stormed out with Drew right behind her.

Rob chuckled. "Wow. She's a real spitfire."

"She shouldn't talk to her dad that way." I paused. "Don't tell her, but I'm proud of her."

✳ ✳ ✳

I finished work early on Friday and went home to change for our second cooking class. Patty swung by, and we strolled over together. "What happened last night? I heard there was another scene at Fiorella's." She grinned. "There's a rumor going around that they're going to ban you from the premises. It took them a month to win back customers after what happened last year."

I poked her shoulder. "They're not going to ban me."

"I wouldn't be surprised if they did. Bad things seem to happen around you."

I brought her up to date. We passed Arianna on the way to our front station. I poked Patty's arm and whispered, "Like she eats desserts."

Gary put on his apron and picked up the recipe. "We'll be making profiteroles tonight. Before we get started, would anyone like wine?"

152

Patty's hand sprung up. Mine was a fast follower. He poured wine in glasses and handed them around the room.

Patty picked up the recipe and started to read. "Wow. It looks like you really have to stir the choux dough." She handed me a wooden spoon. "That will be your job. My arm's still sore from cranking out the pasta."

"Wimp. That was ages ago."

Gary went through the instructions and demonstrated making the dough. Patty did the mixing, handed me the bowl, and a pan, and I stirred the pastry dough over the heat. "You sure you don't want to take a turn?"

She shook her head and held a finger to her lips. A voice behind us rose, "It was quite the scene. Poor Melanie. That brute ripped the necklace right off her neck. Then the police took it. She talked to Detective Ziebold this morning. She decided not to press charges so they let Scott Winters go."

I turned my head slightly. It was Nancy Little. I lifted my hand from the pot to give her a quick wave. Patty smacked me. "Keep stirring."

Nancy's voice rose. "You were there Merry. Wasn't it awful? They should have kept that man locked up. First he kills Jean, and then he assaults Melanie."

I handed the pot to Patty. She grimaced, but started to stir. I turned to fully face Nancy. "I agree that Scott could have handled himself better. I think it was the shock of seeing the necklace. We don't know that Scott murdered Jean. He hasn't been convicted of anything."

"I know your daughter is dating his son."

"So?"

"Maybe that's coloring your perspective." She looked down at her pot and gestured to Gary. "I don't think this looks right."

He strolled over and lifted the pot. "I think you might want to start over."

She sighed and scraped the dough into the trash. "Now look what happened. I really need to concentrate."

I could feel my neck flush. I turned back to Patty. She piped the dough onto a silicone pad. Her left eyebrow lifted. "Take a drink. You'll feel better." I took a sip of wine. "Better?" I nodded. "Then get back to work."

At the end of the class, Gary gave us boxes for our leftover creations. I groaned. "I probably shouldn't have eaten two."

Patty agreed, "They were good."

We started for the door. Arianna stood there waiting. "Merry, I want to talk to you."

Patty asked, "Should I go?"

I shook my head. "Don't be silly." I held the door open for Patty and Arianna followed, both jostling their boxes.

"Drew told me what Jenny said last night."

"And?"

"You know how much I like Jenny, but she shouldn't talk to her father like that."

"I've already spoken to her about it."

"Good. So we can continue to use your garage."

"I objected to the way Jenny spoke to her dad. I didn't object to her message. It's been inconvenient, and you'll need to find somewhere else to store the car."

Arianna stopped. "Where else can we keep it?"

I walked through my garden gate. "Patty, would you like another glass of wine?"

"Love one." We left Arianna on the sidewalk.

I poured us both a glass. We ambled to the living room, sinking down onto the sofa. A few minutes later, there was a rap on the back door. The door opened and shut quickly. I started to rise but Rob rounded the corner. "Is this a closed session, or can anyone join?"

I crooked my finger. "Not just anyone, but you can join us if you like."

He held up his forefinger. "I'll be right back." He returned, empty wineglass in hand. He poured himself a glass and then sat next to me. "How was the cooking class?"

"I have profiteroles in the refrigerator if you want to try one."

"Sounds good. I think I'll have one after I finish this." He sipped his wine. "Jay called me." My eyebrow rose. "Linda decided not to press charges against Scott."

"Old news."

"How did you find out?"

Patty lifted her chin. "We have our ways."

"Then I guess you also know that the necklace did start out as Jim Jefferson's ring."

I sat forward. "I knew it."

"Jay's military buddy was able to get the paperwork, and a jeweler matched the photo that accompanied it to the pendant. They're trying to figure out who gets it now."

"Does Melanie know?"

He shook his head. "Jay's going to tell her tomorrow."

"That's going to be awful." I shuddered. "It's bad enough to have someone murder your husband, but to then find out he's a thief?"

Patty murmured, "We should bring her more food."

"I don't know that it will help, but it will let her know no one holds this against her."

"On that note, I should toddle on home and leave you two lovebirds alone." She stood.

"You don't have to leave."

She tapped my shoulder. "Yes, I do." She left.

Rob pulled me closer. "You smell so good."

"Must be the cream puffs. Would you like one?"

He kissed me and stood. "Yep." I lifted Courvoisier off my lap and gave her an apologetic pet. Rob was already opening the box when I joined him in the kitchen. "These look great." He lifted one and took a bite. "They taste great too. You should make more."

I groaned. "You didn't have to stir them."

"You have to stir them?"

"Never mind. Back to the necklace." I sat. He poured himself a glass of milk, took another cream puff, and slid onto the seat next to me.

"I'm all ears."

"We know that Tom was a thief because he stole the necklace and gave it to Melanie."

Rob bit into the cream puff.

"But we don't know if John was involved. Tom could have done it by himself. We also don't know what any of this has to do with the murders." I took a sip of Rob's milk. "Melanie indicated that, prior to the wake, she had worn the necklace just once this year. What if it was at the VFW. What if Jean saw her wearing it and recognized it?" I sat up straight. "Could Tom have killed her because she saw it?"

"Then who killed Tom?"

I massaged the back of my neck. "I don't know. I'd hate to think there were two murderers wandering around."

Rob stood and paced the length of the kitchen. "What if Jean saw the necklace but didn't say anything? Or, what if she saw it but didn't realize it was the ring? It was a long time ago. Maybe when Scott accosted her that morning, she suddenly knew where she saw it before. And then maybe she told Scott."

"Then why did Jean die? And why was Scott so surprised when he saw Melanie wearing the necklace? Nope. I'm sorry. That scenario doesn't work for me."

Rob sank back onto his chair. "You're right. We need more information. I think we need to talk to John again."

"John and Pete."

Rob caressed my hand. "Why Pete?"

"Just a feeling. I think there's something he's not telling us."

He stood and pulled me into his arms. "Agreed. Now let's do something far more pleasant." He gave me a lingering chocolate-scented kiss.

* * *

The next morning, I turned slowly in my bathroom. I took in the outdated, almost retro, blue and pink tile. *Maybe it's time to get it redone.*

I fed the cats. Spying my phone on the counter, I googled Pete Vassal. Pretty good remodeling reviews. I clicked on his number and turned on the coffee machine. *Rats. Voicemail.* "Hi, Pete. This is Merry March. We met at the VFW a couple of weeks ago. I'm thinking about redoing my bathroom and wondered if you might give me a call to discuss it." I appended my number and hung up.

I pulled over my iPad and googled bathroom remodels. *Do I have enough room for one of those palatial stand-alone soaker tubs?* One looked like a work of art: gleaming alabaster-white with gently sloped sides. That would be perfect for a long bubble bath on a cold rainy day. I sighed. *Should I even be looking at this? Jenny's going to college soon. No harm in looking.*

My phone dinged. It was a text from Rob: "Any bacon?"

"You're so suave. Yes."

"Be there in twenty."

I preheated the oven and took the bacon from the refrigerator. Pulling out a quarter-sheet pan, I lined it with foil and filled it with bacon strips. I deposited it in the oven and washed my hands before sitting back down at my iPad. A few minutes later, Rob bustled through the door. "I come bearing gifts." He handed me a white box tied with string.

I opened it. "Ooh. Pastries." I stood to retrieve a plate and transferred the contents from the box onto it. "I don't know which one I want."

Jenny traipsed into the kitchen, rubbing her eyes. They lit up when she saw the plate of pastries. "Yum." She picked up a bear claw and plopped it down on a plate. She sat at the counter and took a bite. "This is so good. You know what would make it better? A glass of milk."

"The last time I looked, the good Lord gave you arms and legs. I suggest you use them."

She groaned and poured herself a glass. She sat again and scrutinized the screen. "Why are you looking at bathrooms?"

I took the egg carton from the fridge. "I'm thinking of having my bathroom remodeled."

"It's about time. The last time that bathroom was done was probably thirty years before you were born."

I shoved her shoulder. "It's not that bad." I did the math, and my mouth dropped. "You may be right."

"I am."

"What kind of eggs would you like?"

"Scrambled with cheese."

Rob concurred, "Works for me too." He pulled the iPad screen towards him. "This one is nice." He whistled. "Wow. Is that the price of the tub?"

I shrugged. "It looks so luxurious, and I do love baths—" I whisked the eggs and walked around the counter for another look. "It's so expensive. Plus, I don't know if I have the room for a standalone tub."

Rob's eyebrow rose. "What brought on this sudden remodeling desire?"

I poured the eggs into the pan and began to stir them. "Karen Vassal reminded me that Pete is a contractor. He's gotten good reviews online."

"So you thought you'd give him a call."

"Already did. I left him a message." I took the bacon from the oven and added sour cream and cheddar to the eggs. Giving them one last stir, I carried the platter of bacon and eggs to the table. "Jenny, would you bring the pastries? Orange juice, anyone?" I lifted the container. Receiving two nods, I poured the juice.

We sat and filled our plates. I chose a glistening apricot Danish with white zig-zag icing. Rob turned to me. "Are you really going to remodel the bathroom?"

"Depends on the quote."

Jenny frowned. "Then you'd be sharing my bathroom while they remodel."

"It shouldn't take that long. Maybe only a week or two, if we're lucky."

She shrugged. "That's doable." She smirked and poked Rob's shoulder. "After all, I had to share with him for a while last year."

Rob's eyes widened. "Hey, I wasn't that bad. I'm fairly neat."

"I know." She grabbed one last slice of bacon as she stood. "Off to the library after my shower."

I looked up. "The whole gang going?"

"Yep. Researching's more fun as a group." She went back upstairs.

Rob took my hand. "So remodeling has nothing to do with the fact that you wanted to talk to Pete Vassal."

"I wouldn't go that far. It's that whole two bird thing."

My phone rang. "Merry March."

"This is Pete Vassal. You called about a bathroom remodel. I could stop by today around three to talk, if that would work for you."

"Three is fine. See you then." I hung up.

Rob's eyebrow rose. "He's coming by today?"

"Yep."

"Must not be too busy."

"It's a Saturday. It's probably the day he does his bids." I tore a piece off the Danish and ate it. "Heaven."

"Thanks for breakfast. The Presbyterians are having a rummage sale today, and I want to get shots for the paper."

"What would Father Tom say about that?"

He kissed me. "He'd approve, especially since he knows I'll be covering his bake sale in two weeks."

I straightened up the kitchen and put in a load of wash. The cats followed me into the laundry room. "Okay. One only." I tossed them both a treat.

Jenny called out, "I'm leaving." The back door shut.

I took my dust rag into the living room and put in an eighties CD. Turning up the speakers, I danced around the room singing to the Bangles, swiping as I went. In the middle of *Walk like an Egyptian*, complete with hand motions, laughter broke out behind me. I swirled around. My neighbor, Andy, stood there. I shut off the music. "You could have knocked."

"I did. Several times. The back door was open so I came in. I called out, but with the whole dance party thing you didn't hear me. I loved your Egyptian imitation." He picked up the CD cover. "Does anyone still have these?"

I took it from him. "Obviously I do. Was there a reason you came? Or did you just want to give me a hard time about my choice in music."

"The latter definitely. That and, as a side note, Ed and I wanted to know if you, Jenny, and Rob wanted to come for dinner tomorrow. Ed's making his famous garlic chicken."

"I'll need to check with Rob on his plans, but Jenny and I are a definite yes."

"Let me know. Now that I have a better idea what music you like, I'll have to craft a special playlist just for you." He walked out the door.

I turned the music back on and finished dusting the dining room. The doorbell rang. At first I thought it was part of the song, but then it rang again. I opened the door.

Pete stood there. "I hope you don't mind, but I got through with another job I was quoting on early and took a chance that you would be here."

"No problem." I gestured for him to enter.

He stood in the foyer. "Nice house." He caressed the thick molding that cased the opening to the living room. "They don't make them like this anymore."

"We like it, my daughter and me. The master bathroom is up here." I led him up the stairs.

He scanned the space. "Nice size bedroom." I showed him the bath. "This is fairly small. What did you have in mind?"

I pointed to the tub-shower combo. "Would it be possible to have a free-standing tub and separate shower?"

He shook his head. "Not in this space. We might be able to do it if I expanded into your bedroom a few feet."

I went back into the bedroom. "How much space are we talking about?"

He pointed. "See where that window is?" I nodded. "Now move about two feet to the right of it and carry that line all the way across to where the bathroom door is."

I walked back into the bathroom. "Where would you position the tub?"

"I'd center it on the existing window."

I tried to visualize what he was describing. I shook my head. "I need to see it."

"Let me take measurements, and I'll come back with a plan and an estimate."

"I'll be downstairs if you need me." I walked down the stairs, put in another load of wash, and sat on the window seat in the kitchen. *Can I afford this?* A few minutes later, I heard his tread on the stairs. I called out, "In here!"

He joined me. "I'll work up the plans."

"If I decide to move forward, what kind of timing should I expect?"

"Normally I wouldn't be able to start for a few months, but I have a big kitchen job where the owners ordered custom cabinets from Italy. Long story short, the cabinets are stuck on a barge in port, and there's going to be a delay in delivery. I could probably start by the end of this week, if you approve the plans, and don't have anything too fancy that needs to be ordered."

I leaned against the counter. "That's fast."

"There's another job where I could move my crew. But it would mean that I wouldn't get back to your job for at least three months."

"Wow. End of next week or three months?"

"That's right. A lot of people are remodeling right now."

I shook his hand. "Get me the estimate and plan, and I'll give you an answer."

"I'll have it for you Monday night. Eight work for you?"

"See you then." He left, and I leaned against the door. I got so wrapped up in the bathroom I forgot to pump him for information. I sighed.

CHAPTER 19

Jenny and Rob waited for me at the door. I bent over the wine fridge. "Let me grab two bottles of wine. A Pinot Grigio would be nice. That and a Merlot." I pulled out two bottles and handed one to Rob, "Let's go, we're going to be late."

Jenny led the way. "Like it isn't your fault."

We scooted across the alleyway and up the deck stairs. Andy opened the door. "Welcome friends. Ooh and even better, friends who bring wine." He inspected the bottles. "Should be tasty." He retrieved a corkscrew and opened the white. "Let's start with this. Jenny, would you like a soda?"

"Cola, if you have it."

Andy poured her soda, and then poured four glasses of wine.

Ed looked up from peeling garlic. "Be right with you. I want to get the chickens in the oven." The birds were resting on the counter, nestled in a bed of potatoes, celery, onions, and carrots.

I exclaimed, "It looks wonderful! How much garlic do you use?"

"A full head. Don't worry, it gets milder while the chickens roast."

"I love garlic. As long as everyone eats it, no one should complain about garlic breath."

Jenny's hand rose. "I'm still going to complain about your breath, Mom."

I elbowed her. "I had no doubt."

Andy pointed toward the living room. "I have nibbles in there. Let's relocate so Ed can finish working his magic."

We strolled in. Jenny's eyes lit up when she saw the cheese board, "Ooh. Dill Havarti. My fav!" She slid a piece onto a cracker and ate it. "Yummy."

Rob dipped a celery stick into the hummus. He caught my gaze. "May as well go whole hog on the garlic theme."

I poked his shoulder.

He handed it to me and made himself another. "Andy, what's new with you and Ed?"

"The teashop is going gangbusters. And the spillover to the antiques business is just as we predicted. So much fun."

I chimed in, "Isn't it a lot more work?"

"Not really. We come in late on Sunday and take Monday off. Plus, is it really work if you love what you do?"

"True."

He leaned toward me. "Guess who stopped by the house yesterday?"

I shrugged.

"The exotic princess."

Rob's eyebrow rose. I groaned, "That's what he calls Arianna. I'll bite. What did she want?"

"Ed and I are fun people, why shouldn't the exotic princess want to get to know us better?"

"That's undoubtedly true, but somehow I doubt that's what she wanted."

"You're right. She wanted to know if we had room in the garage to store Drew's car. Normally we wouldn't, but since we emptied it out when we opened Ed's business, we had room. So now we have an expensive car in the garage, and they are paying us rent. Win-win."

I sipped my wine. "I wondered where he was keeping it. At least they're paying you."

Andy tapped my arm. "I've been dying to ask. What happened at Fiorella's the other night? I heard you caused quite a commotion."

I held up my finger. "First, I did not cause anything; I was an innocent bystander." Rob handed me a cracker, and I took a sip of wine. "Scott Winters saw Melanie Butler's necklace and went a little nuts."

Jenny gave me a dirty look. "He didn't go nuts. He was just surprised and angry."

Andy asked, "Why was he so angry?"

"Mrs. Butler was wearing a necklace made from a ring that had been stolen from his dead army friend." Jenny tilted her head. "I can see why he was upset."

I touched Jenny's arm. "I need to say this. No matter how upset anyone gets, they should never assault someone."

She rolled her eyes. "I know that, Mom. I'm just trying to explain why he acted the way he did."

Andy tapped his chin with his finger. "Was this an emerald necklace surrounded by diamonds?"

My eyes widened. "How did you know?"

"Tom brought it to me about a year ago. He wanted to sell it."

"He wanted to sell the necklace?"

"He was worried they hadn't saved enough for JJ's college tuition. He wanted me to appraise it and then potentially buy it from him." Andy bit into a carrot.

"What did you do?"

"I told him my field wasn't jewelry, but I had a friend in the business. I asked him to leave it with me, and I would reach out to get it appraised. He refused and told me he would get it done elsewhere." He spread more cheese on a cracker. "It was interesting. He told me not to mention his visit to anyone, especially his wife."

Rob sipped his wine. "Maybe he told you that because it was stolen."

Andy's eyebrow rose. "I thought it was because he didn't want anyone to know about his financial difficulties."

I sighed. "It could have been both reasons."

Ed scooched in between Jenny and Andy on the sofa. "Make way for the chef if you want to eat tonight." Jenny and Andy made room. Ed put cheese on a cracker. "Tom was a jewel thief?"

I shook my head. "For all we know it was one piece, one time."

Andy shook his head. "Uh uh. But he didn't just bring the necklace. He also showed me some antiquities he bought when he was in Kuwait. Again, coins and miniatures are not really my thing. Why is it that no one ever comes to me with a nice Hepplewhite sideboard or even a chair. Now that's something I could drool over." He sat back on the sofa. "And it's something I know about."

A bell rang. Ed stood. "Five minute warning folks."

Andy lifted the cheeseboard. "Who wants to help me set the table?"

Jenny stood. "I'll do it." Andy put his arm around her, and they walked into the kitchen.

I turned to Rob. "Antiquities?"

"That's what I heard."

"Sounds more exotic than the odds and ends Wendy told me went missing."

* * *

Jenny's face was planted in her pillow the next morning. I shook her lightly. "Jenny, it's time to wake up."

She pushed my hand off her shoulder. "It's too early."

"It's not my fault you wanted to play cards with us after dinner. I knew you'd be tired."

She sat up and rubbed her face. "Why did you let me?"

"Because I'm a mean mother. Are you up? I need to leave for the office."

"I'm up." She stood and then sank back onto the bed, pulling the covers up over her. "It's cold out there."

"I turned the heat up. It should warm up in a minute or two." I pulled the covers down. She groaned and grumbled under her breath all the way to the bathroom. I ran down the stairs and out the door.

When I walked into my office, Cheryl was on my heels. "I got a call from the insurance company. They're going to investigate Tom Butler's claim. I bet they think it was his wife too."

I sighed. "They don't think it was his wife. This is standard procedure when someone dies just after purchasing a policy. Hopefully it won't take that long."

"That brings me to the second thing. Melanie Butler called asking when she would get the check. She seemed kind of anxious. That's suspicious, if nothing else."

"Funerals are expensive. I'm sure she's just worried about the money. I'll give her a call. Anything else?"

"Nope that's it for now."

I reached for my phone and punched in Melanie's number. "Good morning. Cheryl mentioned you called about Tom's claim."

She sniffled. "I did. I know you're working on it. I was just wondering when I might receive the check."

I tapped my pencil on the desk. "There's going to be a bit of a delay. Whenever there's a claim so close to when the policy was purchased, the insurance company has a duty to make sure everything was above board."

"Is there a chance they won't pay?"

"They'll see that everything was done correctly, and this was just a horrible coincidence. I'll follow-up with them at the end of the week."

"It's just that we had the funeral expenses and now the mortgage payment is due. I have enough money, but I don't want to spend anything until I have that check in my hand."

"Don't worry. I'll keep you informed as the process moves along." I hung up and made a note to call the insurance company at the end of the week. I had several meetings the rest of the day, and it went quickly.

Rob texted: "Dinner in tonight?"

"Yes. Jenny won't be there."

"My house?"

"No. Meeting with Pete at eight at my place to go over plans."

"I'll pick up dinner and bring it with me."

I ambled in the door, kicked off my shoes, and slid into my slippers. I sat on the window seat and gave the cats some well-deserved attention. Drew and Arianna roared out of their driveway. *Wonder what they are doing for dinner.* I shrugged. *Who cares?* I set the table and poured two glasses of wine. Rob walked in. I gave him a kiss. "What are we having?"

"Since it's cold out, I thought we'd have soup. Gary was offering split pea with ham so I took him up on it." He pulled a large container of soup from the bag. "I also bought a baguette and brownies for dessert." He presented the brownies to me with a flourish.

"Everything looks great. Mind if we eat at the counter?" I handed him a glass of wine.

He sat, while I retrieved bowls, utensils, and plates. "How was your day?"

"Good. I think the cats are getting a bit stir-crazy. They can't wait to go out in the yard again." Both had their noses pressed against the window.

"I see what you mean." He sipped his wine. "I saw John today."

My left eyebrow arched. "What did he have to say?"

"He was complaining about Melanie."

"What? Why on earth would he do that?"

"He implied that it was her fault that the necklace was taken. He felt she should have adhered to Tom's wishes and not worn it out."

"But Tom's dead." I ladled the soup into bowls. He pulled the baguette to him, ripped off two pieces, handed me one, and pushed the butter toward me. I spread some on a piece and popped it in my mouth.

"That he is. John was mad because he feels Melanie ruined Tom's reputation. Now people will remember him as a thief."

"He was a thief."

"I'm just telling you what he said."

I ate a spoonful of soup. "This is good." I winked. "Almost as good as mine."

He elbowed me. "You'll have to make it for me sometime." He buttered his baguette. There's another festival coming up that he wanted us to go to. Are you game?"

"Which one is that?"

"Suds and Grub."

"Oh great. More beer. We'll get treated to another ode to chocolate cherry lager."

"Speaking of chocolate, are you ready for dessert?"

He cleared the dishes and plated the brownies. "Milk or coffee?"

"Milk, please."

He poured me a glass.

I sipped it. "Do you want to go?"

"Yes. You saw the way he drank at the last brew fest we went to. Hopefully we can get more answers from him this time."

The doorbell rang. I glanced at the clock. "It's eight already? That must be Pete."

I led Pete back to the kitchen. "Would you like a brownie? We were having dessert." I extended my hand toward the kitchen table. "Please sit."

He did. "I don't want to trouble you."

"No trouble at all." Rob delivered him a brownie. "Coffee or something else?"

"Java's fine." Rob started the machine. Pete took a bite of the brownie. "This is good. Did you make it?"

I shook my head. "Rob picked them up at Delightful Bites, a shop in town."

"I'll need to check it out." He pulled a blueprint from his case and unrolled it on the table. I sat next to him. We used the salt and pepper shakers and the napkin holder to keep it from curling back up. He pointed. "Here's where we would move the wall in your room. See, it's just a bit past the window, like we discussed. And this is the bathroom. The tub is here under the window. We'll have to get one shorter than a standard tub to fit in a separate shower. I hope that's okay."

"I'm five feet two inches. I don't need a really long one."

"This is the shower. The toilet is tucked out of the way past the shower, and then you have your vanity on the opposite wall here." His finger traced the applicable points on the blueprint as he spoke.

"That looks good, but it's still hard to imagine."

He pulled out his laptop. "Many clients are visual like you. I've created a three dimensional rendering that may be more helpful." He turned it on and pulled up the program. He moved the screen toward me. "Here you go."

My mouth dropped. "It's in color! That is gorgeous. I love the tub. Those sloping sides look perfect for long soaks. What kind of tile is in the shower?"

"That's a tumbled travertine."

"Is that a glass border?" I pointed. "I like how it breaks up the travertine. Such nice greens and blues. That way it's not all beige."

Rob handed Pete his coffee and peered at the screen. "That's a really nice bathroom."

I gulped. "How much?"

"I've prepared an estimate." He handed it to me. "All in, depending on the fixtures you select, it'll run about $15,000."

"That includes moving the wall?"

"I don't think it's load-bearing. If it is, we may have to increase the budget." He put the blueprints back in his case.

I stared at the screen.

"You probably want some time to think about this. Don't forget I have a small window that's opening at the end of the week. If you want to get on the schedule, I need to know by tomorrow."

"I'll take it."

Rob's eyes widened. "Don't you want to think about it overnight?"

I shook my head. "Nope. I want it. It's been ages since I've bought anything for myself. It's time. I can't wait to use the tub." I turned to Pete. "How long will this take?"

"If you select things that are in stock and that wall isn't load-bearing, we should have everything finished up in about a week." He handed me three cards. One was for a fixture and bath place, another for tile, and the last for cabinets. "These are the places I do business with. They know the allowances I have built in and will let you know if you are over or under with your selection. If you go over, you'll pay more. If you go under, you'll pay less. Please make your selections by Thursday night, at the latest, so we can start on Monday."

"That shouldn't be a problem. Do you need money now?"

"At the end of the job." He sipped his coffee.

I held out the plate of brownies. "Would you like another?"

He shook his head. "My wife's been after me about my weight, so I should stop at one."

"I think I've met her. My best friend Patty took me to her bookstore. Isn't it called The Pearl Within?"

"Yes, that's it. Sometimes she brings me home books she thinks I'll like."

"That must be nice." I nudged Rob. "Why don't you own a bookstore." I turned back to Pete. "Did you hear about the stolen necklace?"

"What necklace?"

"The one that Tom Butler gave his wife. He stole a ring from Jim Jefferson when he was in Kuwait and had it made into a necklace for Melanie. You served with him, didn't you?"

His mouth dropped. "He stole Jim's ring? I was just talking to Wendy about that last week." He lowered his voice. "I thought John might have been involved too. Quite a few of us had things stolen. And then there was the whole Kuwait fiasco."

Rob held up his hand to stop him. "What fiasco?"

"We were pushing forward and the Iraqi army was in full retreat. As they left, they took everything that wasn't nailed down. Their main focus seemed to be antiquities. In Kuwait City, we found a trove that hadn't been plundered. The top brass was excited. Then some of what we found disappeared. That made the find not as great a story. They eventually blamed the retreating Iraqi army. That didn't make any sense. They were long gone when the things we found went missing."

"Why would you think that Tom and John took the things?"

"Those two were as thick as thieves. Huh. I guess they were thieves. Too bad Tom died before anyone found out. Thieves in the military should be shot."

Rob asked, "Do you remember what was taken?"

"Miniatures and old coins. I remember hearing that one of the miniatures was a rare copy of the Holy Quran. It was tiny, and the case surrounding it was gold." Pete stood. "I'll see you bright and early on Monday morning. Please clear everything out of the bath by then. Don't hesitate to call me if you have any questions." He left.

I sat at the counter. "Would Tom really have stolen a copy of the Quran?" I shuddered. "Somehow that seems sacrilegious."

Rob crossed himself. "It does."

My stomach clenched, and I put my head on the counter. *The bathroom's expensive. Is it worth it?*

Rob massaged my back. "What's wrong? Buyer's remorse?"

I straightened my shoulders. "Nope. If Drew can buy an expensive car, I can spend a little money on myself."

"I don't understand why that's a good comparison, but if it makes you feel better—"

* * *

The next morning, I texted Patty: "Need emergency consultation. Having bath redone. Know a good designer?" I appended a smiley face emoji.

"What fun. It's about time."

"Contractor gave me list of places to shop. Pick you up at six-thirty."

I swung by Patty's house, Jenny in tow. Patty slid into the back. Jenny hopped out. "I could sit in the back, Mrs. Twilliger."

Patty buckled her seat belt. "No problem, Jenny. I like feeling that I'm being chauffeured."

Jenny sat back down. "If you're sure."

Patty clapped. "This is going to be great. I've been waiting to get my hands on your bath forever."

I shook my head. "It seems so overwhelming: fixtures, tile, cabinets—this is going to take forever."

"No need to panic. I'll steer you through it."

We pulled into the plumbing supply store first. My eyes widened as I walked in the store. "Oh my goodness. So many choices."

A sales person approached. "Patty Twilliger. It's been ages."

She laughed. "Ages and four kids."

"What project are you working on now?"

Patty tagged my shoulder. "My best friend's bath. If your store's still set up the way I remember, the good stuff is this way." Jenny, the sales person, and I followed like ducks in a row. Patty stopped and caressed oil-rubbed bronze fixtures. "I was thinking something like this. It's elegant and timeless."

I gulped. "I'm not sure that's in my budget." I turned to the sales person. "My contractor is Pete Vassal. He told me you'd know his allowances."

She tapped into her iPad. "Here is his information. These are a bit more expensive than what was he usually uses."

Patty huffed, "You don't want something that's going to be builder grade."

"I also don't want to break the bank. Can you work with her to find something that's within the budget?"

The sales person and Patty walked away to confer. Patty marched back. "This way." She moved us through a quick process, and in twenty minutes the sink, tub, faucets, and accompanying fittings had been selected.

We strolled out of the store. I exclaimed, "I can't believe how fast that was! It ended up being two hundred dollars more than I wanted to spend, but I love all the finishes. I'm in love with that tub. Alabaster white. So shiny. I'll feel like a queen soaking in it. I love how the back is higher than the front. And it's just the right size for me; I won't be wasting water."

Jenny elbowed me. "You are going to let me take baths in your room, aren't you?"

"Maybe. But only if you promise to clean it after you use it." I tapped her nose. "Plus, I'm going to have the inaugural bath."

Patty asked, "What's next on the list?"

"Cabinets." I drove to the store. After some back and forth, those were selected.

"Tile store is next." I groaned. "This is probably going to take a while."

Patty smirked. "If you agree with my choices it could be a quick trip."

Jenny and Patty started towards the accent tile, while I went toward the base tile. As I was trying to figure out the difference between regular travertine and tumbled travertine, loud voices arose from the next aisle. "I can't believe you were so stupid as to wear that necklace. Now everyone knows Tom's a thief."

A woman hissed, "How was I supposed to know he stole it? Is there anything else I should be worried about?"

The reply was garbled.

"Well it's not like I can wear those." The voices drew closer. "Stop blaming me. You should have told me the necklace was stolen." They rounded the corner. Melanie's mouth dropped, and she elbowed John. "Merry, what a surprise."

I gave a half-hearted wave. "I'm having my bath redone."

Melanie ran her hand along the tile. "John's going to put in a backsplash for the kitchen; Tom kept on meaning to get to it." She gave a tremulous sigh. "If the insurance doesn't come through, I'll need to think about selling the house. The realtor I spoke with taught me that buyers in my price point expect to see tile behind the sink." She sighed again. "Just another thing that needs to be done."

"Melanie, I'm sure the insurance company will pay. It's only a delay."

"That's my hope, but I need to plan just in case." She held out the tile sample. "This is what I'm going to use."

I touched the tile. "It's pretty."

"And not that expensive. Do we need anything else, John?"

John shook his head. "That's it." He nodded at me. "See you on Saturday for the Suds festival."

"Look forward to it."

Jenny ambled toward me, holding out a sample. "How's this for the accent tile?"

My eyes widened. "It's shimmery. And colorful."

"It's supposed to be." She wiggled it up and down. "It's supposed to look like the water."

I pointed to the red splotches. "What are those supposed to be?"

"Crabs. Aren't they cute?"

"Maybe something with a bit less red."

Patty struggled back with all of her selections. She hoisted them onto the desk, and then plucked the tumbled travertine from my hand. "This for the shower." She placed the accent tile on top of the travertine. "This for the accent tile. And this nice piece of white quartz for the counter."

Jenny caressed the counter sample. "Ooh. Sparkles."

Patty lifted another tile sample. "And this for the floor."

I stood back, examining the mix of tiles and textures.

Jenny put her choice of accent tile back onto the travertine. "What do you think of this, Mrs. Twilliger?"

Patty tapped her chin with her forefinger. "You have a good design sense, Jenny. I'd love what you picked out for a more discerning client, one who wasn't afraid of color." She caressed the travertine. "Your mom is looking for something more Zen." She picked up the accent tile and handed it back to Jenny. "If your mom ever decides to redo your bathroom, we'll use it there."

I touched the tiles Patty had assembled, feeling the texture. "I think I love this combination. Please tell me this is within the allowance Pete gave."

She shook her head. "We are within budget. That's good, because I have other things that would be just perfect."

I shuddered. An expensive bathroom was about to get even more expensive.

* * *

The next evening, I packed everything in my bathroom. I was stunned by the amount of stuff I had accumulated. *Why do I always say yes to the free make-up samples?* By the time I was done, I had a big black garbage bag destined for the trash, worn towels destined for the local animal shelter, and a large bin filled with items I still used on a daily basis. I grinned in the mirror. *Probably not even half of what Arianna uses.*

Feeling accomplished, I floated down the stairs. I checked the freezer and was happy to see ice cream sandwiches. I unwrapped one and sat at the counter, savoring it. There was a quick knock at the door. Rob walked in. "Ice cream? Isn't it cold out?"

"It is. But I worked up a sweat boxing everything from my bathroom."

He shook his head. "If it was anything like your attic—"

I pushed his shoulder. "I don't have that much stuff."

"Whatever. Any more ice cream?"

I pointed toward the freezer.

He retrieved one. "I love the chocolate coating. This is good."

"It is." I took another bite. "You'll never guess who I caught having a fight at the tile store."

His eyebrow rose. "Who?"

"John Little and Melanie Butler."

"A bit random. What were they doing there?"

I explained.

"Interesting. So it looks like John was aware the necklace was stolen."

"That wasn't the only thing stolen. I think we should give Jay an update."

CHAPTER 20

Jay put down the menu and shifted forward in his chair. "I'm still trying to untangle the whole necklace-ring mess, and now you want to hand me another one?"

"What happened to the necklace?"

"It's still in police custody. We reached out to Jim Jefferson's parents. They don't want it shipped, so they are flying here. They're going to arrive early next week."

I leaned back and crossed my legs. "I wonder if Scott knows they're coming to town."

"We haven't told him."

"Would you mind if I did? Jim was his friend, and he may want to reach out to them."

Jay's eyebrow rose. "You do know he's accused of murder right?"

"I know. It's just that the ring was stolen from his dead friend while Scott was being medevacked out."

Jay sighed. "You can tell him."

"Now what about the rest of it."

"Merry, I'm investigating two murders, not a larceny case that's thirty years old. You pulled me into an old army case, and now you want me to get involved in Kuwaiti antiquities?"

I put my hand on his shoulder. "In a word, yes."

"These lunches are just not worth it. I'm getting dessert to go, and you're going to pay for it."

"I'd be happy to spring for dessert."

"Try to get me something else on this. Tom's dead. No one cares about the stolen items anymore. What difference will uncovering the truth make? I can't justify spending my time on this."

"We think John was involved."

"At this point, that's just a guess. You don't have any hard proof. Tom approached Andy looking to sell the necklace. John wasn't with him."

I motioned for the waiter to refill Jay's coffee cup. "Maybe John didn't know that Tom was going to approach Andy. Maybe Tom went behind John's back to sell the stolen goods. Maybe he was trying to cut him out." I sipped my tea. "Might be a motive for murder."

"Maybe for Tom's murder, but not for Jean's." The waiter handed Jay a box of cookies. He stood. "Thanks for lunch." He held up the cookies. "And dessert."

I strolled back to the office. The sun was shining, and the thermometer was projected to hit the fifty degree mark. I smiled. Spring was just around the corner. The afternoon was busy, but I managed to text Scott. He agreed to meet me at the office at five.

"Please have a seat. Would you like some water?" Scott nodded, and I handed him a bottle. "Jim's parents are flying here early next week to get the necklace. I thought you might want to know."

He looked toward the ceiling. "The last time I spoke with them was twenty years ago when Linda and I were on vacation in California. We still send Christmas cards though."

"It would probably mean a lot if you reached out to them. This has to be difficult. I'm sure they're pleased to get the jewelry back, but the reminder is likely painful."

"You're right. I'll call them tonight."

Rob peeked in. "I'm sorry. I didn't realize you were with someone." He started to back out.

Scott stood. "I was just leaving. Thanks for the information."

He walked past Rob, nodding as he left.

Rob sat in the seat Scott had just vacated. "What information?"

"I'll tell you all about it at dinner." I gave him a peck on the cheek and retrieved my coat and purse. "Ready?"

"You are a woman of mystery."

I batted my eyes, as I slid past him out the door.

* * *

Rob picked John up on the way to the Suds and Grub fest. He slid in the back seat. "Thanks for driving."

I turned to face him. "Too bad Nancy had to work today."

"Yep. She likes her beer too."

We drove into the parking lot. Rob's eyes widened. "Wow. There are a lot of people here."

John declared, "It's a great showcase for all the craft brewers in the area."

I led the way. "I can't wait to see what they have to eat."

"I hope you weren't in the mood for something healthy." John pointed to a vendor down the way. "They have the best onion rings. They make them right here and fry them to order."

"That sounds yummy."

"Let's go to the beer tent." The set up was similar to that of the previous festival. John ordered first. "Butterscotch Amber Ale for me." Rob and I studied the selections.

"Butterscotch?"

"It has a creamy mouthfeel with just a hint of butter aftertaste."

I walked up to the bartender. "I'll have the same. Rob?"

"A black and tan for me."

We found an empty high-top table. I took a sip of Rob's beer and winced. "That's bitter."

I gave him a sip of mine. He shuddered. "Too rich for me. I like something with a bit of a bite."

John held the flyer that touted the different beers. He took a long swig. "I may go for the Saint Patrick's Day Green next. It's a bit early for it, but I guess they're testing how well the flavor goes over. It says they use spirulina."

My eyebrow rose. "What's that?"

Rob instructed, "It's a blue-green algae. I guess they use it for the coloring."

I grimaced. "They put algae in beer?"

John tipped his glass back and finished the rest of his drink. "Yep. It's supposed to be good for you. Can I get anyone else one?" Rob and I held up our still full glasses and shook our heads in unison.

The tent had gotten crowded, and people were milling about looking for an open table. I kept on getting accidentally bumped. Rob volunteered, "Let me change places with you."

"Thanks."

John returned. "Would you like a sip, Merry?"

"I'll pass."

John took a large gulp. He coughed.

My eyes widened. "Is it that bad?"

"It went down the wrong way. It just tastes like beer. My next one's going to have to be something more exotic." He picked up the flyer again.

"Spirulina isn't weird enough?"

"Nope. Here's one with nectarines and peppercorns that might do the trick." He downed his beer and again lined up at the bar.

Rob rolled his eyes. "We better get him talking pretty soon. It's too bad they have so many bartenders. The lines are really moving."

John rejoined us. He sipped the beer. "Now that's what I'm talking about. It's nice and smooth with just a hint of nectarine. And there's the heat from the peppercorns. It kind of sneaks up on you. It's good." He motioned with the glass. Some of the contents sloshed out. "Would you like a taste?"

I shook my head. "John, I hate to bring up an unpleasant subject, but it seemed like you and Melanie were arguing in the tile store the other night. Is something wrong?"

He tipped his glass back. "That woman." He looked at his glass. His eyes narrowed. "It seems like I just got this beer. Hold on a minute. I'll need a fresh one to tell this story."

He tottered off back to the bar. Rob turned to me. "This should be interesting."

John returned. "I'm back. What were we talking about?" He sipped his beer. "Oh right, Melanie. What is wrong with that woman?"

I shrugged.

"I know that women like to wear pretty things. Maybe it was too much of a temptation." His voice rose. "But how could she?"

I tilted my head. "How could she what?"

"Tom told her not to wear it. Now, sure, maybe he should've told her why but still."

"Why shouldn't she have worn it?"

He hissed, "You know why, because he stole it. It was only a matter of time till someone recognized it. I told him not to take it. I warned him he might get caught. Did he listen to me? No. He never listened to me." He took a long drink and looked up at the ceiling of the tent. "My best friend. I tried to keep him out of trouble. Like that time with the Kuwaiti stuff."

"Kuwaiti stuff?"

"I'm tired of keeping this a secret. I wasn't raised this way. You won't tell anyone, will you?"

Rob shook his head.

"The troop found some 'antiquities,' at least that's what I think they called them. One piece was pretty cool. It was a miniature Quran. And the cover was gold. It was so pretty. So little." He moved his forefinger and thumb to approximate its size. "I never saw anything like it. I wanted to look at it, sure. But Tom had to have it. I woke up one morning and the platoon was abuzz. The Quran and valuable coins were missing."

He finished his beer and held up his finger. "I'll be right back." He returned with yet another beer. "This one is black walnut." He took a sip. "Tasty." His eyes were glassy. "Where was I?"

"The missing Kuwaiti things."

"Right. The second I heard what was missing, I knew who took it. I confronted Tom. He admitted it. I told him to give the stuff back. He refused. It was bad enough he stole small things from the troops. They searched the barracks, but he must have hidden them well because they never found anything." John drank. "What was I supposed to do? Rat out my brother? Not happening. When he died, I thought his secret died with him. Then Melanie had to wear that necklace. Now everyone knows. Everyone." He shuddered. "It's just not right."

I leaned toward him. "You didn't steal anything?"

His eyes widened, and he staggered back. "Me? No. My mother would have killed me. Tom and I played pranks on people, but that was just to let off steam. Stealing's wrong."

Rob grasped his shoulder. "And you didn't kill Tom?"

His eyes welled. "Kill Tom? I could never have killed Tom. He was family."

I took his arm. "Come on. We're going to see Melanie to get the stuff Tom stole."

"I don't want to see Melanie. I want another beer."

Rob took the glass from his hand and put it on the table. "John, you've had enough. Let's everything returned, so you don't have to worry about it anymore."

"Put him in the car, and I'll be right with you."

Rob was sitting in the driver's seat, with John buckled up in the seat behind him. I slid in, two containers of onion rings in my hand. Rob's eyes widened. I shrugged. "What can I say? I was hungry, and he recommended them." I passed one container back to John and fed Rob one of the rings as he drove.

He took a napkin from my hand. "Greasy but good."

I hurried up the stairs and rang Melanie's doorbell. Her hand clutched her robe at the neck as she let us in. "What's wrong? Why are you here so late?"

John pushed past her into the living room. "I need to sit. The room is spinning."

I touched Melanie's shoulder. "You might want to get him a glass of water." She turned to make her way into the kitchen.

John protested, "Not water. Another beer."

She hesitated. I shook my head. She returned with a large glass of water. I mouthed, "Thanks."

Melanie sat. "What's this all about?"

"Did John have a miniature Quran and Kuwaiti coins?"

Her face paled, and she shot a quick glance at John. He waved his hand. "S'okay, Melanie. I told them everything." His head fell back against the couch, and he started snoring.

She stood and twisted the sash to her robe. "I don't know what to do."

Rob implored, "Get the stuff Tom stole."

Tears flowed down her face as she turned and stumbled up the stairs. A few minutes later she returned with a shoebox. "The police still have the necklace. I think this is everything else."

Rob took it from her. "We'll hold onto this tonight. I'll be taking it down to the station tomorrow. I'll let Detective Ziebold know he should expect a visit from you and John by midday. He'll probably have more questions for you."

She pointed to John. "What should I do with him?"

"I hate to leave him with you, but we can't take him with us. Let him sleep it off on the couch, or give Nancy a call." We left with the box, and Rob locked it in the trunk.

"My car smells like onion rings."

"It should go away once we throw out the trash."

"I'm still hungry."

"We could detour to the diner on the highway."

He put on his left-hand blinker and turned at the traffic light. "Sausage, eggs, and home fries would really hit the spot."

I texted Jenny to let her know we'd be out a while longer. The neon diner sign loomed in the distance. "I'm going to get blueberry pancakes." We pulled in. "And maybe some nice crispy bacon. And a large orange juice."

He held the door for me. "It's an old adage, but it may be true in your case. Your eyes may be too big for your stomach."

We sat in one of the booths and ordered. The old-time jukebox played a song that was equally old. I shrugged. "I guess we should feel good that one mystery is solved." I shook my head. "But all we found was stuff people got used to being gone. Scott's still accused of murder."

Rob reached over the table and took my hand. "I'm sure they've always wondered who had it and who stole it."

I sighed. "But murder is so much worse. Did you believe John?"

He traced a circle on the back of my hand with his thumb. "I think his emotion was genuine. I can't believe he killed Tom. "Strangling someone is personal. You have to be present to do it. The victim doesn't go quietly; he struggles and kicks. Poison is far easier. You can put it in something and leave."

My eyebrow rose.

"I interviewed a criminal profiler once."

"I guess that makes me feel better. Okay. Let's agree he didn't kill John. Maybe he killed Jean."

Rob sipped his coffee. "Why?"

"Jean may have recognized the necklace when Melanie wore it and was startled. Maybe John noticed and decided to kill Jean to protect Tom; he told us they were like brothers."

Then who killed Tom?"

I shrugged. "I didn't say there weren't holes in the story."

Rob paid the cashier, and we left. I must have fallen asleep in the car, because I woke up as Rob kissed my cheek. "Time for sleeping beauty to wake-up."

I yawned as I got out of the car. "Want to come in?"

"You seemed pretty tired. Why don't you get some sleep?"

I came around his side of the car and kissed his lips. "Thanks for the breakfast-dinner combo." His car pulled out of the driveway and headed toward his house.

As I opened my back door, Drew and Arianna roared up his driveway and out into the back alleyway. Andy's garage door opened, the light went on, and the car slid in. Arianna came around behind the car, and Drew joined her a minute later. They embraced as he slid the door shut. I stood silently until they came abreast of my house. "Fun evening?"

Arianna jumped. "What are you doing out so late?"

"Rob and I were at the Suds and Grub fest."

She looked at Drew. He said, "It's an Americanism for beer and food."

"Oh. You have so many colloquialisms; it's hard to keep them all straight."

I leaned over the porch rail. "Andy mentioned he was renting a spot in his garage to you."

Drew glowered. "It's good that one of our friends came through after you left us in the lurch."

I shrugged. "Whatever." I walked into the house, locked the door, and pulled my phone out of my purse. I texted Patty. "Drew says I left them in the lurch on the whole garage thing."

She sent back an emoji that was laughing so hard it cried. I chuckled as I made my way upstairs.

* * *

The next morning, I woke to another fifty degree day. *I could get used to this.* I was enjoying my first cup of coffee when someone rapped quickly at the back door. Rob strolled in. "It was so nice out that I decided to walk over to pick you up for church." He kissed the top of my head, and then walked over to get himself a mug.

I checked my watch. "You're a tad early."

"I am." He poured the coffee. "When you see how lovely it is outside, you're not going to want to go in. I gave us extra time to wander there." He took a sip. "Jay's mad at us."

I smirked. "Why? Because we're solving mysteries no one knew about?"

He shook his head. "Because we're making him come in on a Sunday for something he says is none of his business."

"Poor baby. I wonder how John is feeling this morning."

"Probably not well. You ready to leave?"

I put on my coat and walked out. "Oh, this is delightful. The sun is shining, there's no wind, and no snow on the ground. What a perfect day." I twirled around. "I'm going to enjoy our walk. This afternoon, I'll have to let the cats out. They've been waiting for good weather."

Drew and Arianna waltzed out their back door. She called over, "Are you leaving for church? Drew and I will go with you."

I suppressed a groan. "That would be great." Drew fell into step with Rob, and they began an animated discussion of the basketball season. I asked Arianna, "Any more news on the moving front?"

"Not yet. We're still examining our options."

"You and Drew seem to be going out a lot. Are you enjoying your time in town?"

She flushed. "There's so much to be done if we decide to move. We're trying to, oh how would you Americans say it, get our ducks in a row?"

"Yep. That's what we would say."

We ambled up the church steps and joined a crowd that seemed none too eager to go in. I elbowed Rob, and he followed my eyes. John leaned against the church, barely moving. He looked green. Nancy was next to him. Rob and I sauntered over. "How are you feeling, John?"

He grunted. "Not good. Not good at all. How much did I have to drink last night?"

Rob stroked his mustache. "I lost track after the fourth."

Nancy glared at John. "You told me you only had three beers. You said it was something you ate."

"Don't be such a sour puss. So I'm hungover. It happens."

"You got so drunk that we have to meet with Detective Ziebold after church."

He turned even paler, which I hadn't thought possible. "Don't remind me."

"It would serve you right if they locked you up." She grabbed his arm and led him into the church.

Patrick and Patty joined us on the steps. "What was that all about?"

I slid my arm through hers. "I'll tell you later." Patrick filed in the pew, then Patty, then Rob and I. Drew shooed us farther, so he and Arianna could join us.

Patty's eyes widened. "Isn't this cozy?"

I picked up the hymnal, gritting my teeth. Rob put his arm around me and began to sing. Father Tom's homily was about forgiveness. I scanned the congregation. Some people are going to have to work on that one. My eyes landed on Drew. *Especially me.*

Strolling out of the church, Patty turned to me. "Do you want to join us at Delightful Bites?"

Drew agreed, "We'd love to."

She glared at him. "I wasn't talking to you." Arianna's mouth dropped.

I tapped Patty's shoulder. "Forgiveness is divine. Drew, would you and Arianna care to join us?"

She groaned. "Drew and Arianna, you are certainly welcome."

I led the way. We ordered, and then pulled two tables together. Rob and Patrick retrieved a couple of extra chairs. Everyone sat. Patty lifted her coffee. "So, Drew, have you and Arianna decided where you are moving?"

He coughed. "We haven't decided if we are going anywhere."

Patty's eyes rolled. "Let me rephrase the question. If you were to move, where would you go?"

Arianna divulged, "We've been thinking about quite a few places. My place in Miami, Nouakchott, Mauritania, or even Brunei."

Patrick blinked. "Where is Mauritania?"

"It's on the western coast of Africa."

My eyes widened. "Why there, or Brunei? Isn't Brunei on Borneo in the South China Sea?"

Drew's mouth formed a perfect circle. "High marks on geography, Merry."

Arianna interrupted, "Mauritania because it would allow me to be closer to the people I serve with my charity. Brunei because it is so beautiful with its beaches and rainforest."

"They're both so far away. Drew, you told me you wanted to help with Jenny's college tours this summer. How would you do that from there?"

He smirked. "Planes. A wonderful invention. Plus, it broadens what's available to her. Who knows? Maybe she'll decide to study abroad."

I gulped. Luckily breakfast came, and everyone was hungry. After the meal, Drew and Arianna left for the library, and Patrick and Patty decided to window shop.

Rob held out his hand. "What are your plans for the afternoon?"

"You may think it's silly."

"Nothing you do is silly."

"It's so nice out. It sounds strange, since I didn't know her that well, but I want to visit Jean's grave."

His eyebrow rose.

"She didn't have anything to do with the stolen goods, and yet somehow she's dead."

"I'll come with you." He took my hand, and we walked toward the cemetery. We came abreast of the supermarket.

I paused. "Let's pick up flowers. I know they're nowhere near what Jean would put together, but I think she'd appreciate the gesture." I purchased a bouquet of multi-colored daisies and rejoined Rob. "Ready?"

He held out his hand.

We strolled to the cemetery. It was on a bit of a hill with large oaks that would provide good shade come summer. Gravel paths meandered along the soon to green grass. Rob took the flowers as I shrugged off my windbreaker and put it on the grass next to the raised mound of Jean's recent grave. I knelt on the windbreaker, and Rob gave me back the flowers. I placed them on her headstone. "Thank you for your service, Jean. We miss your flower shop and your sense of humor. I feel I've gotten to know you better now than when you were living, and I wish that were different. One mystery is solved, but I want to make you a promise. We'll figure out who killed you, and the police will bring that person to justice."

Rob helped me to my feet. I brushed off my windbreaker and put it back on. He hugged me. "Feel better?"

"It was something I had to do."

We ambled back to the house. Rob put his arm around me. "Kind of a shock about Drew and Arianna."

"It is. For some reason I thought all of the places they'd be considering would at least be on this continent."

"It's interesting that two of the places they are considering have no extradition treaty to the United States."

CHAPTER 21

My head still spun when I woke Monday morning. I poured my coffee and slumped at the counter, glaring at it. If they picked a place far away, what would it mean for Jenny? She'd be so upset. And what about me? She'd leave for the summer, and I wouldn't see her. Then she'd be away at school. I gulped. Could I take that?

The doorbell rang. Pete and two of his crew stood on the stairs. "Good morning. Are you ready for us to start?"

I shifted from one foot to another. "As ready as I'm going to be."

Pete reassured me, "It'll be painful at first, but then you'll see. It will be beautiful."

"I'll take your word for it."

I led them up the steps. He pointed to the wall. "We'll be taking down the wall today and demoing everything in the bathroom. Were you able to get everything out?"

"Yes. I can't believe how much stuff I tossed."

Jenny waltzed in. "Wow. Are you getting ready to start?" I introduced Jenny to Pete and his crew. She shook hands. "Do you think I could hit the wall or something? I've watched it on TV, and it looks like so much fun."

Pete smiled. "It's not that much fun if you do it every day." He handed her goggles and a hard hat. Then he gave her a sledgehammer and made her take a few practice swings. Next he showed her where to hit. I backed up. She swung, and the drywall imploded. Pete clapped. "Nice hit."

She beamed. "That was fun. Mom, you should try it."

I shook my head. "I need to get to work, and you need to go to school."

She pouted. "One more swing?"

"One more but then we need to go."

She connected, and more drywall fell.

"You'll be late. Let's go."

Jenny lagged behind me on the stairs. "We should remodel something else." She touched the wall to the kitchen. "We could take out this wall here."

I held the door. "You have a choice. Kitchen remodel or college."

"It was fun to hit that wall but college, definitely college."

I came home at noon for lunch to check the progress. Unfortunately, the crew was on break, and the house was empty. I hurried up the stairs and turned the corner to the bedroom. My mouth sagged. The wall was gone, and a heavy-duty plastic sheet hung from one end of the room to the other. *Must be for the dust.* I pushed forward through the zippered opening. The tub and vanity were gone. I hazarded a glance out the window and saw that the small dumpster was filling up. They were moving fast.

I finished my sandwich just as the crew returned. Pete asked, "What did you think?"

"I can't believe how much you got done this morning."

"It is a small space. The real time will be spent in making it beautiful."

"I need to get back to the office. My plan is to be home around four today. Do you think you'll still be here?"

"We'll probably work till about five tonight."

Hurrying back to the office, I texted Jenny: "What time will you be home today?"

"Four thirty. Shooting some hoops. Why?"

"Don't want you home alone while workers are there. I'll be home by four." Tonight we'll talk about what to do the rest of the week."

"Sheesh."

Midway through a busy morning, Cheryl poked her head in. "Detective Ziebold called. He said you owe him lunch."

I laughed.

She shook her head. "I don't think he was kidding."

"I know."

"Scott Winters also called." She checked her notes. "The Jefferson's are arriving tomorrow, and he is taking them to lunch."

"That's nice."

She continued. "He wants you to join them. His wife's aunt is ill so she had to go out of town." She sat. "The bottom line was he didn't want to go on his own" She paused. "I checked your calendar. As long as you return by two, I can move things around."

I tapped my pencil. "Okay. I'll meet Scott and the Jefferson's. It seems like the right thing to do. Please let him know I'll be there. Would you also call Detective Ziebold back, and see if he can come for dessert tonight? Tell him I'll defrost a cheesecake for him."

"Will do." Cheryl walked to the door and stopped. She turned. "Only if you bring me a piece tomorrow."

"No problem."

Just before four, I gathered the things I needed to work on at home. I waved at Cheryl as I left. "Call me if anything comes up." I stopped as I walked out the door. The sun was shining, and the air, while still crisp, felt fresh. I took a deep breath and slowed my step. The days were getting longer.

I turned into my gate. Arianna was beating a beautiful Moroccan area rug on Drew's front porch. "Good afternoon. Beautiful day."

"It is. I'm sorry that I spent most of it in the office. Nice rug."

She pointed to the dumpster. "What are you remodeling?"

"My bathroom. It was time to say goodbye to the fifties."

She left the rug on the porch and walked across the driveway. "Can I see?"

I shrugged. "I don't think there's much to see yet. They were just finishing demo when I stopped by for lunch." A package was lying on the front porch. I picked it up. It was heavy. Balancing the package, I extended my arm for her to precede me into the house. I put it down inside the door. We ambled up the stairs and into the bedroom. I pointed to the zippered opening. She slid through, and I followed. The new wall was in place with what looked like the first coat of mud.

Pete stood outside the new bathroom and held up his arm. "Hold up. I just poured the floor leveler and don't want you to step in it."

I looked down. A gray wet substance was near my feet. "Sorry."

"No problem. Just didn't want you to get it all over you." His eyes widened as he saw Arianna. "Hello. Are you the building inspector?"

She gave a throaty chuckle. "I'm just nosy. I live next door."

"Pete. I'd shake your hand but—" He displayed his hands, which were dirty.

"I quite understand. It's nice to meet you."

I inched back against the plastic sheathing and pointed to a roll of orange mesh that stood in the corner. "Is that for the heated floors?"

He shook his head. "Yes. We'll install it once the leveler dries. It should keep you quite toasty for what's left of this winter."

I backed out of the plastic opening. Arianna followed. "Can I see the plans?"

"Sure. Let's go back downstairs."

The package again caught my eye. It was stamped fragile in quite a few places.

I picked it up. "Do you mind if I open this?" She shook her head. I took a scissors and sliced through the outer packaging. The inner box displayed a small round Swarovski crystal chandelier.

Arianna leaned over my shoulder. "Is that for the bathroom? How elegant. I envy you."

"I'm not sure it's me. I think Patty sent it for me to consider." Arianna's carefully tweezed eyebrow arched. I explained. "She used to be a designer."

I moved the box and retrieved the plans, unrolling them, and anchoring them to the table. I pointed out where everything was going to be.

She sat. "Is the chandelier going above the tub?"

I shrugged. "I guess so."

Arianna sighed. "Heated floors. I wish we had them. It's so cold here."

"It's starting to get nicer out."

"I love it when it's in the nineties."

"Won't get that here for a while yet." The cats pawed the door. "Would you like coffee?"

"I'd love some."

"Let me let the cats out first or they'll start vocalizing." I opened the door, and they were out like a shot. The button on the coffee machine pushed, I plunked down two mugs and sat. "You surprised me last night."

"How so?"

"I hadn't thought you'd be moving so far from here. I'm worried about how Jenny will react." The coffee machine whirred. I stood. "You take cream as I remember." I put the container on the table and poured the coffee.

"As Drew told you yesterday, we haven't made any decisions."

I sat across from her. "I'm still not clear on what's driving this decision. It seems pretty odd. Miami, the west coast of Africa, or someplace on the China Sea. It's so random."

"It's not. I told you that I like the beach. All of those places have beaches." She stirred cream into her coffee, turning it a rich mocha.

A flash of yellow at the window startled me. Then it disappeared. I leapt up. "What is that?" I walked to the window. Two eyes stared back at me. I jumped.

Arianna touched my arm. "What is it?"

"There's someone out there." I hurried to the back door, yanked it open, and rushed to the driveway. A tan Ford pickup peeled out.

"Who was it?"

"I don't know. It all happened so fast."

Rob's Audi zipped into the driveway. He got out. "A welcoming committee. You shouldn't have."

I poked his shoulder. "Get over yourself. Someone peered in the kitchen window when Arianna and I were having coffee."

He turned toward the street. "Did you see who it was?"

"No, but the person drove a tan pickup."

Arianna touched my shoulder. "Thanks for the coffee, but I better get back. Your bathroom is going to be lovely. Promise you'll give me a tour when it's done." She crossed the driveway and retrieved her rug.

Rob and I walked back into the house.

Pete was in the kitchen washing his hands. "I hope you don't mind, but your bath upstairs no longer has water."

I picked up my coffee mug. "That's fine."

"Who was that woman? She could be a model."

I rolled my eyes. "She was. What time will you be here tomorrow?"

"Eight if that's not too early. The leveler should dry overnight. I want the guys to get another coat of mud on the drywall, and then we'll start tiling the floor." He left.

The coffee was cold, so I put the mugs in the sink. Rob pulled me to him. "Are you okay?"

"It was just creepy seeing someone looking in. It startled me. I wish I had more than just a glimpse to go on. Whoever it was had to be tall to look in that window. Hold on a minute—" I picked up my phone and texted Patty: "Know anyone with a tan pickup."

My phone binged. "Nope. Why?"

"Peeping Tom."

"Be careful."

I handed Rob my phone, bent over the freezer, and pulled out a cherry covered cheesecake.

"Mm. That looks good. What's the occasion?"

"Jay's coming over for dessert. I figured I ought to make it special since we've been asking him to swim pretty far out of his lane lately."

"We keep life interesting for him." Rob uncorked the wine. "I'm surprised Patty didn't know who the truck belonged to. She usually knows everything happening in town."

"Maybe whoever it was doesn't live here."

Jenny walked in the door. "Ooh. Let's have that for dinner."

I wagged my finger. "That's dessert, young lady. We're having salmon for dinner."

"Roasted salmon with mustard and garlic?"

"You bet."

"You're the best, mom." She picked up the package from the floor. "What's this?"

"A chandelier."

"You're going to have a chandelier in your bath? How cool." She ran up the stairs.

Rob poured us both a glass of wine and motioned toward the ceiling. "How does your bathroom look?"

"Destroyed. Want to see?"

"Of course." He picked up the chandelier. "May as well bring this up with me." We walked into the bedroom; Jenny's back was to us.

I warned, "Don't go in there. The leveler is still drying."

She turned. "I'm not stupid." She prattled to Rob, "I got to swing the sledge hammer and made a big hole in the wall right about here." She pointed to a place on the plastic sheet. "Well, farther in there, where the wall old wall was."

"I'll have to start calling you slugger." Rob slid through the zippered opening and peered through the door frame on the new wall. "It looks bigger. Moving the wall really made a difference."

"It did. I can't wait till it's done." We had dinner, and the back door opened right on time.

Jay walked in and went straight for the cheesecake. "This looks good." His eyes narrowed. "I'm not sure it's going to make up for all the extra work you caused me." I cut him a large wedge, and Rob poured coffee. Jay took a bite. "Yum. Nice and creamy. I like the graham cracker crust too."

"I'm glad you like it. Scott told me that Jim Jefferson's parents are going to be here tomorrow."

"They're coming to the station at eleven to pick up the necklace."

"Scott's going to lunch with them and asked me to tag along." Jay's eyebrow rose. "He didn't want to go alone, and his wife's out of town."

"Are you going?"

"I'm curious to see what their plans are for the necklace."

Rob touched my shoulder. "Maybe I should go too. It'd make a great story for the paper."

I shook my head. "I don't know these people, so I'm not sure how they'll feel about a newspaper story. Do you trust me?"

He tilted his head. "Of course."

"I'll broach the subject at lunch. If they are willing, I'll text, and you can meet us." I turned to Jay. "Before I meet with them, I wanted to get an update on where you are with everything."

Jay sipped his coffee. "My army buddy helped me out. He took the personal items that were stolen and is working with the MPs to identify the rightful owners. The Kuwaiti treasures were more complicated. The State Department is involved, and they are working to return them to Kuwait."

"I'm glad that everything is getting back to its proper place. What's going to happen to John?"

"Nothing. He admits that he knew about the thefts, but says he didn't help Tom. Plus, the statute of limitations on theft ran out some time ago." He took another bite of the cheesecake and sighed. "So everything is coming up roses on the thefts. Now if Scott Winters's trial was just scheduled earlier, I could put these murders to bed."

My mouth dropped. "You haven't charged Scott with Tom's death."

"Not yet. The investigation continues." He stood and put on his coat. "I wouldn't get too close to him, Merry. That man's a cold blooded killer." The door shut behind him.

Rob cleared the table. "He may not be wrong. You should be careful around Scott, just in case."

✳ ✳ ✳

I talked to Pete and his worker, Ben, as I left the next morning. Pete told me their plan was to lay the floor tile, and then grout later the following day.

I worked my call list until it was time to leave for lunch. The sun felt warm on my back, and my pace slowed on the way to the Golden Skillet. I took a deep breath as I opened the door. Scott waved to me from across the room. An older couple was seated with him. They smiled in unison as I approached, reminding me of Mr. and Mrs. Claus with their silver-tinged hair and rosy cheeks. Scott and Mr. Jefferson stood as I approached. "Merry, I'd like you to meet James Jefferson and his wife Cathy."

I shook their hands and sat. "It's nice to meet you. Please accept my condolences on the loss of your son."

Cathy wiped a tear from the corner of her eye. "He was such a good person. I know it's been nearly thirty years, but it still seems so fresh. The ring brings it all back."

James put his hand over hers. "Scott was just telling us that you helped find the stones. Thank you. They were family heirlooms."

I shifted in my seat. "I don't know that it was because of me. Scott's been trying to find the ring for a long time. I wouldn't have known about it if it weren't for him."

"Either way, we're happy the stones are back in the family. We were showing Scott pictures of Jim's fiancée. Would you like to see them?"

"I'd love to."

He pulled an old snapshot from his breast pocket. "This is one of Heather and Jim. It was taken right before his last deployment." They looked so young. Not that much older than Jenny. Heather sat on Jim's shoulders, grinning down at him, her long brown hair caught mid-swing. He grinned at the camera.

"So young."

"The benefit of photos. They capture a single, sometimes sublime, moment in time. Such a fun day. This was his going away party." He tucked the photo back in his jacket and pulled out his phone. "We're still close. I took this one last week." He handed it to me. A slightly more weathered Heather peered out, grinning, arms around two good-looking teens. "Those are her two kids." He pointed. "Mark and Morgan. Her husband Duncan wasn't home that day, but he's a real pip. She married him about two years after Jim died."

Scott stuttered, "She's happy?"

Cathy touched his arm. "Yes, she's happy. Jim's dying broke her heart. Even in my own grief, I was worried about her. Then, one day, she met Duncan. After a while they fell in love, and then later, the little ones came. Her life is full. I'm happy for her, though I still think about what might have been." She wiped away another tear. "Do you have children, my dear?"

I beamed. "One. She's seventeen and the light of my life."

"The same age as little Arial, our youngest granddaughter. She's a real pistol."

"If you don't mind me asking, what are you going to do with the stones?"

James leaned forward. "We're going to have them made back into a ring. Our other granddaughter, Debbie, is getting engaged to such a nice boy, and we want her to have it. If Jim had lived, he would have been her godfather." He wiped away a tear. "My two children were so close." He stared at the necklace. "It will mean so much to my daughter for Debbie to have it."

"What a lovely thing to do, and what a great ending to such a sad story. I hate to ask, but my friend runs the local newspaper. He was wondering if you could spare him a few minutes. He'd love to write about your son."

Cathy twisted her napkin. James whispered in her ear. She straightened her shoulders. "I'd love to have the world know more about my son. We need to leave soon though. We have a bit of a trip in front of us."

"Let me text him to meet you here."

Rob's reply read: "I'll be there in four."

A few minutes later, Rob hurried in the door, camera in hand. I waved, and he joined us. I introduced him. "I'm afraid I need to get back to the office." I stood.

Scott moved to join me. "I guess I should leave you alone with Rob."

Cathy took his hand. "Please stay."

I hurried back to the office for a meeting. At four, I packed up my things and strolled back to the house. Country music played. I turned to run up the stairs. Loud voices echoed down the hallway. Pete yelled, "That's not funny. I hate practical jokes. They get people injured on a job site, or worse. You're fired."

Ben brushed past me on the way down the stairs, face aflame. "That guy's nuts." He slammed the door behind him.

I continued up the stairs and into my bedroom. Pete's face was flushed, and his trowel seemed glued to the mortar. His eyes widened as he saw me. "I didn't know you were home. We went on break, and when I got back my trowel was like this. He thought it was funny." He scowled. "I hate practical jokers."

I backed up a few feet. "Are you okay?"

He took a deep breath. "I am. No need to worry. I run a tight crew. That guy was new and didn't know the ropes. I'll just get another trowel and more mortar. We're almost done. Take a look."

He left, and I peered through the hole in the plastic. I had selected a gray, wood-look porcelain tile for the floor, and it was beautiful. *That's going to be great with the travertine.* Pete pounded back up the stairs. I turned. "It looks good. You're almost done."

"Thanks. I would have been done if not for the unplanned delay."

"I'll let you finish."

I started down the stairs when there was a quick knock, and the back door opened. Rob called out, "Anyone home?"

I turned the corner into the kitchen. "I'm here."

He hugged me. "What a great story. I can't wait to write it up."

I pointed toward my office. "Why don't you set up in there, and I'll start dinner."

"Are you sure?"

I kissed him. "Yep." I texted Jenny: "Home now."

"Okay if stay at Cindy's for dinner?"

"Fine. Be home by nine."

I poured myself a glass of wine and sat on the window seat. Leaping up, I scouted to make sure no one was outside looking in. *Silly.* I sat back down. Arianna came out of Drew's house with a large box. She looked right and left, and then scurried to Andy's garage.

Glancing around again, she opened the door, slid the box in, and hurried back to Drew's house. *What's that all about?*

"All done for today." I jumped, and the wine sloshed in my glass. Pete stood near the door. "Sorry. I didn't mean to startle you. What were you looking at?"

I stood. "Just woolgathering. How long before you can grout?"

"Twenty-four hours. Please make sure no one walks on the floor until I come back. Later tomorrow, we'll work on that, and the next day, we'll be able to start on the shower."

"Can't wait." He walked out the door. I ambled to the front of the house and pulled the drape to the side. Pete talked to someone sitting in a tan pickup. I couldn't see who it was. I shifted to the left and then to the right. Pete looked up and waved. The pickup drove away.

Rob came up behind me. "What are you looking at?"

I jumped and spilled my wine. "Why does everyone keep doing that to me?"

He got a towel and wiped it up. "Doing what?"

"Sneaking up behind me."

He kissed my forehead. "The problem is that you concentrate too hard. When you do, the world melts away." He held my arms. "Now what were you looking at?"

"Pete was talking to someone in a tan pick-up. It looked just like the one the peeping Tom used."

Rob's eyes darted from one car to the next. "Where is it?"

"Gone. Along with Pete. I'll have to remember to ask him who it was tomorrow."

He hugged me. "You do that."

My stomach rumbled.

"Someone's hungry. What's for dinner?"

"I didn't take anything out yet. Jenny's eating at the Twilliger's. Maybe we should call for pizza."

He took the wine glass from my hand, sipped, and put it down on the coffee table. He lifted my hand to his lips and kissed it. "How hungry are you? Do we have to call for the pizza right away?"

I shook my head. "What did you have in mind?"

He led me to the bedroom.

* * *

As we remade the bed, I pointed out, "This is easier at your house."

"We didn't have to make it. You're only going to get back into it in a few hours."

I pushed Rob's shoulder. "You know Jenny's going to come in here the second she gets back. She's even more excited about this remodel than I am."

Rob smoothed the comforter and tripped as he rounded the bed. He pulled a box from under the bed. "What's this?"

"It's the chandelier for the bath."

"I remember carrying it up here, but that's not where I left it. What's it doing under the bed?" He turned the box so the picture faced him. "Looks fancy."

"It is. I still haven't decided if I'm a chandelier kind of girl."

"Too luxurious for you?"

I caressed the box. "Maybe."

He strolled down the stairs in front of me. "I'll call for the pizza. What do you want on it?"

"Sausage, please." I picked up my wine from the table and brought it into the kitchen. "I saw something strange today."

His eyebrow lifted. "What?"

"Arianna took a large box out to Andy's garage."

"So?"

"Why would she do that?"

"Maybe they're giving clothes away to Goodwill."

I shook my head. "I don't think so. She looked furtive."

"One thing I know for sure. There's no way they could fit a large box into Drew's car."

"That is a small car. I wonder if Andy knows what's going on."

CHAPTER 22

I wrapped the leftover pizza in aluminum foil and put it in the freezer. Rob poured us both coffee and handed me a mug. "Any leftover cheesecake?"

"There might be a piece with your name on it." I took the plate from the refrigerator and cut two slices."

Jenny walked in the back door holding a large package. "This was at the front door. Cheesecake? Cut me a slice too please."

"What are you doing home early?"

Jenny pointed to the clock.

I felt my face flush. "Oh. I guess we ate later than I thought." I took the package. "I have a horrible feeling this is something else Patty sent." I opened it up. Lovely soft rose-colored drapes were carefully arrayed. The sashes were brocade with a mix of rose, turquoise, and silver.

Jenny yelped. "Those are beautiful. If you don't use them in the bathroom, I want them for my room."

I pulled the package to me. "You have two windows in your room. This is for one."

Rob jumped to his feet. "I forgot something in the car. I'll be right back."

I put the package by the stairs, cut another slice of cheesecake, and carried the plates to the table. "What did the Twilliger's have for dinner?"

"Chicken and rice. It was good." She pointed at the pizza box. "I can't believe you had pizza without me."

Rob stood in the doorframe, a big smile on his face, one hand hidden outside. My eyes widened. "What do you have there?"

He brought his hand into view. "A sledge hammer." It was three feet long with a solid steel head. A large pink bow was tied to it. He presented it to Jenny with a flourish. "I figured you might want your own."

"It's perfect!" She leapt to her feet and took it from Rob. She swung it a few times. "It seems lighter than the one the contractor had."

Rob grinned. "I got the one with the fiberglass handle. It makes it lighter, but it still packs a punch."

She swung again. I stood. "It never occurred to me that I would have to say this, but stop playing with the sledgehammer in the house."

Jenny pulled it toward her body. "I'll take it up to my room so you don't have to see it." She ran upstairs before I could take it away.

I turned to Rob. "Thanks, I think." I caressed the kitchen wall. "I'm not sure how much time this wall has left. She was talking about taking it down earlier, and now she has the tools."

"Every woman should have her own tools." He pulled me close. "I'll see you tomorrow." He kissed me and left.

I put the plates in the dishwasher. *A sledgehammer?*

I paced for a moment or two, pulled on my coat, and turned out the back light. I scurried across to Andy and Ed's garage and peered in the window. My mouth dropped. I must have missed several of the trips Arianna or Drew made. There had to be nine or ten boxes stacked by their car.

* * *

Frost was on the window the next morning. I sighed. *Winter's still here.* I took a quick shower, and then scooted back down the hall to my room. I peered through the zippered opening. *Looks dry. Hopefully they'll be able to grout today.* I bundled up and made my way downstairs.

The cats pawed at the door. "Not today. It's cold out." I poured food in their bowls and gave them fresh water. I opened the front door and picked up the paper. The headline read, "Hero's jewelry returned." I read the article as I ate breakfast. Rob had a great photo of the Jefferson's with an inset picture of their granddaughter and her fiancé. *What a lovely article.*

Pete knocked and walked in. "Cold out there today."

"Sure is. Would you like a cup of coffee?"

"I wouldn't say no. Here, I have my own travel mug."

I topped him off. "Alone today?"

"Grouting is a small job. I have the rest of my crew on another site. I'll bring them back tomorrow when we set the tub and start work on the shower."

Jenny ran through. "Running late. See you, bye."

Pete's eyes widened. "She's like a mini-tornado."

"You have no idea." The clock chimed. "I need to get moving too. Help yourself to the rest of the coffee."

I walked out the door and straight into Andy Perkins. He grabbed me. "Whoa, what's your hurry?"

"Sorry. I didn't expect you to be standing there."

"I was going over early to the shop and thought we might walk together." He shivered. "It's a bit colder out than I thought it would be. I should have driven."

"This isn't that bad. It's got to be in the high thirties."

"I was spoiled by the fifties."

I smiled. "Don't worry; spring will be here soon. What are you up to today?"

He sighed. "Inventory. Need to check that everything is where I think it is. I hate doing it. It should have been done in January—New Year and all that—I've procrastinated long enough."

"When was the last time you were in your garage?"

He stopped. "Last week sometime. It's been so nice out, we haven't used the car." His eyebrow arched. "Why?"

"Just curious." I continued walking.

He put his hand on my shoulder. "Why would you ask that question?"

I squirmed. "Because I saw Arianna putting a big box in it the other night. And, to tell you the truth, I looked in the window last night. There was more than one box."

"That's strange. The exotic princess didn't say anything to me about boxes. I agreed to the car but there's not enough room for them to store their cast-offs. I'll check tonight."

"This is my stop."

He looked up. "So it is."

"Would you call me tonight to let me know if the boxes are still there?"

He tapped my nose with his finger. "Merry, haven't you learned that poking your cute nose where it doesn't belong is dangerous?"

I made as if to bite his finger. He withdrew it. "Have a pleasant day. I'll call you later, Ms. Busybody."

I quickly prepped for my staff meeting. One of our insurance companies was downsizing, so I knew there would be questions. Cheryl stopped me on the way into the meeting room. "Good news. They're going to pay on Tom Butler's life insurance claim." She hesitated. "I still think they should be looking into Melanie. She had something to do with this. It's too big of a coincidence."

I sighed. "There's a reason why coincidence is a word in the English language. It's because they do happen. I'm glad to hear the company wrapped up their investigation. And faster than I thought. I'll call Melanie after the meeting."

Patty texted me. "Meet for lunch? Delightful Bites at noon?"

"Sold."

Patty's back was toward me as I walked in. She was intent on the menu. I touched her elbow. "I need soup."

"You're in luck. They have Italian wedding soup today. I'm going to have that and a thick slice of their nine grain bread slathered in butter." She stepped up to order.

When she finished, I moved to the counter. "What she's having." We sat and caught up on each other's lives. I surveyed my soup bowl with disappointment. "It's empty."

She shrugged. "It happens. Luckily I have one more mouthful left." She ate it. Her eyes narrowed.

"A bad bite?"

"No." She pointed behind me. I turned around. A tan Ford pickup pulled into a parking spot. Pete's van rolled in beside it. "Didn't you say that you've been on the lookout for that kind of truck?"

Karen Vassal hopped out of the pickup. Pete exited his van, took her hand, and they strolled into the café. Karen's mouth sagged. "My two best customers. Pete told me about this place, and I just had to check it out for myself."

Patty pointed to the menu board. "Get the soup of the day. Believe me it's worth it. Would you like to join us?"

Karen gave Pete a quick glance; he gave a curt nod. "We'd love to." They ordered and returned to the table.

I introduced Pete to Patty. "He's doing a great job on my bathroom."

"I can't wait to see it."

Pete picked up his spoon. "I'll finish grouting this afternoon. The mortar was set when I checked earlier. That means we can load in the tub, cabinets, and sink tomorrow. I'll have the tile guy working on the shower at the same time, and then we'll be out of your hair late Friday. We'll likely need to come back on Monday for any touch-ups on the paint."

"I hate to ask, but someone who shall remain nameless sent me a small chandelier the other day. It seems silly to have one in the bathroom, but my designer tells me it will look great over the tub."

Patty nudged me with her elbow. "Look at you getting all elegant on me. I wasn't sure you were going to keep it."

I felt my face flush. "It is pretty."

Pete broke off a piece of bread. "No problem. There's a pot light over the tub. I'll just change it out for the chandelier. Leave the fixture by the bathroom, and we'll install it."

"One more thing."

He looked up.

"I was also the happy recipient of lovely rose colored drapes. They're going to look great on the window behind the tub." I grimaced. "I'm going to hate it when I start getting these bills."

Patty shot me a smug expression. "If you are going to do something, you should do it right."

Pete buttered his bread. "You can have anything you want. It's your bathroom. I'll put the rod up for you. Leave it with the chandelier." He popped the bread in his mouth. "Anything else?"

I eyed Patty. She shook her head.

"You heard the boss. I can't wait for it to be finished. And, now, I need to get back to the office." Patty and I rose and walked out together. I elbowed her. "Why do you think Karen was peeping in the window?"

"Maybe she thought she'd catch you and Pete together."

I shivered. "It's creepy. Just plain creepy."

The rest of the day was uneventful. I left again at four, in case Pete had any questions. Following my new routine, I hurried up the stairs as soon as I got home. The plastic wall was down, and someone had done a good job vacuuming. I peered through the door. The grout was finished. *Progress.*

A step creaked. "You up here?" Rob came into the bedroom.

"Look. No more plastic."

"It looks like the grouting is done. These guys are moving fast." He nudged me. "I don't think you're ever going to leave this bathroom, once it's finished."

We ambled back downstairs. I poured two glasses of wine and handed him one. "Guess who I saw today at lunch?"

"Patty."

"Yes, her. But that's not who I meant."

His eyebrow rose.

"Karen Vassal. And she was driving a tan Ford pickup."

He whistled. "Who was she spying on the other day? Pete? Or you?"

I sipped my wine. "I don't know. It creeps me out."

He put his arm around me. "She was probably just looking for Pete, and you startled her."

"I startled her? Why didn't she just come to the door?"

"Maybe she didn't want him to know she was checking up on him."

"That could be true."

"Are you free tomorrow night?"

I checked my calendar. "Why?"

"John called. He and Nancy wanted us to go to dinner with them at the VFW. He wants to thank you for making him go to the police. He saw the article in the paper yesterday and mentioned it's like a huge weight has been lifted from his shoulders. I guess the stress of keeping secrets was hard for him."

"I thought he'd still be mad at me."

"Quite the contrary."

"Fine. We'll go." I tapped the entry into my phone.

Jenny texted. "Dad and Arianna want to take me to dinner tonight. Okay?"

"Fine."

"Looks like it's just us tonight."

"Want to go to my place for a movie?"

I kissed his nose. "Thought you'd never ask."

* * *

The next morning was the usual rush. Pete arrived just as I finished my coffee. I handed him the carafe, and he refilled his mug. I picked up my purse. "I'm glad I ran into you. Something strange happened earlier in the week."

His eyebrow rose. "I hope it wasn't something one of my workers did."

I shook my head. "It was your wife."

"What?"

"Arianna and I were sitting on the window seat the other day." I pointed toward it. "A flash of yellow caught my eye. Someone was peeping in the window."

"Who was it?"

"It happened too fast for me to recognize the person. Arianna and I raced out the door, and we were almost too late. We saw a tan Ford pickup truck. Its tires squealed as it pulled away from the house. It looked exactly like your wife's truck."

He shook his head. "I can't believe she'd do that. Are you sure?"

"Yep."

"That's a pretty common truck."

"It is."

"I'll talk to her."

✳ ✳ ✳

Rob and I strolled into the VFW a few minutes early. John and Nancy were already there, talking to Scott and Linda. Scott scowled at John and stormed off into the dining room. Linda hurried to catch up. Rob and I turned quickly to study the Veterans' photos.

John joined us. "It's prime rib night in the dining room." He led the way, asking the host for a table on the other side of the room from Scott and his wife.

"No wonder it's so crowded." We ordered.

I turned to John. "Your conversation with Scott seemed a bit intense."

He scowled. "He doesn't believe I didn't help Tom steal from the troops. I admitted that I knew about it afterward. He declared that made me just as guilty." His head hung. "Maybe I am."

Nancy took his hand. "Nonsense. You were just protecting a friend."

He took a sip of water and changed the subject. "Rob, I really liked the photos you took of the hall. Can you tell me what you did to get them looking so crisp?" They started a technical discussion full of f-stops and other things.

Nancy rolled her eyes and engaged me in chatting about the upcoming church fete and what she was cooking. A movement over her left shoulder attracted my eye. Pete dipped a mozzarella stick in marinara and fed it to Karen. They were a few tables behind us. *That looks yummy.* Scott Winters stood, phone pressed to his ear. He hurried toward the entrance.

Rob and John were now onto the benefits of UV filters. I picked at my salad, as Nancy droned on about one of her neighbors. John stood and excused himself from the table. He wandered to the alcove containing the restrooms. Rob joined our conversation and told an amusing story about when he was young and in Paris. He and a friend were dining, and he ordered veal with sweetbreads thinking that they were sweet breads. He was appalled to find out he was eating a lamb thymus.

I grimaced. "That's not a pleasant surprise."

"It makes for a great story though."

Nancy twisted her napkin and glanced toward the restroom. "What could be taking John so long? I hope he's not ill."

Rob stood. "Would you like me to check on him?"

"If you don't mind."

Rob strolled toward the restroom. In a minute, he waved to me from the alcove. I exclaimed, "What on earth?" I patted Nancy's hand. "I'll be right back."

Rob motioned for me to hurry. "Call an ambulance. John's been injured."

I called 911 on my way back to the table. I motioned for Nancy. "John's been injured."

Her eyes widened as she stood. "How could that happen?" She rushed to the alcove and pushed open the men's room door. I was right behind her. Rob knelt next to John, who was lying on the floor. A golden cord lay next to him. John coughed. Nancy fell to her knees and pulled his hand to her, patting it. "John, are you okay?" She gasped. "What happened to his neck?" There was an indentation, and it looked chafed.

"I'm not sure. I walked in, and he was lying there." He pointed to the drop ceiling. One of the cross tees that made up the grid was broken and swung drunkenly. John coughed again. His eyes fluttered.

Nancy leaned closer. "John, what happened to you?"

A croak came from his throat, but his voice failed, and his eyes rolled back.

Detective Ziebold strode in. "What happened here? Give the man room." He shooed Rob away. The EMTs arrived a short while later and loaded John onto a stretcher.

Nancy tossed me her keys. "I want to ride with John. Would you bring our car to the hospital?"

I caught them. "No problem. See you shortly."

The EMTs wheeled him out. Nancy gripped John's foot, and she scurried to keep up. Jay called over to the two patrolmen who had just arrived, "No one leaves till I talk to them."

He gestured for Rob and me to follow him back into the men's room. He pointed to the floor. "What is that?"

I explained, "It's an aiguillette." Jay's eyes widened. "It's from the military. They have them displayed in the front room."

"What's it doing here?"

"I don't know. Rob?"

"It was around John's neck when I found him. I know it's bad to touch anything, but he was gasping, so I pulled it off." Rob pointed toward the ceiling. "If I had to guess, someone tried to strangle him. Then they hung him from the ceiling. Luckily, the cross tee wasn't strong enough, and it broke."

The crime scene technicians hurried in. Jay declared, "We need to clear the room." We walked out. Jay scribbled in his notebook. He looked up, and his eyes narrowed. "That's the first person I want to talk with. I'll meet up with you at the hospital." He told the patrolman we were cleared to leave, then swiveled and marched straight over to Scott and Linda.

I retrieved my purse and coat. We hurried to the door. Rob was in the process of opening it, when I stopped in my tracks. His eyebrow arched as I turned back to the room. "What are you looking for?"

"Pete. He was here with Karen. I don't see them now."

"Maybe they finished dinner and left before everything happened."

I shook my head. "Doubtful. It's prime rib night, and they were just on appetizers before John left for the men's room. They're not here now. I'll need to tell Jay."

* * *

We waited in the hall outside John's hospital room. I sat in a chair while Rob paced in front of me. "How does this guy do it?"

"What do you mean?"

"The dining room was crowded. Anyone could have come in. The murderer must be a risk taker."

Nancy came out of John's room. I returned her keys. "The car's in the emergency room parking lot. How's John?"

She sank onto the chair next to me and rubbed her face. "He's okay. The doctor advised he'll be pretty bruised. You saw his neck. The nurse is icing it right now. He's uncomfortable, as you might expect." She sighed. "He was lucky. I can't believe someone tried to kill him. And in such a public place. My money is on Scott Winters."

I shifted in my seat. "Did John say it was Scott?"

"He doesn't know who it was. He was facing the wall when someone came up from behind and hit him on the head. The next thing he knew, the aiguillette was around his neck. The only thing he's sure of is that the guy was taller than him."

That didn't narrow it down much. John was small in stature, only about three inches taller than me.

Nancy continued, "He lifted him up and must have looped the rope around the ceiling struts." She felt her throat. "John whispered he couldn't breathe. He heard the door close. The next thing he knew, he was laying on the floor. He could breathe again. He's never been more thankful for saving money on ceiling hardware." She stood. "I should get back. Thanks for bringing me my keys." The door closed behind her.

Jay came around the corner. "Good, you're still here." He sprawled on a chair. "What a night. I arrested Scott. His wife says he just left the table for a quick phone call."

"That's true. I saw him walk toward the entrance."

"When was that?"

I groaned. "Not too long before John left the table."

"Did you see him return?"

"No, I didn't, Rob?"

He shook his head.

I turned my plastic chair toward Jay. "You should probably know that Scott and John got into it before dinner. They didn't come to blows, but it was pretty tense."

"I knew it. I've got the right man."

I stood. "He may not be the right guy."

Jay's eyebrow rose. "How's that?"

"I saw Pete and Karen Vassal having dinner. They were both gone when we left for the hospital."

He shrugged. "Maybe they were done. They must have left before my guys got there."

I stretched my legs out. "It just seems strange. Why would they leave after having appetizers? I would think they'd want their entrees."

I touched my neck as I trudged into my house. *Poor John.* The answering machine light was blinking. "Hello Ms. Busybody. It's your neighbor. I didn't get a chance to look in the garage last night but rectified that tonight. There weren't any extra boxes there. Let me know if you need me to investigate anything else." Andy chuckled and hung up.

Where did the boxes go?

I ambled up the stairs and knocked on Jenny's door. She declared, "Enter."

I sat on the edge of the bed. "Did you hear about Scott's dad?"

"Jacob texted me. They didn't believe his mom about the phone call." She put her hand in mine. "His mom wouldn't lie. Why would the police think that?"

"He was in the wrong place at the wrong time. Don't worry. If Mr. Winters didn't do it, they'll set him free."

Jenny plumped her pillow. "It just seems so unfair."

I lay down next to her. "How was dinner last night with your dad and Arianna?"

"It was fine. Except Dad kept on giving me all kinds of advice, like how to pick a school. Not to get serious about boys too soon, that kind of stuff. I think he was catching up on the years he missed." She yawned. "I'm tired. Anything else?"

"Nope. Just curious. Love you." I kissed her nose.

I walked into the new bathroom and stood looking out the window at Drew's dark house. *What's going on?*

CHAPTER 23

I shook Jenny's shoulder the next morning. "It's time to get up sleepy-head. You went to bed early enough last night."

She turned over and scrunched down farther under the covers. "Jacob was freaking out. He texted me all night."

"How many times do I have to tell you to put the do not disturb on your phone?"

Her eyes widened. "Mom, his dad's in jail. What kind of friend would I be if I didn't answer his texts?"

I pulled the covers down. "You're a good friend. But now I'm afraid it's time for you to get up. I'll defrost you a muffin."

The cats still had water, so I refilled their food dish. I pushed the button for coffee, and then rummaged in the freezer for muffins. *Almost time to make more.* I pulled out two carrot ones and placed them in the microwave to defrost. There was a knock at the back door. Pete strolled in. "Good morning."

I pointed to the coffee pot. "You missed all the excitement last night."

He poured coffee into his travel mug. "Really? What excitement."

"At the VFW."

He looked up. "There wasn't anything going on when I was there."

"Someone tried to murder John Little."

The coffee splashed on the counter. "What?"

"He went to the restroom, and someone attacked him."

Pete wiped the counter with a paper towel. "It's hard to believe the VFW isn't safe."

Jenny came running in, talking a mile a minute. "That's not the worst of it. The police arrested Mr. Winters. Just because he was there. It's so unfair." She downed a small glass of orange juice, grabbed the muffin, and raced out the door.

A slight smile played on Pete's face. "They arrested Scott. Too bad for him."

"Why did you and Karen leave?"

Pete fixed me with a stare. "We were done eating. We must have left before everything happened."

"You were eating mozzarella sticks just before he went into the men's room. There wasn't time for you to have dinner."

His eyes narrowed. "We weren't that hungry. I didn't know we'd have to account for our food intake." A knock sounded at the front door. "Must be my crew with the tub. Thanks for the coffee."

I walked out the door. Standing on the back stoop, I hesitated then scurried to Andy's garage. I peered in the window. Drew's car was there. I exhaled. They hadn't left.

✻ ✻ ✻

Patty and I bundled into Delightful Bites ten minutes early for class. Tonight was chicken. We moved to our usual station. Gary poured us both a glass of wine. "We have a new student tonight. Would it be too much to ask that she join you?"

I lifted my glass. "The more the merrier."

Other students filed in, taking their places. Gary filled more wine glasses. He gestured with the wine bottle. "Karen, you're up front with Merry and Patty."

Patty elbowed me. I turned.

"It seems like I'm turning up everywhere you are. When Pete and I had lunch here the other day, Gary told me about the class." Karen shook our hands. "I love Mediterranean recipes. They're so good for you. I just had to sign up."

"Glad to have you."

She gave me a sidelong glance. "Pete mentioned that you thought you saw me looking in your window earlier this week."

"I couldn't tell who it was. Then my neighbor and I saw a tan truck pull out."

"So you didn't know that it was me."

I raised my eyebrow. "I just said I saw your truck."

"I go down that street all the time. But I don't make a habit of peering into people's windows. Pete was really hot about it when he came home. I think you should tell him that you were mistaken."

"Was I?"

Gary tapped on his wine glass. The class came to attention. "First we're going to learn how to cut up a whole chicken. The most important item is to make sure you have a separate cutting board for meats to avoid any cross-contamination." He held up his wood cutting board. "The second most important thing is to make sure your knife is sharp, like this." He ran his blade against the honing steel four times. Then he walked the room making sure we were doing it correctly. "That's right."

"Now let's remove the leg." His instructions followed.

Karen picked up the knife. "I'll do it." She inserted the knife between the breast and the thigh. With a sharp stabbing thrust, they separated.

Patty's eyes widened, and she poked me in the ribs.

Gary walked by. "That's perfect Karen. Keep it up." He strolled back to the front of the room and gestured with his knife. "Now the next one."

With Gary's instructions, we passed our knife back and forth until all of the parts of the chicken lay displayed in a neat row in front of us. I whispered, "That wasn't as hard as I thought it would be."

Patty tittered. "I'm still buying pre-cut ones from the supermarket."

Gary called out, "Let's take a break. When we get back, we'll talk about a super Mediterranean chicken recipe with loads of olives. Everyone wash up please before touching anything." He handed out recipes and topped off wine glasses.

I leaned against the counter. "You missed the excitement last night."

Karen's eyebrow arched. "How so?"

"Someone tried to murder John Little."

She coughed and gasped, "Sorry, wine went down the wrong way. What did you say?"

"Someone tried to murder a man Pete served with in Kuwait."

"I knew John. He was one of those awful practical jokers who tormented Pete." She took another sip of wine and traced the recipe with her finger. "Someone tried to kill him? Does that mean he's okay?"

"He's in the hospital, recovering."

"That's good, I guess. At least for his wife."

Patty gasped.

"I'm not going to apologize. He and his friends were evil." She sipped her wine. "I can't believe it happened at the VFW." Her eyes widened. "And while we were there."

"I'm curious about something."

"What?"

"It seemed like you and Pete left early."

She chuckled and pushed my shoulder. "You know what it's like. Pete wanted to get busy, if you know what I mean."

Gary tapped on his wine glass again. "Please turn your attention to the recipe. We're about to begin."

* * *

Patty and I strolled back to the house. She slowed. "Did you see Karen with that knife? If Jean, Tom, and John had been stabbed she would have been my first suspect."

I slowed my pace. "She didn't admit to being my peeping Tom. But she insisted she was on my street a lot. It's not like it's a through street, and she doesn't live here." I stopped at the crosswalk. "Maybe she meant because Pete's been working on my house." I kicked a pebble. "It surprised me that she knew John. And she knew Pete was cheating on her with Jean. If she knew them, it's not that much of a stretch to say that she knew Tom. Maybe she's mixed up in all this. She's certainly acting suspicious enough. Plus, she and Pete gave different reasons for leaving the VFW."

"Maybe he didn't want to tell you he left to get amorous with his wife. I have to say, though, her comment about John being evil seemed over the top."

"How would you feel if someone left Patrick with scars?"

She shuddered. "I'd rather not think about it."

I continued walking. "Pete seemed uneasy with my questions."

Patty stopped. "Pete and his wife have been pretty sketchy. But it was probably Scott who tried to murder John. He was there, he had a mysterious phone call, you saw him walking to the front room where the decorative ropes were, and you told me he argued with John. Plus, he has a connection to the two murders."

I opened my garden gate. "You're starting to sound like Jay."

"Sometimes the police are right." Patty put her hands on my shoulders. "Merry, promise me you'll be careful. Whoever is doing this is dangerous."

I shivered and hurried into the house.

Jenny was lying on the sofa. "What did you cook tonight?"

"Mediterranean chicken. It was good. Lots of garlic and olives."

"Sounds better than my leftovers."

I moved her feet and sat down. "I'll make you something good tomorrow. Are you hankering for anything?"

She licked her lips. "Shrimp scampi with angel hair pasta."

"Done."

"With lots of lemon."

"Is there any other way? How was Jacob today?"

She put her phone down. "He's still pretty upset. I remember what it felt like when Dad was accused of murder." She shuddered. "I hope they figure out who did this soon."

"Is it too late to talk to Jacob's mom?"

She typed on her phone. "He says she's still up."

"Ask if we could come over for a few minutes."

Her phone display read: "Come ahead."

I stood and pulled her up. Jenny slid into her shoes and grabbed her purse. "Can I drive?" I tossed her the keys.

Jacob answered the door. He was pale. Jenny hugged him. "How are you?"

He flushed and looked at his feet. "Okay, I guess. Thanks for coming over." He opened the door wider. "Come in."

He led us to the living room and sat next to his mother, who seemed shrunken. Jenny sat next to Jacob, and I took the chair opposite. "Linda, I'm so sorry."

"I can't understand it. How could they think Scott would do this? He didn't even go near the restroom." She stood and walked to the window, drawing the curtains. "Why don't they believe me?"

"I'm sure they'll be asking other people at the restaurant to find out if anyone can confirm when he came back to the table."

"Why would they remember? No one was paying attention to us."

"I saw Scott take the phone call. He was headed for the entrance. Unfortunately I didn't see him return. Someone else might have." I paused. "I know it's painful, but would you take me through what happened that night?"

She stood and paced the length of the living room. "We walked into the VFW. John Little and his wife were standing there. Scott and John argued about the thefts; Scott thought John should have turned Tom in. I wish he'd just let it go." She sat heavily. "Then we had dinner. We were talking about the schools Jacob's been looking into. Scott got a phone call and told me he was going to take it in the lobby so he could hear. He came back just after I saw Rob go to the restroom. Then all of a sudden, the police were there, and they took John away on a stretcher."

"What happened next?"

She sighed. "You and Rob left, and Detective Ziebold made a beeline to our table and arrested Scott."

"Did you notice anything else?"

Linda stared at the coffee table. "There was one thing. I saw that guy who served in Kuwait with Scott. You know the one I mean. The well-built guy with the limp. He and his wife seemed to be in a hurry to leave. I can't believe how tall she is. She's like a mountain."

"Pete and Karen?

"It was Pete. I don't know the woman though. "

"When did they leave?"

"A little while after Rob went to the restroom. Pete stumbled a bit when he stood. That's why I noticed him. He pulled her up, and they hot footed it to the door."

I leaned forward. "His wife implied he was feeling amorous."

She snorted. "Didn't look like it to me. I've seen people hoping for a room, and it wasn't them. I'll agree they were in a hurry, but they were also talking a mile a minute as they left."

Jenny and I drove back in silence. She pulled into the garage. "What does it all mean?"

I got out of the car. "It means there are questions. I'd feel a lot better if I had seen Mr. Winters return to the table. The way it stands, he better hope someone else did."

"What are you going to do?"

I gave her a one-armed hug. "I'm going to talk to Detective Ziebold."

As I traipsed up the stairs to my room, I texted Rob. "Would you see if Jay could meet us for lunch tomorrow?"

"Will do. Have a good night's sleep." He added a hug emoji.

The bathroom door had been rehung. I took a deep breath and walked in. The tub shimmered in the moonlight. The vanity was in and the sinks had been set. They still needed to install the fixtures, chandelier, and drapes. I hugged myself. By tomorrow night, this should be finished. *It's already lovely. It will be over the top when it's done.* I slid between the sheets.

CHAPTER 24

I was awake before my alarm went off. I checked my phone. A text from Rob read: "Meeting Jay at noon. Golden Skillet."

Jenny was reading a book when I poked my head in to wake her. My mouth dropped. "This is unusual. Should I make scrambled eggs to mark the occasion?"

She hopped out of bed. "I'll be down in five."

I fed the cats and gave them both rubdowns. Coffee poured, I started on the eggs.

Jenny sat at the counter.

"Now isn't this more civilized?" I put the catsup on the bar. "I'll never understand why you eat eggs with catsup."

"It's the best."

"The workers will be finishing up today. I'll let you know when they leave so you can come home."

She groaned. "Mom, it's Friday night. I have a date with Jacob. Where am I going to get ready? It'll be easier if I just come home."

I shook my head. "Nope. Go to Cindy's. Don't worry, I'll call in plenty of time for you to get dressed." I touched her chin. "I mean it."

"Okay. I guess." She picked up her backpack and trudged out the door.

I'm such a mean mom. I finished putting the dishes in the dishwasher and went to work.

* * *

Just before noon, I left for the Golden Skillet. As I walked in, Rob and Jay waved me over.

Jay eyed me over his reading glasses. "This better be good."

I gulped. "You had to eat anyway. It's my treat." I turned to Rob. "What are you getting?"

"Meatloaf sandwich. You?"

"A hamburger. But I'm getting a side salad instead of the French fries."

He patted my hand. "Don't worry. I'll give you some of mine."

We ordered. "I know that everyone needs to get back to work, so I'll try to make this brief. I don't think Scott Winters is the killer."

Jay rolled his eyes. "Merry, we've been through this already. Scott's the guy. But you're buying lunch, so I'll listen. What have you heard?"

I leaned forward and recounted how Pete and Karen's stories differed, and that Linda had seen them leaving just before John was discovered. Our food arrived.

Jay put his burger down and wiped his hands on the napkin. "I appreciate all the work you're doing, but what you're telling me doesn't change my mind." He dipped a fry in catsup. "Several people, including you, saw Scott leave the table. Only Linda and one other witness could say when he came back to the table, and they both mentioned that it was after Rob left your table to check on John. That means he could have done it."

"I'll admit it looks bad. I still think it was suspicious that Pete and Karen left when they did. Plus, Karen stated that John was evil."

He sighed. "If I promise to talk to the Vassals, will you let me finish my lunch in peace?"

I chuckled. "You got it."

* * *

At four I packed up and hurried home. I couldn't wait to see my new bathroom. Hopefully they'll be done. I dropped my purse and briefcase on the kitchen stool and draped my coat over them. "Anyone home?" No one answered. I picked up the note that was propped up on the coffee maker. It read: "Left to get more paint for touch-ups, Pete."

I ran up the steps. The door to my room was open. A slight whiff of fresh paint came my way. I beamed. *This is going to be great.* I opened the door to the bathroom and waltzed in. The faucets were on the sink, the grout was done in the shower, and my chandelier was hung. Patty was right. It was the perfect touch. And someone had placed a planter with a peace lily in it next to the shower. *How nice.*

The tub beckoned me. The drapes hung on the window behind it; such a great pop of color. I stopped. That was strange. The left sash was tied and looped in place, but the right drape hung free. What happened to the other sash? Maybe it had fallen into the tub. I walked farther into the bathroom and bent over the tub. It wasn't there. I moved the drape aside, expecting the sash to be on the ground. It wasn't.

I straightened up and the sash came down in front of my face. It pulled tight around my neck, and I choked. I couldn't breathe. I clawed at the sash. My eyes teared. The sash pulled tighter. I raked my attacker's hands with my fingernails. The pressure on my neck increased. *I am not leaving my daughter!* I braced against the tub and launched myself backwards. My head slammed up under the person's chin.

My attacker stumbled. The tie loosened. I could breathe. I greedily sucked air into my oxygen-starved lungs. I pulled on the sash with all my might and twisted toward my attacker. It was Pete Vassal. I croaked, "You."

He pulled tighter. I stomped on his bad foot, and he lost his balance for a minute. There was a crash. I gasped for air just before the sash tightened again. I felt myself losing consciousness. Then my eyes widened. Jenny stood behind Pete, pulling back her sledgehammer. She swung hard and connected with his arm. A sickening crack echoed through the small space. He screamed. Pete crashed to the ground, arm at an impossible angle. I ripped the sash away from my neck, clutched my throat, and sank onto the floor, gulping in air, my back against the tub.

"Mom, are you okay?" Jenny skirted Pete and rushed to me. I nodded, unable to speak.

I glared at Pete as my chest heaved, fighting to regain my breath. I motioned for Jenny to get behind me. She hissed, "No way," and stood guard over Pete, sledge at the ready.

I held my throat and croaked, "Why did you do it?"

He moaned. "Call an ambulance."

Jenny stood in front of me, facing Pete. She rested the sledge hammer on her thigh, and pulled out her phone.

I kicked his bad foot. "Talk."

"Revenge," he sobbed. "All through my childhood I was picked on and bullied. I was scrawny back then." He wiped his face with his good hand. "When I was seventeen, I started to work out and lift weights. Then I had a growth spurt. Finally I was the one who was the big kid. I swore no one would bully me again.

"After high school, I joined the army. Most of the guys were great. They saw I could hold my own. Then I ran into the practical jokers. In high school, the bullies were all about brute strength. In the army, it was all about wits. You needed to be aware of your surroundings at all times. What made it worse was that they were friends with the NCO—non-commissioned officer." A tear rolled down his face. "He thought they were hilarious. When I complained, he'd give them some small punishment and tell me to buck up." Pete tried to lift his bad arm and screamed again. His face went even whiter.

"Then it escalated. I was barely awake and had to use the restroom. One of them put a caustic agent on saran wrap and stretched it across the toilet. I could hear them laugh as I ran screaming into the showers. I still have the scars."

He shifted position slightly. Jenny clutched the sledgehammer tighter and held it up.

He recoiled and waved with his good hand. "No need. You've done enough damage."

"That time was bad. The NCO couldn't prove who did it. But I knew. I never forgave and I never forgot. I bided my time. A few months ago, I walked into the VFW and saw Jean sitting at the bar. She didn't remember me at first, but I sure remembered her."

"I thought you really cared for her."

"She did too." He grimaced. "While I was talking to Jean that night, John joined us. He mentioned that Tom also lived in town. Something just snapped. All three of them back together. They were probably playing their miserable tricks on some other sad sack. You know that leopards don't change their spots. I decided right there and then to get back at them."

He grimaced "I started with Jean. I wooed her. And then I killed her. She was so surprised. It was easier than I thought. I passed her shop on the way to a job and saw her fracas with Scott. I waited till she closed for the day and knocked at the back door to her shop. She let me in, and I killed her with some ribbon she had been using to decorate a vase."

"What about your wife?"

"What about her?"

"Was she in on it?"

"She didn't know anything about this." He shifted again and squealed. After a moment or two, he continued. "She had some pretty hard questions after you told her about John at that cooking class."

Rob called out, "Merry, where are you?"

Jenny yelled, "Up here! In Mom's bathroom."

He pounded up the stairs. His eyes widened as he ran into the bathroom. "I heard your address on the police scanner. What happened?"

Jenny started to explain.

Jay rushed into the room, just ahead of the EMTs. I pointed to Pete. "He tried to kill me." I massaged my throat.

Rob lifted me up. He felt the lines on my throat. "Are you okay?" He gave me a fierce hug.

"I'm good now, thanks to Jenny."

Jay harrumphed. "We need to make room in here so that we can get this piece of garbage out." He glared at Pete, as he Mirandized him.

I motioned for Jenny to leave. She hesitated, but then lifted her sledgehammer and exited to the bedroom. My foot slipped, as I started to follow her. Dirt from the broken peace lily planter littered the tile. Rob steadied me. We sat in a row on the bed.

Jay helped the one EMT with Pete, while the other EMT checked me out. "You're going to be bruised, but you were very lucky. If you use ice, twenty minutes on every hour, you're going to be a lot happier. Do you want to come with us to the hospital to get checked out?"

I shook my head. "I'm fine here." The EMT hesitated. "I'll go to my doctor in the morning. I promise."

The EMTs wheeled Pete out the door. Jay stood in front of me. "Are you up to answering questions?"

I motioned with my hand. "Downstairs."

Rob held me close as we negotiated the stairs, then he made tea. Jenny started to shake. I hugged her. "Thanks for saving my life."

"Your face was all red. I thought he was going to kill you. So I hit him. Hard." She shook her head. "That crack. I think I broke a few bones. I can't believe I did that." She collapsed on a chair.

Rob brought her tea and heaped two spoonsful of sugar into it. He wrapped her hands around it. "Jenny, drink this. You'll feel better."

Next he handed me an icepack wrapped in a blue-striped kitchen towel. I placed it against my throat. Jay started the coffee machine and sat, taking out his pad and pen. "What happened?"

"Pete confessed."

He sighed. "Take me through it step by step." I did.

Rob handed him a mug of coffee. He sipped it. "Jenny, do you feel up to talking?"

"I guess so."

"Same thing, just tell me what happened."

"I wasn't supposed to be home. Mom told me to go to Cindy's." She gulped and tears ran down her face. "What if I had? What would've happened then?"

I rubbed her back and handed her a tissue. "You were here, and you saved the day."

She wiped her eyes. "I just wanted to be home. I snuck in and tiptoed up to my room." She sniffed. "I locked my door."

"Good for you."

"I was listening to music with my headphones and realized it was almost time for me to get ready for my date with Jacob. It was so quiet in the house; I thought everyone was gone. I was applying my makeup when there was a strange sound. Then I heard a crash. It came from Mom's room." She touched my shoulder and shuddered. "I didn't know what happened so I grabbed the sledgehammer and crept along the hallway. I peeked into the bedroom but no one was there. I turned the corner to the bathroom, and Mr. Vassal was strangling Mom. I was terrified." She straightened in her seat. "I couldn't let him kill her. I gripped the sledgehammer and swung like Mr. Vassal taught me. He dropped the sash and went down like a sack of potatoes." A tear dripped from her chin, as she grabbed my hand. "I was so scared. What if you died?"

I hugged her. "I didn't die. You did great. I love you."

CHAPTER 25

The grapevine must have worked overtime, because the house was soon full of people. Patty was the first one to arrive. She burst through the back door. "Are you okay?" I waved, holding ice against my neck. She pulled my hand away. Her face paled. "That must hurt."

"It does."

Her finger wagged in my face. "You have got to stop putting yourself in harm's way."

"I hear you."

"Good." She held up new sashes. "I had these sent to me early this week in case you didn't like the other ones." She shrugged. "These will work even better. Plus, who needs the reminder?"

I chuckled and caressed them. They were pretty, a soft weave of rose, aqua, and sage.

Rob uncorked a bottle of wine.

The back door swung open again, and Andy and Ed piled in. "We heard what happened, are you okay?"

I whispered, "Yes."

Ed held up a bag. "I brought munchies. I figured you needed sustenance." Rob handed him a platter and got to work filling glasses.

I stood and motioned. "Let's go into the living room. It will be more comfortable."

Jenny led the way. Ed came in last and placed the platter of goodies on the coffee table. I sipped the wine and eyed a breadstick. *Nope, too rough. A mini-quiche might be soft enough.* I lifted one and nibbled.

The front doorbell rang; Jenny bounced up and opened the door. Jacob's whole family stood on the stoop. Scott mumbled, "I'm sorry. I didn't realize you were entertaining."

Jenny beckoned them forward. "Come in, it's an impromptu kind of thing."

He hugged her. "They let me go. I know you and your mom were responsible for that. Thank you." Jenny and Jacob grabbed dining room chairs and brought them to the living room. They sat on the fireplace hearth, shoulders touching, talking quietly.

Rob stood. "Time for more ice."

I groaned, as he handed me the wrapped pack.

"Trust me, you'll be happier in the morning if we keep doing this." He turned to the assembled crowd. "Who wants pizza?" Everyone raised their hands.

By the time the pies arrived, Ed's hors d'oeuvres had been thoroughly picked over. Rob took them into the kitchen and brought back paper plates and napkins. I was able to snag some mushrooms off my slice to eat. Rob touched my shoulder. "Aren't you hungry?"

I waved my hand. "I'm good. I think pizza may be too ambitious for my throat."

He jumped up. "I should have thought of that. Do you want me to make you eggs?"

I shook my head. "Later maybe. Eat something. I had a few of Ed's mini quiches."

The guys collected the empty pizza boxes and put them in the kitchen.

Rob strolled back into the living room. "Time for this little lady to get to bed. We'll see you tomorrow." There were hugs all around, and everyone departed. Rob and I collapsed on the couch.

Jenny held up her phone. "It's blowing up. News travels quickly." She stood. "Mr. Jenson, do you think you could stay here tonight? I know Mom would sleep better." She shifted from one foot to another. "And I would too."

"I would be happy to."

Jenny kissed the top of my head. "I'm going to bed. I can't believe how tired I am." She passed Patty coming down the stairs with a trash bag in her hand.

My eyebrow rose. "I thought you left."

Patty pulled rubber gloves from her hands. "Since the police released your bathroom I thought I'd clean it. It's beautiful, by the way."

I hugged her. "You are the best friend ever."

"Yes, I am. Call me in the morning to let me know how you're doing."

Rob nudged me. "Almost time for more ice."

The back door slammed. Jay asked, "Where is everyone?" I stood and we went into the kitchen. Jay pointed toward the pizza boxes. "Any left?"

"You're in luck. I stored some in the refrigerator. And we have goodies from Ed." He popped two slices into the microwave and handed the container with Ed's leftovers to Jay.

I sank onto a chair. "Were you able to talk to Pete?"

Jay grabbed a breadstick. "Just for a few minutes. They took him into surgery. His arm was broken in two places, plus he cracked a rib." He grinned. "Your daughter should have gone out for softball. She has a heck of a swing."

Rob handed him a plate with two steaming slices of pepperoni. "Here you go."

Jay took a bite. "Good."

I took the ice from Rob and placed it on my neck. "Did he say anything?"

"His story matched yours. He was quite talkative. He wanted to make sure I understood that he was the injured party. That what he did was justice."

"I feel kind of sorry for him."

Rob flinched. "He killed two people, attacked John, and almost killed you."

I clutched the ice to my neck. "I know. But he was a kid who got bullied. He grew up and was bullied some more. The power structure did not help him."

Jay shook his head. "I guess that's for the jury to decide." The clock chimed. "It's late. I'll be in touch. Thanks for the pizza."

Rob cleaned the kitchen. I rested my head on my hands. He shook my shoulder. "Come on sleeping beauty, time for you to go upstairs. I'll take care of making up the guest room bed."

He half carried me up the stairs, I was so exhausted. I put my finger to my lips outside Jenny's door, and then opened it. Her soft snores greeted us. I blew her a kiss and eased the door shut.

Rob smiled. "She did well today."

"She sure did."

CHAPTER 26

I woke early the next morning, the sun not yet cresting the horizon. I pushed the covers off and walked to the bathroom door, hesitating as I reached for the handle. I straightened my back, threw it open, and scanned the room. I let out my breath. No one there.

I locked the door behind me and walked into the bathroom. The tile floors were so warm. I caressed the tub's curve. The new sashes held back the curtains. How pretty they were. Plenty of time for my inaugural bath. I closed the curtains and filled the tub. A bottle of bubble bath adorned with a bow sat on the floor. The label touted the aroma as a stress reliever. I chuckled as I poured some in, and turned on the spigots. Wonder why Patty thought I'd needed this. I slid in, dipped the washcloth into the water, and draped it over my face.

Every piece of my body relaxed. *He may have been a murderer, but he was a good contractor.* My mind floated. The bath was so comfortable. I added more hot water. The morning light began to infiltrate around the edges of the washcloth.

Someone was hammering somewhere. I wished they'd stop. Don't we have ordinances about doing work this early? It droned on. And it sounded like people were shouting. *What on earth?* I stood and peaked between the drapes.

Agents in navy jackets labeled FBI swarmed Drew's yard. They hammered on his door. I cracked the window. "Drew March, open the door. We need to talk with you. If you do not open the door, we will be forced to break it down."

My mouth dropped.

A loud crack sounded as the door splintered. The FBI agents strode in. Intermittent shouts of "Clear" rang out.

An agent exited and spoke to a man in a suit. "No one's here."

"We'll canvas the neighborhood."

I shut the window, praying it wouldn't make a noise. It didn't. I shivered. The bath had gone cold, and I was standing in it. I toweled dry and donned sweats, t-shirt, and hoodie.

I crept to the guest room. Rob was snoring softly. I shook his arm. "Rob. It's the FBI. They've come for Drew."

He started awake. "What?"

"The FBI. They're storming Drew's house."

He rubbed his eyes. "What's he done now?"

I shrugged and handed him his pants. He put them on and followed me back to my room. We edged around either side of the tub, and I parted the drapes. The FBI agents were still there, and the property's owner, Melissa, had joined them.

Jenny ambled in, rubbing her eyes. "What's going on?"

I hurried over and hugged her. "It's the FBI, and they are looking for your dad."

She ran to the window and yanked the drapes open. "What do they want now?"

I joined her at the window. "I'm not sure, honey. It looks like your dad and Arianna aren't home. Get dressed."

I walked back into the bedroom and peeked out the front window. A small crowd gathered across the street. They seemed intent on the happenings at Drew's house. *Great. More damage control.* I turned to Rob. "I'll put the coffee on."

"Do you mind if I shower in your bathroom while Jenny's in hers?"

"Have at it."

I trudged down the stairs and petted each cat. As I fed them, there was a rap on the door. I unlocked it. Jay strode in. "Coffee ready yet?" He sat at the counter.

I put a mug in front of him and filled it. "What's going on?"

"They're looking for Drew."

"That part I got. Why are they looking for Drew?"

"Two reasons. Remember when Drew's previous girlfriend got mad at him and called the FBI?"

"But she was killed. I thought they dropped that."

He shook his head. "Nope. They followed the money he hid with his girlfriends and built their case. It led right back to Drew. He should have reported it when he went to prison four years ago."

I snorted. "Like that was going to happen. Why do you think he hid it in the first place?" I poured myself a cup of coffee and joined him at the counter. "Wait. You said two things."

Rob came around the corner. "Any coffee for me?" I pointed to the carafe, and Jay brought him up to date.

"The second thing was that he was up to his old tricks. He created a new scam that he ran out of the library."

Rob put the mug down with a bang. Coffee sloshed out. "That man! What's next?"

"He wasn't home. They'll try to trace where he went."

Jenny pounded down the stairs. "Did you see the crowd on the sidewalk?"

I groaned. "It's gotten bigger?"

"Oh yeah!"

Jay stood. "Better get back. Thanks for the java." The door shut behind him.

Jenny's phone dinged. Her eyes widened as she read the text. "Mom, it's from Dad and Arianna. They're in Brunei." She looked up and smiled broadly. "And they left me his car."

ABOUT THE AUTHOR

Eileen Hammond is an author who retired from a successful marketing career in the insurance industry. She and her husband share the house with two cats that are determined to train them.

For those of you who have read this page before, you know that it contained a description of the pet koi and shubunkins. Unfortunately they did not fare well this year. A hungry heron ate them on his way to warmer climes. Eileen and her husband will be looking to restock their pond in the spring and will be enhancing their hungry critter defense system.

The author looks forward to this summer where she will continue writing and rescuing the frog population from drowning in the pool.

ALSO BY EILEEN CURLEY HAMMOND

Murder So Sinful
Murder So Festive

www.ingramcontent.com/pod-product-compliance
Lightning Source LLC
Chambersburg PA
CBHW052046240626
47153CB00006B/2243

9 781732 546059